THE SEVEN SEEDS

SHEPHERD OF SOULS

By

Neil Perry Gordon

ISBN: **979-8-9875632-7-4**

Contents

CHAPTER ONE
A RIPPLE

The rhythmic sound of footsteps echoed softly through the ancient halls of the Vatican, their resonance absorbed by centuries-old stone. Pope Gregory moved steadily through the corridors, his nightly walk meant to bring him peace. Yet, tonight, an unease settled over him—a restlessness he couldn't shake. His cassock, heavy with the responsibilities of his position, felt oppressive, and the golden cross hanging over his neck brought no comfort. The Vatican had always been his sanctuary, but tonight it felt different as if the air itself carried a warning.

The silence pressed in around him as he turned into a narrow corridor he rarely traveled, the archives lying just ahead. This place, filled with relics of the Church's long and tangled history, had always been a refuge—a sacred space away from the demands of the papacy. Yet tonight, a strange compulsion pulled him deeper into the shadows of the Vatican, urging him to move toward something unknown.

His fingers drifted over the spines of forgotten tomes, the scent of old parchment mingling with the faint chill of the archive. As he let his hand wander, his fingers brushed against a particularly worn volume half-hidden in the shadows. Intrigued, he pulled it from the shelf and wiped a thin layer of dust from the cover. The leather binding was cracked with age, its edges softened by countless hands that had once sought its contents. Pope Gregory felt an inexplicable pull, a strange sense of recognition, as though this book had been waiting for him. Drawn in, he opened it slowly, revealing dense lines of mostly indecipherable Latin script illuminated by the dim lights of the archive.

Pope Gregory observed the manuscript, its ancient leather cover cool beneath his fingertips. The text was dense, archaic, and strange; he could make out only fragments: phrases that spoke of a "Shepherd from beyond" and a time when faith would be rekindled in an age of darkness. His brows knitted in concentration as he deciphered cryptic lines foretelling a guide who would "bridge two realms" and "restore the lost path." The words sent a chill through him—a sense of fate lingering on each leaf.

The pages whispered as he turned them, the ink pulsing faintly under his gaze. Symbols danced on the parchment, shifting subtly as if resisting his attempt to grasp their meaning. Each new line stirred something deep—a tingling in his fingertips, a quickening in his chest. Shadows flickered across the words, adding layers to the obscure text, weaving images of distant landscapes and shadowed figures into the edges of his vision. He felt pulled in as though a hidden thread connected him to the ancient words, binding his fate to theirs.

Without fully realizing it, he slipped the manuscript into the depths of his vestment, his fingers lingering on its surface for a brief, solemn moment. It felt right there, as though it had always belonged with him, patiently waiting for his arrival.

Then, a strange light flickered at the end of the corridor, drawing his attention. Pope Gregory froze, his heart skipping a beat. This was a place of quiet shadows, not shimmering lights. Yet there it was, unmistakable and insistent—a glow that pulsed with a life of its own.

At the far end of the hallway, a wall that had been solid stone moments before now rippled with a faint luminescence, like the surface of disturbed water. He approached cautiously, each step tightening the knot of unease in his chest. His hand reached out almost involuntarily, brushing against the glowing stone. It was cold but shifted beneath his fingers instead of remaining firm. The wall slid away, revealing a narrow, spiraling passage that descended deep into the earth.

Pope Gregory hesitated, every instinct telling him to turn back, but an invisible force pulled him forward. He gathered his robes, took a deep breath, and stepped into the unknown. The further he descended, the stranger everything became—the air grew colder, almost suffocating, and the stone walls seemed to move and twist as if they were alive. He stumbled as a sudden dizziness overtook him, his vision flickering and blurring.

Then, as abruptly as it began, the vertigo ceased. Gregory stood at the base of the passage, staring at an archway of rough-hewn stone. Unlike the rest of the Vatican, this arch was engraved with symbols he did not recognize—pagan symbols that seemed both familiar and entirely foreign. At the top of the arch was a strange emblem, reminiscent of a cross but incomplete, as if it had been left unfinished on purpose. Compelled by a force he didn't understand, he stepped through the arch.

For a moment, everything went black. There was no noise, no light—only the faint vibration of something immense and unseen. Then the world snapped back into place, and he found himself standing outdoors. But he was not in the Vatican's familiar courtyards. No, this was something entirely different.

The spires of St. Peter's Basilica were gone, replaced by a massive square dominated by towering marble columns and grand temples. Statues of what appeared to be ancient Roman gods stood proudly where the saints and angels of the Vatican had once been. This was Rome, but not the Rome Gregory had known his entire life. It was a city alive with reverence, apparently not for Christ, but for the old gods—Jupiter, Mars, Venus. It was as if he had stepped back in time, yet the cars and electric lights told him this was no ancient era.

The panic clawing at his mind was slow, almost gentle at first. He instinctively reached for the golden cross at his neck, gripping it tightly, seeking some sense of familiarity. But the more he looked around, the more he saw the truth. Christianity had never existed here; Rome was devoted to a different kind of faith; a faith he thought had been left behind centuries ago.

With a racing heart, Gregory approached a passerby, a middle-aged man dressed in a tailored suit with intricate symbols of Jupiter embroidered on his cuffs. "Excuse me," Gregory began, his voice trembling as he struggled to maintain composure. "The Vatican… where is the Vatican?"

The man paused, frowning as if Gregory had spoken in an unknown tongue. "I'm sorry, I don't understand what you mean," he said, polite but detached, his tone tinged with the slightest edge of impatience.

"The Vatican!" Gregory's desperation seeped into his voice, growing louder and more pleading. "St. Peter's Basilica! The Holy See, the center of Christendom!" He held onto each word like a lifeline, hoping for some glimmer of recognition.

The man only looked more puzzled, and perhaps even a bit concerned. "Vatican, you say," he repeated slowly, tasting the unfamiliar word. "I'm not sure what you're referring to, sir. Are you lost?"

Gregory's hands shook as he staggered back, his breath coming faster. "You've never heard… of the Vatican?"

"No," the man replied firmly, his brow furrowed in pity and discomfort. "Never heard of such a place. Perhaps you should seek guidance at the Temple of Jupiter if you need a certain type of help."

Gregory's mind reeled, the alien nature of this world pressing down on him. In a desperate gesture, he reached for his cross, holding it out in a trembling hand. "Look! This must mean something to you," he said, almost pleading.

But the man's face twisted in horror. His gaze locked onto the cross with revulsion, and he took a hurried step back, his hand rising instinctively as if to ward off some grim specter. "Are you mad?" he hissed, his voice tense with alarm. "Why would you carry such a symbol openly? Hide it, for your own sake, before someone else sees and mistakes you for a condemned man."

The words struck Gregory like a physical blow. He stumbled away, nearly colliding with another passerby, who shot him a strange look. Desperation overtook him, and he tried again, stopping a young woman in flowing robes. "Please," he pleaded. "Tell me you've heard of Christ, of the Church… of God!"

Her eyes narrowed, confusion giving way to wariness. "Christ? Don't know that name," she said, stepping back as if he were a madman. "Is this some new religion?"

"No, it's not new!" Gregory's voice cracked with panic. "Christ— the Savior, the Son of God!"

The woman shrugged and turned away.

Gregory staggered back as the full magnitude of the world's transformation hit him like a blow to the chest. He wandered through streets that felt both ancient and strangely modern, his eyes wide as he tried to make sense of the scene unfolding around him. Some of the familiar architecture of Rome remained, but now temples to Jupiter, Mars, and Venus dominated the skyline, their columns gleaming under the afternoon sun.

Gregory's footsteps slowed as he noticed a change in the atmosphere—a subtle, shifting tension. A soft murmur swept through the streets, growing louder with each passing second. People were gathering along the sides of the promenade, some craning their necks and others standing on their toes for a better view. He hesitated, unsure what was happening, but the crowd's anticipation was palpable, drawing him closer.

A faint, rhythmic thudding reached his ears, almost imperceptible at first, like the distant echo of a heartbeat. The sound grew stronger, reverberating through the cobblestones until Gregory could feel it thrumming in his chest, each beat heavy and deliberate. He scanned the street, searching for the source, when the first low notes of a drum reverberated through the air. A deep, resonant sound made the hairs on his arms stand up. The crowd shifted, parting like the sea, to make way for something unseen, and Gregory moved to the edge of the gathering, his back pressing against the cold, unyielding stone of a nearby building.

The drumming grew louder, each beat echoing through Gregory's chest as the rhythm quickened, becoming a relentless, hypnotic pulse that filled the air. His breath caught in his throat as they appeared— figures at the far end of the avenue, moving in perfect time with the drums. Priests emerged from the shadows, their crimson robes flowing around them like blood on the wind. Their steps were slow, measured, and unified, swaying in unison with the powerful beat.

Each priest wore a crown of laurel leaves upon their brow, the green leaves stark against the deep red of their robes. They moved with an almost ethereal grace as if the ground carried them forward. A heavy silence fell over the crowd, drawn to the procession by an unseen force. Gregory watched, captivated, as they came closer, their faces calm and impassive, eyes fixed ahead as though gazing into a reality beyond this world.

The priests' chanting began—a low, rhythmic murmur that ebbed and flowed with the drumming. Gregory strained to understand the words, feeling the familiar tones of Latin in their cadence. Yet this was not the Latin he knew, not the comforting prayers of his Church. The phrases were older, infused with a sense of ancient power, and the meaning was elusive, just beyond his comprehension. It was as if he were hearing echoes from a time long forgotten; the language slipping through his mind like grains of sand through his fingers.

The words rose and fell like the waves of a restless sea, each phrase building upon the last, swelling in a strange and alien harmony. Gregory's heart beat faster, the rhythm pulling at something deep within him. It was a call to something primal and powerful, a language older than the faith he devoted his life to, a language that spoke directly to his basest desires.

But then, as he listened more closely, the strange language began to coalesce, its meaning slowly unfurling in his thoughts. It was an older Latin, a dialect buried in the depths of history that he had only read about in the margins of dusty manuscripts and ancient inscriptions. The sounds became clearer, the words more distinct, and he found himself piecing together their meaning.

This was not a language of salvation or grace but of power and the raw forces of nature. The cadence was unlike any Mass he had known, flowing with a wild and untamed rhythm. Yet, despite its foreignness, there was a magnetic pull to the chant—a power that stirred something deep within him, drawing him into its ancient pulse.

As the parade of priests passed, Gregory's gaze focused on their symbols: banners emblazoned with the wolf of Rome, the spear that pierced through the heavens, and a shield stained with the deep, rich red of freshly spilled blood. They held the standards high, and the crowd pressed closer, whispering prayers and lifting their hands in gestures of reverence.

Then came the followers, a mass of men and women moving in unison, their eyes alight with fervor. Some carried garlands of flowers, others bore offerings of bread and wine, and all seemed to move as if guided by a single, unseen force. Gregory watched them pass, feeling the power of their devotion settle over him like a heavy cloak. There was a beauty to it, a raw and untempered reverence that pulsed in time with the drums, and for a fleeting moment, he felt the stirrings of something he had not expected—admiration.

Yet it was wrong. He knew it was wrong, for there was no Christ here, no redemption or salvation, only the primal and unyielding faith in mythological gods of power and war. And at the head of it all, towering above the procession, was the emblem of Mars—bold and unrelenting, a god of bloodshed and glory who would not be denied.

Gregory's fingers instinctively tightened around the cross at his neck, feeling its edges press into his palm. Remembering the stranger's horrified reaction, he slipped it beneath his robe, unwilling to draw attention to it or himself. The stranger's response had been a chilling reminder that his symbol of faith held a different, darker meaning in this world. Even as he concealed it, Gregory could not look away from the unfolding celebration, a display of belief so alien yet compelling, painted in a vibrant, terrible splendor. He felt adrift, his faith both his guide and his exile in this unfamiliar land.

The celebration swirled around him, a river of beliefs he could not comprehend, flowing past without a single ripple to acknowledge his presence. He was alone—a solitary figure in a world that had forgotten him, a world where even God had gone missing.

CHAPTER TWO
LOST

As the night settled in and exhaustion gnawed at his limbs, Gregory felt the burden of his confusion and despair pulling him down. His vision blurred, and the city's unfamiliar celebrations, full of laughter and ritual, grew oppressive. Each step was heavier than the last, and he hadn't the strength to search for answers.

In the shadow of a tall marble building, Gregory noticed a narrow alley that offered a temporary escape from the noise and strangeness of this world. The alley was dark, a sliver of shadow wedged between two massive stone structures. At its end, he saw a small, forgotten passage, partially hidden behind a crumbling archway. Without contemplating the dangers, Gregory slipped inside, his heart pounding. The coolness of the stone walls pressed close around him, muffling the sounds of the pagan celebrations in the distance.

He sank against the cold, damp wall, the exhaustion enveloping him like a suffocating wave. The cross around his neck pressed heavily against his chest, a reminder of the world he'd left behind of a faith now distant. His trembling hands instinctively pulled his cassock tighter, the familiar fabric offering a fragile sense of solace in the foreign emptiness surrounding him.

Gregory's mind swirled with images as he closed his eyes, his situation pressing harder with every breath. He could imagine Jose, his ever-faithful assistant, pacing anxiously in the papal apartments, his face pale with worry. The silence of his absence would have grown unbearable, the unanswered questions ricocheting through the Vatican halls like a storm.

He thought of the Cardinals gathering in frantic whispers, their red robes swaying like restless waves. The Vatican's carefully ordered world would collapse, panic spreading as speculation turned to dread. He could picture the staff and the Swiss Guard, their stern expressions cracking under the strain of a crisis unlike any they had prepared for.

Then the scene shifted in his mind: the police arriving, their somber faces betraying the seriousness of the situation. The Apostolic Palace's corridors would echo with investigators' clipped voices. Theories of kidnapping would be floated, darker suspicions of assassination creeping into the corners of every whispered conversation. He almost heard the hushed, incredulous words: "Pope Gregory has vanished."

And then the news. It would ripple out from Rome to the world's farthest reaches, spreading like wildfire. Gregory saw the headlines flashing: "Missing Pontiff—Mystery Shrouds Vatican." The faithful would weep, their prayers rising like a lamenting chorus. The press would descend like vultures, cameras flashing, questions hurled into the void.

A missing Pope. The thought sent a chill coursing through him, the enormity of it pressing heavily against his chest. Such a thing had never happened in modern history—never in living memory. The image burned into his mind: a Church left leaderless, a world plunged into uncertainty. And he, stranded here in another existence, could do nothing to stop it.

As sleep finally claimed him, his dreams were haunted by the familiar—a grand cathedral bathed in Christ's light, prayers echoing softly in the hallowed sanctity of the Vatican. But even in the dream, it felt impossibly distant, like a memory slipping through his grasp with every passing breath. The Vatican, his purpose, and his people were all slipping further and further away.

Suddenly, a rough shake jolted him awake. Gregory's eyes shot open, squinting against the blinding light of dawn streaming into the passage. A coarse voice rang out above him, half-amused, half-irritated.

"Get up! You can't sleep here, old man," a city guard barked, pulling him roughly to his feet. "You can't loiter here like some mad beggar."

Confused and disoriented, Gregory stumbled, his legs weak. He tried to explain, to say anything that would make sense of his presence, but the guard's eyes only filled with pity and mild disdain. To the guard, he was no more than a homeless lunatic, babbling in an ancient tongue about things no one understood.

"Move along," he snapped. "Before I report you."

Gregory quickly tucked the cross under his rope, his heart pounding with the fear that the guard might catch a glimpse. Glancing cautiously at the guard, who seemed indifferent but imposing, he straightened, the weight of loss and secrecy settling heavily on his shoulders. Taking a steadying breath, he turned away from the shadowed passage, resolved to keep moving, even though every step reminded him of how far he was from home.

The morning sun unveiled a city both familiar and strange, its architecture echoing a Rome Gregory had once known yet now cloaked in alien indifference. The arches and columns of imposing buildings loomed overhead, grand in construction but devoid of the sacred resonance he sought. He moved with the crowd, his steps hesitant, hoping for some remnant of the faith that had defined him.

As Gregory walked, his vestments bore down on him like an unspoken truth. The immaculate white robe, pristine yet heavy with meaning, swept the ground as he moved, its fabric catching the light in contrast to the world around him. A crimson sash cinched at his waist—a band of deep red that once symbolized sacrifice and authority—now pressed against him like a silent reproach. The soft cap perched atop his head felt less like a crown of humility and more like an awkward relic of a forgotten throne.

His red leather shoes, worn but unblemished, whispered of tradition and power with every step, though the path they trod no longer recognized him. Children gawked, their fingers pointing as mothers tugged them away, and others paused only to chuckle or dismiss him with skeptical glances. Each thread and stitch carried the weight of a world without a place for him—an exile robed in forgotten glory.

The crowd parted for him begrudgingly as though his presence was an affront to their daily routine. Gregory caught a man's glare, his expression a mixture of confusion and disdain. To them, he was no longer a figure of authority or Divine purpose—just a stranger wrapped in outdated finery, a relic of a forgotten era.

A group of young men leaning against a wall whispered and laughed as he passed. He could almost hear their unspoken thoughts: What kind of fool walks the streets dressed like that?

The faith he carried within him felt heavier under the guise of their judgment, and yet Gregory pressed forward. His gaze remained fixed ahead, scanning the horizon for the Church he once knew, for any sign that sanctity still lingered in this strange reflection of Rome. The streets twisted and turned, and with each step, the faint hope in his heart burned dimmer. The city was vast, unknowable, and indifferent to his search. Here, his vestments held no meaning. What had once been a symbol of Divine authority was now reduced to the costume of a man out of place, out of time.

Still, Gregory walked on, the whispers and stares trailing behind him like ghosts.

His heart skipped as he approached a structure that looked like a sanctuary. It was an imposing building he associated with holy places—

tall columns flanking a wide entrance and arches that seemed to beckon him inside. The air around it felt cool, the shadows deep, offering a glimmer of hope. Perhaps here, he would find a quiet corner to pray, catch his breath, and remember.

But the moment he stepped inside, the sting of disillusionment struck him. Instead of the comforting sight of a crucifix or the familiar scent of burning incense, he was met with the cold gaze of marble statues, tall and forbidding. At the center of the room loomed a massive effigy of Jupiter, his stern face staring down from a throne of stone. Other statues surrounded him—Minerva, with her helmet and shield; Neptune, holding his trident; Venus, her marble form radiating serene beauty. This was not a church but a temple, and the realization hit him like a physical blow.

The room was dimly lit, sunlight filtering through narrow windows and casting elongated shadows over the faces of these ancient idols, relics of a world that worshipped what he saw as false gods. Gregory felt a strange chill as he gazed upon the stone forms. The statues seemed alive in the dim light, their expressions carved with pride and dignity as if challenging him to understand the grip they still held on Rome. To Gregory, they were more than mere stone—they were echoes of a lost faith, symbols of a Divine order that had led people away from the true path.

Priests in traditional Roman attire—simple robes pinned at the shoulder with brooches—moved through the chamber with a quiet, practiced grace. They seemed to glide rather than walk, their movements calculated, their expressions serene. Gregory's presence in his heavy, foreign vestments caught their attention, and he felt the intensity of their stares.

"Where is Christ?" he blurted, his voice desperate, breaking the silence that seemed to hum with an ancient, unfamiliar energy. "Where is the Church?"

The priests exchanged amused glances, their eyes narrowing slightly in disdain. One of them, a tall man with a lined face, stepped forward, his brow furrowed in a mixture of curiosity and pity. "What strange god do you speak of, old man?" the priest asked, his tone condescending. "We serve the true gods, the eternal ones who rule the heavens and the earth."

Gregory tried to explain, the words tumbling out in a torrent—he spoke of Christ, the Son of God, of the Church that had risen to spread His message of love and redemption. He pleaded for understanding, for some acknowledgment that his world had existed. But the priests only listened with bemused expressions, as if he were a child recounting a fanciful tale.

"Madness," the tall priest said with a shake of his head. "You speak of dreams and shadows, of myths that never were. The gods are eternal; their power has shaped our world since time began. There is no place here for your strange beliefs."

Gregory's voice broke, his desperation pouring out in a final plea. "Please," he begged, his eyes wide with a grief that felt like it would consume him. "Please, tell me that Christ lived, that the Church—"

"Enough!" the priest snapped, his voice harsh. "Leave this sacred place. You insult the gods with your madness."

Gregory stumbled back, his throat tight with unshed tears, his hands trembling. He had hoped to find a sanctuary, but this was a house of strangers, of false gods he had never believed in, in a world that had never known the one true faith.

He turned and fled, his steps uneven, feeling the disdainful eyes of the priests on his back until he was outside, in the open air once more. The city buzzed with life around him, but he felt utterly alone.

Christ had never walked these streets, and the Church had never risen from the dust of the Roman Empire. He was no longer a shepherd of souls in a world guided by faith, but a lone man lost in a sea of ancient gods, relics of a time he thought he had left behind. The familiar symbols of his devotion—the cross, the saints, the cathedrals—were not missing; they had never existed.

Gregory wandered, his steps faltering, until the glare of sunlight and the bustling noise became too much to bear. The scenes around him stirred memories of the homeless souls he had once tended, those who drifted along the edges of society, retreating into the shadows for a moment of respite from a world that had no place for them. Now, like them, he slipped into a dim alley, the city's pulse dulling to a distant throb behind him. Here, away from the relentless gaze of a sun that seemed alien in its warmth, he sank to his knees, a wave of utter defeat washing over him. His faith, his purpose, all that he had once believed in, felt fragile and broken, as though crushed beneath the weight of something ancient and immovable. The ancient gods of Rome had claimed this world, and he was but a lost soul in their dominion, a stranger seeking solace in the forgotten corners where no light dared to intrude.

CHAPTER THREE
A KINDNESS

The coolness of the shadowed alley offered little comfort as Gregory knelt on the cobblestones, his shoulders slumped in utter defeat. He had never felt so lost, so stripped of everything that defined him. The sounds of the city—a city he once knew—faded into a muted blur. Somewhere in the distance, chants of Roman prayers echoed, punctuated by bursts of laughter and life from a world that had forgotten Christ, forgotten the Church, and forgotten him.

He remained hidden in the alley's depths, his breath shallow, his grip tightening around the cross, which now seemed more like a relic of a lost time than a source of comfort. A jolt of panic surged through him as he realized he was no longer alone. A pair of stern eyes glared down at him—an official dressed in the attire of this strange, pagan Rome. The man's lips curled into a disdainful frown, and with a harsh voice, he barked something Gregory did not fully comprehend, gesturing for him to move.

It was clear what the stranger saw: a lost, disheveled figure of a costumed madman crouched in the corners of the city like a discarded memory. With bitter humiliation, Gregory pushed himself to his feet and fled the alley.

The world beyond the shadows seemed harsher, the noise sharper. He moved like a wraith among the crowd, half-forgotten in his own mind. The vastness of Rome enveloped him—a city where the gods of old were alive in the hearts of the people and where he, the Pope, was an anomaly. Desperation and exhaustion weighed down his steps, and he moved without direction, hoping to find anything that might make sense.

The sun climbed higher, bathing the city in harsh light, and Gregory's aimless wandering took him through grand forums where marble statues cast imposing shadows. He moved among the crowds, his cassock dragging in the dust, his eyes haunted by the sight of towering temples that mocked his faith with their grandeur. Every stone, every statue of Jupiter, Venus, or Mars, reminded him that he no longer belonged. The feeling of isolation tightened around his chest.

And then, amid the rush of a city that had passed him by without a second glance, a voice reached him—soft, gentle, cutting through the cacophony like a ray of light. "Excuse me, sir?" The voice carried a note of genuine concern, so out of place amidst the indifference that Gregory almost did not respond. But he turned, and there, standing in the sunlight, was a man who looked at him not with disdain or curiosity but with a quiet, understanding sympathy.

The stranger appeared to be in his late forties, neatly dressed in a scholarly yet approachable manner. His face was framed by wire-rimmed glasses that caught the sunlight. A satchel hung over one shoulder; his expression was of sincere curiosity, almost compassion. Gregory blinked, his gaze locking onto the stranger's calm eyes, and at that moment, he felt something he hadn't felt since arriving in this strange world—a glimmer of kindness.

"Are you lost?" the man asked, his voice gentle yet cautious. Gregory was too stunned to respond at first, but the stranger's calm demeanor felt like a lifeline. "I'm Dr. Marcus Taylor," the man continued, extending a hand. "Professor of philosophy at the university. You look… like you need help."

For the first time since he had stepped through the archway, Gregory felt a flicker of hope. He took the man's hand, his grip desperate and hesitant. "I'm Gregory," he managed, his voice weak.

Marcus's eyes were sharp, taking in Gregory's attire. "You don't seem to be from here," Marcus observed gently. "How about an espresso? You look like you could use a moment to rest."

Gregory hesitated, the strangeness pressing down on him, but something about the professor's sincerity broke through his isolation. He allowed himself to be led to a nearby café, a modern structure that felt entirely out of place in his confused mind. Inside, the hum of conversation filled the air, students chattering about their studies and lives, untouched by any sense of the sacred.

They sat in a quiet corner, and Marcus handed Gregory an espresso, his eyes patient and attentive. "Would you like to tell me what's going on?" he asked softly, his voice free of judgment. "You seem like someone who has lost his way."

Gregory's gaze was fixed on the foam, his thoughts spinning. He took a deep breath, feeling the cross hidden against his chest. "I used to be Pope Gregory," he began, his voice shaking. "I lived in a world where Christ was our Savior, where the Church guided our lives. But then… something happened. I stepped through a doorway, and now… everything is gone. The Church, Christ, all of it vanished."

Marcus's brow furrowed as he listened, intrigued but cautious. "You believe you've come from another world?" he asked, his tone carefully neutral. "A world where a savior existed?"

"Yes," Gregory said, his voice firmer. "Jesus Christ. I devoted my life to Him. But now I am here, and everything I believed in and knew has vanished."

Marcus's expression softened. "It sounds like you've experienced something profound," he said, though his skepticism was evident. "But why was this Christ figure so central to your world?"

Gregory's eyes filled with grief. "Christ wasn't just a figure," he said. "He was the Son of God. He taught us love, forgiveness, and redemption. His teachings were the foundation of everything—our laws, values, and hope."

Marcus leaned forward, his curiosity genuine. "And now you're in a world that has never known him," he said softly. "What makes your Christ's message so different, so irreplaceable?"

Gregory leaned forward. "Because without Him," he said, his voice breaking, "there is no salvation. No forgiveness. There is no hope of redemption. He was the light that guided us, the reason we believed in something greater than ourselves."

Marcus sat back, absorbing Gregory's words, his fingers tapping lightly against the table. "What if people don't need salvation?" he asked gently. "What if they can find hope, morality, and love in other ways?"

Gregory looked away, his face pale with the enormity of his loss. "I don't know," he admitted. "I only know the world I came from. And now it's as if I've been erased."

The professor's eyes softened with understanding, even if his beliefs remained unshaken. "Perhaps there is a reason you are here," Marcus said thoughtfully. "Perhaps there is something to discover, even in a world that feels so different."

Marcus watched Gregory intently, his brow furrowing with curiosity and concern. He leaned forward, his voice gentle but probing. "Gregory, where do you live? Do you have a home nearby? Family?"

Gregory shook his head slowly. "Like I said, I live at the Vatican," he said, his voice wavering. "That's my home. It's where I serve, pray, and lead the Church. There is no other place."

Marcus's expression softened, but his eyes showed a hint of doubt. "You say you live at a place called the Vatican, but… do you remember anything else? Family, friends? Is there someone I could contact for you? Perhaps you have a place to return to, someone who can help?"

"My family," Gregory began slowly, his voice heavy with recollection. His gaze drifted to some unseen point as if reaching through time to pull at the delicate threads of memory. "They lived here in Rome a long time ago."

Marcus leaned forward, concern etching lines into his brow. "That's something, at least. And you have no phone? No contact information? Someone we can call?"

Gregory's expression darkened, his face etched with anguish. Marcus's questions seemed to deepen the chasm of his isolation. "No," he whispered, the word barely audible. "There's no one left. My family… they perished in a fire. Many years ago."

Marcus froze, the casual frown replaced by a shadow of understanding. "I'm… I'm sorry," he said gently. "But, Gregory, are you certain you haven't been elsewhere since then? A home for the elderly, perhaps? Sometimes trauma—especially something like that—can confuse. Memory loss, even. You may be disoriented."

Gregory's shoulders sagged further. "No," he repeated, quieter this time. "I remember the flames. I remember what I lost. And now…" He let the words trail into the silence, his voice hollow as though the fire had burned through more than just his past—it had scorched the roots of his very being.

Marcus exhaled, watching Gregory carefully, unsure whether he was unraveling, holding on by a thread.

Gregory's eyes flashed with a spark of indignation, his voice rising slightly as he responded, "I was the Pope, leader of the Church. I remember everything clearly. I lived in the Vatican, walked the halls of St. Peter's, and prayed in the chapel. I am not confused. It is the world that has changed, not my mind!"

Marcus sat back, absorbing the passion and certainty in Gregory's voice. For a long moment, he said nothing, scratching at his stubble as he weighed his response. "I believe you're telling the truth, Gregory," he said slowly. "At least, the truth as you know it. But we are here, now, in this world. I want to help you, but I need you to try and accept that things might differ from what you expect."

Gregory nodded, his movements slow and hesitant. "I don't understand any of this," he whispered, his voice barely audible. "But if there is a reason I'm here, then I need to figure it out."

Marcus leaned forward, his voice gentle and reassuring. "Come home with me, Gregory," he offered, his eyes steady and calm. "We don't have to solve everything right now. You need a safe place to rest and clear your mind; I can offer you that."

Gregory hesitated, glancing at Marcus's outstretched hand. It was a simple gesture, but in this bewildering world where nothing made sense, it felt monumental—a lifeline in a sea of confusion. Slowly, he reached out. He grasped Marcus's hand, feeling the solid warmth of another human's touch, a tangible connection that grounded him.

"Bless you," he said, his voice catching on the words. Marcus's quiet generosity was a glimmer of grace in a world without the familiar faith that had defined his life.

"Let's go," Marcus said softly, guiding him from the table. Gregory followed, the heaviness in his chest lifting just a little. They walked out of the café together, the city's bustling life sweeping past them—a blend of ancient temples, modern buildings, and a rhythm that still felt alien. But with Marcus beside him, Gregory felt less alone, even if the path ahead was uncertain.

As they moved through the busy streets, Gregory's eyes lingered on the temples and statues of the old gods. He felt the strange pull of a world that honored a pantheon he had once dismissed as myth. He glanced at Marcus, who walked with calm assurance, his shoulders relaxed and his steps sure.

They arrived at Marcus's modest and welcoming home, which seemed to exhale warmth and stability. Gregory paused at the doorway, his hand resting on the frame as his shoulders sagged. He stepped inside, the door closing softly behind him, and for the first time since he had crossed the threshold into this strange world, he allowed himself to take a deep breath.

CHAPTER FOUR
REFUGE

In the warmth of Dr. Marcus Taylor's modest home, tucked away on a peaceful street not far from the University of Jupiter, Gregory felt a strange mixture of disorientation and relief. The golden afternoon light streamed through the windows, casting soft shadows over the worn floors and simple furnishings. It was a world far removed from the grandeur of the Vatican, yet its simplicity offered a sense of safety he had not felt since arriving in this unfamiliar version of Rome.

As they stepped inside, a woman emerged from the kitchen. Her hands, dusted with flour, stilled as she took in Gregory's appearance. She shot a questioning glance at her husband, her brow furrowed with concern, but Marcus gave her a gentle smile—the kind that spoke of quiet reassurance, even when answers were scarce.

"Maria, this is Mr. Gregory," Marcus said softly, placing a calming hand on her arm. "I found him at the university. He's… not from here. He needs to rest."

Gregory observed Maria, noting the flicker of uncertainty in her eyes as Marcus introduced him. There was a subtle wariness as her gaze swept over him, pausing on his clothes. The white robes, though clean, bore faint smudges of dust and creases from travel, their heavy layers draping over him like remnants of an era long past. The crimson sash belt, tied tightly at his waist, its edges frayed ever so slightly. Her eyes caught on the intricate gold stitching that bordered the hem—a detail that whispered of craftsmanship foreign to anything she'd seen.

The zucchetto perched atop his head seemed ceremonial, its pristine surface glowing faintly in the dim light. Finally, Maria's gaze fell to his feet, where polished red leather shoes peeked out from beneath the robes. It was as if every piece of his attire had been lifted from the pages of a forgotten history. Gregory felt her hesitation; her eyes lingered, searching for a sign, a clue that might explain this peculiar stranger—someone who, despite his dignified appearance, seemed profoundly out of place in the world she knew.

Gregory's heart beat a little faster. *Not from here*. How strange it sounded, yet how accurate. He was under examination; Maria's curiosity mingled with concern.

Finally, Maria nodded, her expression softening into a tentative smile. "Of course," she said, though her voice held a note of wariness. "You must be hungry. I'll prepare some food."

Gregory exhaled, his shoulders sagging as her words settled over him like a warm blanket on a cold night. His stomach growled faintly, the thought of food stirring a long-dormant hunger. For a moment, he stopped glancing over his shoulder, his grip on the frayed edges of his coat relaxing. Though still uncertain, the world felt less like it was slipping through his fingers and more like it had offered him a handhold, however temporary.

Gregory stood awkwardly, his robes pressing down on him. Everything about the scene was comforting and disorienting—a domestic warmth that made his heart ache with memories of when the world still made sense. As Marcus gestured for him to sit, he sank into the sofa's soft cushions, the house settling into a gentle quiet.

The crackle of a small fireplace and the scent of baking bread filled the air, and for a moment, Gregory closed his eyes, allowing himself to breathe. But the respite was short-lived as the light sound of footsteps approached. A young boy appeared in the doorway, peeking around the corner with wide, curious eyes. He couldn't have been more than seven or eight, his dark hair slightly tousled.

"This is my son, Joshua," Marcus said gently, a note of pride in his voice. "Joshua, say hello to Mr. Gregory."

"Why are you wearing those clothes?" he asked, his voice innocent and direct, a small finger pointing at the unfamiliar attire.

"These are my vestments," he replied quietly, though the words felt strangely empty. The explanation lingered in his throat, but he couldn't offer it—not here, not now.

With a gentle gesture, Marcus beckoned Gregory toward the kitchen, signaling with a quiet encouragement that eased the tension in the room. The soft clinking of dishes and the kitchen's warmth enveloped him, offering a solace he hadn't anticipated. The simplicity of the setting, so unlike the grandeur he had known, wrapped around him, grounding him in a moment of quiet acceptance.

Gregory eased himself into a chair at the small wooden table. Moments later, Maria placed a simple plate of bread, cheese, and fresh fruit before him. "I wasn't sure what you'd prefer," she said gently, a hint of caution in her tone.

Gregory looked down at the meal, its simplicity striking him deeply. This was no lavish feast, no ornate spread like those that graced the Vatican halls—just humble offerings presented with a warmth that pierced through his weary heart. He glanced up at Maria, his voice soft and unsteady. "Thank you," he murmured, meeting her eyes with a gratitude that words could scarcely convey.

For a time, the house settled into a gentle rhythm. Maria and Joshua moved about the kitchen, their soft murmurs providing a soothing backdrop as Gregory ate, his movements slow and deliberate. The food, plain and wholesome, felt like a blessing, each bite grounding him in a reality that still felt surreal.

Marcus watched Gregory from across the table, his expression thoughtful. "You seem so certain about where you came from," he said eventually, his tone quiet, almost cautious. "It's as if you've stepped out of another reality."

Gregory set down his fork, his hands trembling slightly. "Exactly," he said, his voice barely above a whisper. "I came from a world where Christ's teachings shaped everything—our laws, our morals, our culture. But now… it's all gone."

Marcus leaned forward, his brow furrowed. "And you believe it's gone for everyone, not just you?"

"Yes," Gregory said, his gaze dropping to the floor. "In this world, no one knows of Christ. It's like… like He was never born."

His words settled over the room, and for a moment, Marcus was silent, lost in thought. Then his eyes softened. "I can see this is real to you," he said gently. "But you are here now, in this world, and you must find a way to live in it."

Gregory swallowed. "I don't know if I can," he admitted. "Without the Church, without my faith… I don't know what's left."

There was a long silence. Marcus's expression remained gentle, but his eyes held a firmness, a determination to understand. "You don't need to figure everything out now," he said softly. "You're welcome to stay here as long as you need."

Gregory looked up sharply, caught off guard by the offer. His eyes searched Marcus's face, but he found no hint of mockery or deceit, only kindness. "Why would you do that?" he asked, his voice raw with disbelief. "You don't know me?"

Marcus's smile was soft, almost wistful. "Because sometimes we all need a place to belong. And right now, it seems like you're searching for something to hold on to."

Gregory's eyes burned with unshed tears, emotion swelling within him. In this strange, godless world, Marcus's kindness was like a lifeline—a fragile thread in the darkness. "Bless you," he said, his voice barely a whisper.

The evening passed in a quiet, companionable silence. Maria calmly moved through the dining room, glancing occasionally at Gregory as she cleared the dishes. Sensing the strange air tension, Joshua remained close to his mother, his young eyes flicking curiously between the adults.

As the fire crackled softly and the last light of day faded beyond the windows, Gregory allowed himself to sink back, exhaustion pulling him down like a lead weight. He was lost and adrift in a world that made no sense, but for the first time since stepping through the archway, he was not alone.

And that, he realized as his eyes fluttered shut, was a kind of solace he had not expected to find.

CHAPTER FIVE
UNIVERSITY OF JUPITER

Gregory awoke with a start, his heart racing as he emerged. For a fleeting moment, he clung to the hope that this craziness had been a nightmare—some strange, terrible dream conjured by an exhausted mind. But the room around him was not the opulent chamber of his Papal apartments. There were no tapestries rich with sacred symbols, no heavy velour curtains to shield him from the morning light, and no crucifix hung over the fireplace. Instead, simple linen drapes let the pale dawn seep through, illuminating a modest, unfamiliar space.

Reality crashed back in as he lay there, each memory sharpening with brutal clarity. The archway that had swallowed him and transformed the city, the sudden absence of everything he had once known, was real. The luxurious Pope's bed with its memory foam mattress was replaced by a firm, metal-frame cot. There were no sacred chalices, no ivory rosaries draped delicately across a velour-covered altar—only the quiet hum of an ordinary household stirring to life. The air held no trace of myrrh or lingering candle smoke, only the faint aroma of breakfast from the kitchen. He was far from the Vatican and the world where his faith had reigned supreme.

Gregory's breath caught in his throat, the cold, new reality settling heavily. There was no escaping it. Everything he had known was truly, irrevocably lost.

He sat up slowly, running a hand over the rough blanket, and listened. From downstairs came the gentle clatter of dishes and the alluring smell of toasted bread mingling with the rich aroma of coffee. Gathering his resolve, Gregory dressed in his robes, descended the wooden staircase, and found his way to the kitchen, where the mundane warmth of family life greeted him.

Maria was humming quietly as she moved around. Joshua sat at the table, spreading butter on his toast, and Marcus looked up with a welcoming smile. But there was an awkwardness in the air—a sense that they were all trying too hard to act as if nothing was out of the ordinary. Gregory was an intruder in this simple domestic scene, a relic of another time and place.

After breakfast, Marcus pushed his chair back, his gaze steady as he looked at his guest. "Gregory," he began, a note of gentle insistence in his voice, "perhaps a visit to the university would do you some good. It's the center of knowledge and philosophy—a place that might ground you, give you some sense of… context." He paused, choosing his words carefully.

"Maybe seeing it will remind you of your surroundings and, who knows, perhaps help you snap out of what you're experiencing." Marcus offered a small, encouraging smile.

Gregory looked up, a mixture of confusion and wariness in his eyes. Before he could speak, Maria interjected, her brow furrowed with concern. "The university? Marcus, are you sure that's wise? He's been through so much already. Maybe setting up an appointment with one of your psychologist friends would be better. He clearly needs help."

"I don't need a psychologist," Gregory barked back.

Maria's brow furrowed in concern as she glanced at Gregory, her worry deepening. "Maybe you hit your head recently?" she asked cautiously. "It could explain… everything you've been saying."

Gregory's eyes flashed, and he leaned forward, his voice sharp with frustration. "I did not hit my head!" he snapped, his tone laced with defensiveness. "I am not delusional!"

The intensity of his outburst startled Maria, and she stepped back. Marcus put a calming hand on Gregory's shoulder, his eyes filled with quiet reassurance. Gregory's anger faded almost as quickly as it had flared, leaving him raw and exposed.

But deep inside, a small seed of doubt began to grow. *What if I am losing my mind?* he considered. *What if everything I knew was just some figment, and this strange world is my only reality?*

Marcus's voice broke through his spiraling thoughts, gentle but firm. "Not to worry. We'll get to the bottom of this," he said. "One step at a time."

Gregory forced himself to nod, though the uncertainty gnawed at the edges of his mind, refusing to be silenced.

Maria's expression softened, though doubt still lingered in her eyes. "Fine," she agreed with a hesitant nod. "But at the very least, he should wear something more suitable. These robes…" she said, gesturing to Gregory's heavy ecclesiastical attire, "look out of place here."

Marcus gave a reassuring smile. "Of course. You're right. We'll find something in my closet," he agreed. Then he turned to Gregory. "What do you think?"

Gregory hesitated, glancing down at his Pontiff's attire. It was his last tangible link to the life he had left behind, but he understood the practicality of the suggestion. Reluctantly, he allowed Marcus to lead him upstairs, where he traded his flowing cassock for a simple tunic and trousers. The unfamiliar garments felt strange against his skin but were soft and practical. He glanced at his reflection in a small mirror, barely recognizing himself without the distinctive robes of his office.

"Ready?" Marcus asked, his tone gentle but firm.

Gregory nodded, feeling exposed and uncertain, yet he trailed behind Marcus, determined to face this bewildering reality. As they weaved through the bustling streets, Gregory's gaze roamed over the cityscape. What he saw stirred something deep within him—a mixture of awe and disbelief. The ruins he once knew as forgotten footnotes of history had been perfectly preserved, not as monuments to a republic but as functioning, integral parts of the city.

A bathhouse stood just ahead, its once-crumbling walls now smooth and polished, and its marble facade gleamed with intricate carvings. Steam rose from the building's rooftop chimneys, and Gregory caught the faint scent of herbs carried on the breeze, hinting at its use as a sanctuary for the city's elite.

Nearby, a sprawling marketplace bustled with energy. A structure Gregory vaguely remembered as an ancient granary, its roof half-collapsed in his world, now towered proudly over the square. The building hummed with activity, its soaring arches framing merchants trading goods, coins clinking as citizens bartered for silk, spices, and wine.

At the edge of the square, a smaller temple, previously an overlooked ruin, loomed with an understated dignity. Once forgotten in the shadow of grander structures, it had been transformed into a courthouse. Gregory noticed toga-clad figures ascending its broad steps, their serious expressions suggesting matters of justice within its halls.

Even the tenement buildings, which he recalled as uneven piles of brick and faded plaster, now stood proud and uniform. Their rows of terra-cotta roofs created neat lines across the skyline. Residents bustled in and out of the courtyards, their hurried movements underscoring the life these ancient buildings now supported.

Gregory faltered as the scope of what he was seeing settled upon him. It wasn't just the grandeur of the maintained architecture that struck him—it was the purpose these buildings now scrved. They weren't relics of a forgotten past; they were alive, embedded in the rhythms of daily life, and a testament to a civilization that had never crumbled.

Statues of the gods and heroes stood proudly on every corner, the expressions on their stone faces resolute and commanding. It was as if these figures weren't merely monuments but vigilant sentries, overseeing the city with an almost living presence. Gregory's gaze drifted further, half wondering if the Colosseum—likely in pristine condition along with everything else—might still serve its original purpose. The thought unsettled him. This was Rome, and yet it wasn't; it was something both ancient and strangely immediate, a vision of the past brought vividly into the present.

As they approached the university, Gregory's awe only deepened. The campus sprawled across several blocks, a labyrinth of grandiose buildings that merged the architectural spirit of ancient Rome with subtle modern elements. Massive stone columns rose proudly at the entrances, adorned with intricate carvings depicting mythological scenes and wisdom figures. Marble steps led up to towering doors crafted from polished wood, each handle glinting with the unmistakable touch of modern metalwork, melding the historical with the functional.

Students flowed through the courtyards and corridors, an eclectic blend of the past and present. They wore clothing that evoked the grace of classical Roman attire—tunics, robes, and cloaks that flowed with each step—yet woven from materials Gregory recognized as distinctly modern. Linen and wool were seamlessly mixed with fabrics like denim and jersey, creating a strange harmony of ancient silhouettes and contemporary comfort. Some students carried scrolls and leather-bound notebooks, while others held sleek, transparent tablets, their surfaces shimmering with digital text and symbols. It was as though the institution had not simply adapted to time but had molded time, creating a place where the ancient and the futuristic intertwined.

The air buzzed with animated discussions, the voices of students and professors filling the halls with debates that seemed familiar and foreign. Gregory caught snippets of conversations in Latin interspersed with modern Italian phrases and technical jargon. He felt as if he'd stepped into a world suspended between epochs, where philosophy, theology, and science were given equal weight, woven together in an intellectual tapestry that honored the mysteries of the cosmos.

Marcus led him down a broad hallway lined with statues of philosophers. Each had a tablet at its base displaying rotating holographic text—quotations from the ancient thinker's works illuminated for all who passed. Gregory paused, looking at a hologram beneath a statue of Marcus Aurelius: "You may not command the storms, but you can steady your heart. In this lies the greatest empire a man can rule—himself."

The words seemed to shimmer with timeless wisdom, resonating deeply in the corridor's silence.

Nearby, a tablet beneath a statue of Seneca flickered to life, displaying: "The measure of life is not counted in years or victories but in the seeds we plant in others. Goodness outlives the man who sows it."

Gregory felt the impact of the words settle within him as if the ancient philosopher was whispering a truth he had always known but never fully grasped.

Further down, the quote beneath Cicero's statue appeared: "The welfare of the people is the highest law." Gregory noted the juxtaposition of this ideal with the grandeur and ambition he had already seen in this alternate Rome. Was this wisdom a guide or a relic of a forgotten ethic?

It was a place where ideas were meant to be seen as living entities, evolving and expanding across time. Gregory felt a strange sense of reverence. These were not just monuments to the past but active dialogues, inviting reflection and challenging the viewer to consider how such wisdom could guide the present and shape the future. This was no ordinary institution; it was a temple of knowledge, a sanctuary where minds from across centuries gathered, conversing silently through stone, sculpture, and light.

"This is our main hall," Marcus explained as they climbed the steps. "Here, education is considered sacred—just as it should be."

Inside, Gregory's eyes widened at the sight of the vast interior, lined with towering columns and frescoes depicting the deeds of the gods. It was both a temple and a place of learning, a strange fusion of the sacred and the intellectual. The murals displayed scenes of Jupiter hurling thunderbolts, Venus rising from the sea, and Mars leading legions to victory—stories Gregory had known as the ancient myths. Still, here they were celebrated as the guiding truths of a modern society.

As they walked down the corridor, Marcus gestured toward an open doorway. Inside, a group of students leaned in over a table, voices animated as they dissected the ethics of Roman Stoicism. Gregory slowed, listening with intrigue.

A scholar with silver hair, a figure of authority, spoke passionately. "Virtus, pietas, dignitas, gravitas—these are our virtues," he declared, his voice steady. "Living in harmony with nature, fulfilling our duty to family and the gods, and embracing fate is the Stoic way."

Gregory's brow furrowed, torn between fascination and confusion. The teachings felt distant and oddly familiar, resonating in a way he couldn't fully understand. He whispered to Marcus, "If there's no Divine salvation, what becomes of you when you die? Where does your soul go?"

Marcus's gaze softened, his voice calm but carrying the weight of his beliefs. "For those who live with honor, courage, and adherence to virtue, there is Elysium. It is a paradise of endless peace and beauty, where the soul finds rest among heroes and sages. It is a place of harmony reserved for those whose lives were guided by wisdom, justice, and the gods' favor. There, the spirit thrives in a state of eternal fulfillment, basking in the fruits of a virtuous life.

"But not all spirits find their way to Elysium. For others—those who neglect virtue, forsake honor, or defy the natural order—there are the Inferi, the shadowy depths where the unworthy confront the consequences of their misdeeds. This underworld is not merely a punishment but a realm of reckoning, where the soul must acknowledge its failings and the harm it caused in life. Here, souls wander, awaiting the judgment of the gods.

"Yet our beliefs go beyond these destinations. To us, the afterlife is not just about the soul's destination but the legacy left behind. Living a life of significance ensures the soul endures through memory and the impact of one's deeds. Guided by virtue, we seek not only to gain the favor of the gods but to weave ourselves into the fabric of our family, community, and Rome itself for as long as the world stands."

Marcus's voice grew quieter, almost reverent, as he continued. "It is not enough to simply live; one must live in a way worth remembering. To honor the gods and embrace virtue is to ensure that the soul carries the light of one's life into the next realm, where it becomes part of a grander story—woven into eternity."

Gregory exhaled softly, his mind swimming with the vastness of the Roman belief system. He glanced at Marcus, feeling a strange mixture of wonder and longing for the clarity of purpose embedded in such convictions. "It's… a beautiful way to see existence," he admitted, his voice tinged with both admiration and melancholy. "To think that every act, every choice, could ripple so far beyond this life—it's humbling."

Marcus leaned back slightly, his gaze steady as he considered Gregory's words. "Yes, but it's more than that," he replied, his tone measured and thoughtful. "It's about accepting the impermanence of life and finding strength in what we leave behind. Honor isn't just for the self; it's a gift to those who come after us. Memory ties us together, across time, like a thread that cannot be broken."

Gregory absorbed the words, feeling as if the walls around him echoed the Stoic ideals he struggled to understand. "So… it's about honor and memory, not forgiveness or redemption?"

"Redemption?" Marcus said with a grimace. "Our pursuit is a life worthy of remembrance. That is our highest calling, not redemption."

The answer left Gregory silent as he followed Marcus through the halls. They entered a grand lecture hall where a professor offered a perspective on Roman history.

Gregory's eyes narrowed as the professor described Rome's far-reaching power—legions marching to conquer distant lands, grand temples rising in foreign cities, and forums establishing the pulse of Roman life across continents. He spoke of Roman culture's remarkable ability to assimilate and reshape itself, absorbing the traditions of those it subjugated while leaving its own indelible mark.

Gregory's expression tightened as he listened and glanced at Marcus with a sense of urgency. "Am I to understand there were no Dark Ages?" he asked, his tone edged with incredulity.

Marcus frowned, clearly puzzled. "Dark Ages? I've not heard that term before. What does this mean?"

Gregory's eyes widened, a heaviness settling over him as he tried to explain a time he never thought he would have to justify. "It lasted about five centuries, beginning with the fall of Rome," he began slowly.

Marcus's face shifted, eyes widening in shock. "The fall of Rome?" he interrupted as though Gregory had just spoken a blasphemy. "Rome never fell, Gregory. Our empire has stood firm, evolving and growing over two millennia. We may have faced challenges, but we endured. You're telling me that in your world, Rome—collapsed?"

"Yes," Gregory replied. "In my world, the Roman Empire fell in the fifth century. The power vacuum left in its wake was filled by the Church, which rose to absolute authority over Europe." He paused, struggling to put into words the enormity of the transformation. "This era became known as the Dark Ages because scientific progress, the exploration of new ideas, and discoveries were suppressed—often sacrificed to protect and preserve the Church's dominance. Learning became more guarded, and libraries fell into disrepair. Knowledge that didn't align with the Church's teachings was cast aside, sometimes brutally."

Marcus shook his head, disbelief shadowing his expression. "Collapsed," he murmured. "Rome never experienced such a fate. Even during the chaos of Caligula's reign, when the empire nearly crumbled beneath his madness, Rome stood resilient. Brave men fought to resurrect the Senate and restore balance to our republic before it could fully spiral into ruin."

Gregory leaned forward, sensing Marcus's pride in his empire's ability to endure. "In my world, it was not an emperor but time that brought Rome down. The strains of internal corruption, invasions, and division broke it apart piece by piece. But your Rome…" he paused, his voice filled with awe and curiosity, "your Rome found a way to survive, to evolve into something unbroken."

Marcus met Gregory's gaze, his tone softening but remaining firm. "Our survival was the will of those who refused to see the empire fall. Men who saved Rome were more than its rulers. It was its people, ideas, and unyielding desire to endure." He paused, his eyes narrowing slightly. "And that endurance shaped everything that came after."

Gregory exhaled, a flicker of understanding passing between them. This Rome had stood not just because of power or fortune but because of the determination of its people—a testament to a legacy neither man could fully grasp, but that defined the worlds they called home.

Gregory met Marcus's gaze, the sincerity of the question compelling him to respond thoughtfully. "In my world, the Church rose to prominence in a time of chaos, when the fall of Rome left people searching for order, for meaning. The Church became the answer for many, a beacon of stability in a fractured world."

He paused, his tone growing heavier. "But with that power came fear—fear that unbridled and unchecked knowledge might challenge that authority's foundation. Ideas questioning doctrine and offering alternative paths to understanding the Divine were seen as threats. The Church wasn't suppressing knowledge for its own sake—it was protecting a version of truth it believed was sacred, though the cost was immeasurable."

Gregory glanced at the statue of a Stoic philosopher nearby, its features etched with wisdom. "In suppressing certain ideas, they hoped to preserve unity, but in doing so, they silenced voices that could have propelled humanity forward. Libraries burned, scholars persecuted, and fear replaced curiosity. What you describe here—the encouragement of wisdom, the celebration of truth—is what we lost in that time."

Marcus listened intently, his brow furrowing as he absorbed Gregory's words. "So the suppression of knowledge wasn't out of malice but out of fear of losing control?"

"Yes," Gregory said softly. "Fear can be a powerful force, Marcus—blinding even noble intentions."

Gregory's gaze dropped, his fingers curling around the cross hidden beneath his tunic. He felt a pang of guilt, a sense of responsibility for the legacy of an institution he had once served so loyally. "Because with knowledge comes power," he said softly. "And power… is never shared freely. At that time, the Church feared that too much understanding and questioning would unravel the very foundations upon which it stood. So they kept a tight grip on what people could know and explore."

Silence settled between them for a moment, a chasm created by the weight of two worlds and the choices that shaped them.

The professor continued his lecture, unaware of the whispered conversation at the back of the hall. Gregory felt a wave of grief for the lost centuries in his world—centuries that had never been dimmed in this reality, untouched by the shadow of the Church's influence.

Gregory's breath caught at the image the professor painted—an empire that had endured, untouched by the collapse that deeply defined his knowledge of history. There was no mention of Christ or the Church; the Roman gods had remained the unchallenged guides of human destiny.

They moved on to a smaller classroom, where a lesson on astronomy was in progress. The walls were lined with star charts, and at the front of the room stood a man in flowing white robes with intricate purple and gold borders. A laurel wreath encircled his head, and rings depicting various gods glinted on his fingers as he gestured to the constellations.

Gregory's eyes were drawn to the priest's commanding presence. His voice was steady and authoritative as he explained the influence of the planets on human affairs. "The stars," he said, "are the manifestations of the gods' will. Their movements are not random but messages, offering favor or warning to those who know how to read them."

Marcus leaned close to Gregory, his voice barely above a whisper. "That's an Augur—a Roman priest. The laurel wreath and the robe mark him out. Augers are skilled in interpreting omens from the heavens."

"Omens?" Gregory repeated. This was a world where faith, reason, religion, and science had merged in ways he could hardly fathom. And yet, despite himself, he was intrigued.

They ended the tour at a large auditorium where Marcus was scheduled to lecture. He invited Gregory to sit at the back, and the former Pope watched with a mixture of awe and discomfort as Marcus spoke to eager students about the role of civic duty and virtue in their society.

"There is no greater calling than to serve the government and honor the gods," Marcus proclaimed, his voice carrying a quiet intensity. "Our strength comes from our shared dedication to the mos maiorum—the customs of our ancestors. These traditions, not a single doctrine, bind us together. We are guided by duty, reverence for the Divine order, and the values that have shaped our people."

The students leaned in, captivated, and Gregory felt a pang of envy. There was a unity here, a conviction that felt foreign yet compelling. He felt both drawn in and adrift in this world, where humanity's purpose was to serve the state rather than the salvation of one's soul.

Marcus continued, unwavering. "For Romans, life is about leaving behind a legacy worthy of memory. The gods do not save us but guide us. When we pass on, our deeds live on, held in the hearts of those that survive us."

A student raised his hand, eager. "So, master, our lives belong to Rome and to the gods?"

Marcus nodded. "Yes, our lives are not solely our own. We are bound to each other and to our duty. Virtue is about honor, resilience, and the commitment to the common good."

Gregory listened, feeling both admiration and resistance. He had entered a world shaped by ancient resolve, where the gods watched over lives lived with honor, not as saviors but as silent witnesses.

As the lecture concluded, Marcus found Gregory, his expression conflicted. "What did you think?" he asked gently, eyes searching Gregory's face for some sign of understanding.

Gregory took a deep breath. "I don't know," he admitted. "I understand the wisdom you teach and the strength in your traditions. But it is not my faith—it is not the truth I know."

"I understand," Marcus said softly. "But perhaps it is a truth worth considering, even if only to understand the world you now find yourself in."

Gregory nodded slowly as Marcus's words settled over him like a shroud. He was lost, searching for answers, but something here spoke to him, even if it was in a language he could not fully understand. For now, it would have to be enough.

CHAPTER SIX
THE PSYCHOLOGIST

Marcus glanced at Gregory over breakfast, noting the silent intensity in his guest's eyes. "I think it might help for you to speak to someone about all this," he said gently. "You've been through… something extraordinary. Maybe a professional could help you process."

Gregory hesitated, his mind whirring with the implications. In his world, priests offered guidance, not psychologists. Yet, a conversation with someone trained to understand the mind could provide some grounding amidst his disorientation. "Very well," he replied, uncertain but willing.

Later, as they entered the office of Dr. Elena Marcellus, a psychologist who specialized in existential crises and philosophical therapy, Gregory felt a strange mix of relief and anxiety. Dr. Marcellus, a woman with a calm demeanor and piercingly observant eyes, greeted them warmly.

"Marcus has told me you're going through a… shift in perspective," she said, gesturing for Gregory to sit across from her. "I'm here to listen, Gregory, to understand what you're experiencing."

Gregory settled into his chair, and after a moment of silence, he spoke, his voice filled with a reverent sorrow. "I don't know how to convey what Christianity means—what it means to be part of something greater than oneself. I am… was… Pope Gregory. A religious leader, a shepherd to the faithful. I led people in a belief that extends beyond life's fleeting joys and sorrows—a promise that, through Christ, there is salvation, forgiveness, and eternal life. In our faith, God became man, sacrificing himself for humanity. We are redeemed, cleansed of sin, and given hope of life everlasting."

He paused, studying Dr. Marcellus's expression, searching for disbelief or dismissal, but her gaze remained steady, welcoming him to continue.

"This faith is everything to me," he continued. "It shapes not only how we live but how we love, forgive, and endure hardship. The conviction that each soul matters and that no one, regardless of sin, is beyond redemption is at the heart of it all. In Christ, we find both mercy and strength. And yet, here I am, in a world where He never walked, where His sacrifice is unknown. The Vatican, my basilica, the Church itself… all has vanished. I am a stranger in a world devoid of the hope that once filled me."

He took a breath, his voice trembling. "How can I carry on in a place where the light of my faith has been extinguished?"

Dr. Marcellus leaned forward slightly, intrigued. "You believe you've traveled to a world without this…" she asked, pausing to look at her notes. "Christianity?"

"Yes," he replied, a flicker of desperation in his eyes. "It's more than belief; it's my reality. But now I am in a world where Christ was never born, where Rome still stands proud, with temples to gods I once thought were relics. It's… unthinkable." He ran a hand through his hair, his voice trembling. "How do I exist in a world that has erased my life's work?"

Dr. Marcellus paused thoughtfully. "Tell me more about your role as Pope. What did it mean to you to lead?"

Gregory's gaze softened, memories filling his eyes. "It meant everything. It was a calling. I led believing that I was shepherding souls, offering them salvation. Now… now I am told salvation doesn't exist here. You speak of honor, legacy, and duty to Rome and the gods, but… there is no forgiveness, no redemption."

She nodded, absorbing his words. "Perhaps this absence of salvation challenges you because it asks something different of you—a way to find meaning without that certainty. Have you found anything here that resonates with you?"

Gregory thought of his conversations with Marcus and the Stoic philosophies he had begun to explore. "There is… something," he admitted slowly. "Marcus speaks of living with virtue, of pursuing honor not for Divine reward, but because it strengthens the soul. It's difficult to accept, yet I can acknowledge that there's a purity—a power."

Dr. Marcellus leaned back, carefully choosing her words. "Maybe this world offers you a chance to explore a different path, Gregory. You might discover that meaning doesn't need salvation as you once believed. It could lie in the life you create here and the values you uphold."

Gregory's brow furrowed as he turned over Dr. Marcellus's words, a question forming in his mind, pressing at the edges of his consciousness. He glanced up at her, hesitant but curious. "But… what happens when someone here sins? How do they bear the burden of their wrongdoings without the path to forgiveness and redemption? Without the promise of absolution, how do they move forward?"

Dr. Marcellus tilted her head, her expression thoughtful. "Perhaps in this world, Gregory, the concept of sin doesn't hold the same weight as yours. People make mistakes and are punished for them, but redemption comes through actions and the effort to live with integrity and honor afterward. We believe one's worth is shown in how they handle their errors—whether they seek to restore balance and honor or let their transgressions define them."

Gregory felt a pang of unease but also a spark of curiosity. "So there is no confessional? No chance to kneel, to unburden one's soul to a priest, to be granted forgiveness?"

Dr. Marcellus shook her head gently. "Responsibility rests within the individual. If possible, they must reconcile with those they've wronged and with themselves. The Stoics believe that virtue is found in discipline, resilience, and self-awareness. No Divine hand is waiting to wipe away the misdeed—only the person, left to reflect, grows and makes amends through their subsequent actions."

Gregory let the words sink in. Without the promise of Divine mercy, the path seemed harsher and lonelier. Yet he couldn't deny the strength within it—the belief that one must carry one's burdens, that redemption was not a gift freely given but something one had to carve out through daily actions, through living in harmony with a personal code of honor.

"It's… difficult to grasp," he murmured, the concept both foreign and challenging. "But I can see a power in it, a resilience. It asks more of the congregant, doesn't it?"

Dr. Marcellus nodded, her gaze steady. "I suppose it does. And perhaps that is what makes their sense of morality unshakable—there is no external forgiveness, no shortcut to grace. Only the choices they make and the legacies they leave behind."

Gregory felt pangs of hope and sorrow. He had come here hoping someone would help him find a way back to his world, but her words suggested a different journey that demanded a painful transformation. "So, you're saying… I must let go of my old beliefs?"

"Not necessarily," she replied gently. "But perhaps open yourself to the possibility that they may evolve. Transformation doesn't mean abandonment; it means growth."

Dr. Marcellus paused, a flicker of concern crossing her face. "Gregory, you mentioned that you feel you've… crossed into another reality. In our field, sometimes disorientation can signal deeper conflicts within the mind—a disconnection from reality. Hypnosis could help us explore whether something internal or unresolved is keeping you… blocked."

Gregory frowned, wary yet intrigued. "You think I'm imagining this?"

Dr. Marcellus met his gaze with calm reassurance. "I'm not dismissing your experience. But exploring your mind further could reveal truths you may not yet understand. Hypnosis might help uncover the root of this experience—whether it's a way to heal or a path to accepting this new reality."

After a brief pause, Gregory nodded, agreeing to try. Dr. Marcellus moved her chair closer, her voice soft and calming. She instructed him to lie on the nearby chaise, close his eyes, and breathe deeply. "Focus on each breath, letting it carry you to a place of calm," she murmured, guiding him slowly into relaxation. "Let go of the present with each breath, allowing yourself to drift back in time."

Under Dr. Marcellus's guidance, Gregory's breathing slowed, each word drawing him deeper into his memory. "You're back in the Vatican," she murmured, her tone as steady as his heartbeat. "Feel the marble beneath your feet, the vastness of the space around you. Picture yourself walking through those hallowed halls, a place you know so well."

As Gregory sank into the trance, the sensory details flooded in like the pages of a familiar book, each line vivid and charged with emotion. He imagined the cool stone under his feet, the echo of his footsteps reverberating softly against the towering columns. He felt the warmth of candlelight on his face and smelled the faint scent of incense clinging to his robes.

"Where are you now, Pope Gregory?" Dr. Marcellus prompted, her voice gently guiding him.

Gregory's brow relaxed as his surroundings crystallized in his mind. "I'm standing on the balcony… overlooking St. Peter's Square," he whispered. He could see it clearly now—the vast sea of people stretching out before him, their faces upturned in reverent anticipation, candles flickering like stars in the early evening light.

In his vision, he raised his arms, clad in the rich vestments of the papacy. The golden cross around his neck caught the morning light as he recited the Christmas blessing. His steady and full voice resonated across the square, giving each listener a powerful wave of shared faith. As he spoke, he felt a profound connection with the people, a unifying energy that transcended words, binding him to each person gathered below.

Dr. Marcellus's voice brought him further inward, urging him to describe his emotions. "How do you feel, Pope Gregory?"

"Purposeful," he replied, his voice thick with feeling. "I feel… a duty that transcends my own life. Standing there, I am not just a man but a vessel, a shepherd guiding my flock. They look to me with hope, trusting me to keep their faith alive in a turbulent world."

He could almost feel the weight of the papal ring he had left behind—a solemn reminder of the authority and duty once entrusted to him. It was a strange absence, a symbol of his position and purpose now lost, left behind in a world no longer reachable. And yet, standing here in memory, the crowd before him seemed as real as the devotion in their eyes, their collective faith filling the void left by the ring's absence. In that moment, he felt bound to them still, lifting his hand in blessing, drawing strength from their adoration, even across the divide of worlds.

As he stood on the balcony, overlooking the immense crowd gathered in St. Peter's Square, the resounding chimes of the basilica's bells echoed behind him, resonating with centuries of tradition. The people below raised their faces in adoration, their eyes fixed on him with trust and devotion. In that moment, he felt their faith flow toward him, an unbroken bond that united them all in purpose and reverence. His heart swelled, and he lifted his hand in blessing, the air heavy with their shared hope.

Dr. Marcellus's steady voice kept him grounded as the sorrow poured out. "And now, Pope Gregory, how does it feel to remember this?"

He exhaled, a tremor in his voice. "It feels like a loss… a wound that still bleeds. Yet, even in that loss, I sense there might be a reason I was brought here, something I have yet to understand."

She encouraged him to linger in the silence, letting the memories settle. After a pause, she guided him back, her voice gently anchoring him to the present. "With each breath, feel yourself returning. Let the past recede as you come back to this moment."

Gregory's eyes fluttered open. The memory lingered in his chest like an ache, a bittersweet reminder of what he once was and what he might still be called to do. He lay there momentarily, absorbing the depth of his journey into memory.

Dr. Marcellus observed him, her professional calm betrayed by a glimmer of fascination. "Gregory, everything you described during the session—every vivid detail—aligns with an unwavering belief within you. There's no indication of delusion, nothing that suggests your mind is playing tricks. Scientifically, I can't make sense of it, but your conviction… it's extraordinary."

Gregory exhaled. "So, I'm… sane, then?"

She nodded, though uncertainty lingered in her expression. "You're as sane as any person I've ever worked with. But that doesn't mean what you remember can exist as you believe. Still, your mind holds onto it as though it were absolute truth."

They sat in quiet, profound understanding, with Gregory feeling validated yet more lost than ever and Dr. Marcellus wrestling with the limits of her knowledge as if trying to bridge a gap between two worlds neither could fully see.

CHAPTER SEVEN
THE HIDDEN SHRINE

Days after the session, Gregory drifted through his usual wanderings in the city, still grappling with the strange truths he uncovered about himself. One afternoon, his steps carried him to the edge of the city's bustling center, and he found himself amidst a secluded grove of ancient oaks. Nestled within was a small, hidden shrine untouched by time or modern reverence. A stillness hung over the place, reminding him of the sanctity of sacred spaces he once knew, an echo of a world that was out of reach.

This shrine was humble, unlike the imposing temples devoted to gods of power and glory. It was dedicated to Vesta, goddess of the hearth and home, a deity revered for her quiet strength rather than grand displays. Simple offerings—bundles of herbs, clay oil lamps, and hand-carved stones—lay upon the altar, evidence of quiet devotion rather than lavish ritual.

Gregory felt something stir deep within. The simplicity and sanctity of the grove resonated with a whisper of the holiness he once knew. He approached the shrine tentatively, recognizing it as a vessel where people reached beyond themselves, hoping to touch the Divine. Kneeling before it, he hesitated, then allowed his head to bow, feeling the loss and isolation pressing him down.

His prayer rose, but not to Vesta nor any Roman deity. Instead, he reached out to the God he'd long served, the one who now seemed so distant. "If you are there," he murmured, "if you can hear me, show me how to make peace with this world. Guide me, even here, where I feel so far from you."

He paused, the silence around him heavy yet sacred. His voice grew firmer, though it trembled with vulnerability. "I ask for the strength to carry out your will. If there is a purpose in this exile, reveal it to me. Let me be its instrument if there is a way to bridge the chasm between this world and the truth I have known."

Tears welled in his eyes as he clasped his hands tighter, his words spilling out in desperation. "And if I have been sent here to learn, then teach me. Teach me how to bring light where there is darkness, to sow unity where there is division, and to carry hope even when I feel abandoned."

The air hummed momentarily with an unspoken response, but Gregory could not tell if it came from within or some higher realm. He bowed lower, his heart a mix of longing and resolve, and whispered, "Thy will be done, even here."

In the silence that followed, Gregory felt a surprising calm settle over him. Though his God remained silent, the act of prayer—of reaching out—left him with a faint sense of connection, as if the sacred, though unseen, could transcend even this strange new reality. He felt a glimmer of hope that the Divine was not gone, merely hidden, waiting to be found.

When he rose, Gregory felt transformed, a shift settling within him. The boundaries between his lost faith and this new world began to blur, and he wondered if, perhaps, the sanctity to which he had once devoted himself was not as distant as he had feared. He left the grove feeling lighter, as though, in that quiet place, he had glimpsed a bridge between his old world and this one.

As Gregory walked away from the grove, a sense of calm washed over him, a comfort he had not felt in this strange world. Yet beneath this tranquility simmered a fire of guilt, a gnawing sensation that he was drifting from the path he once knew. He had tasted something sacred here, but it felt foreign, like he was letting go of the faith that once defined him. His visit to the shrine brought peace and confusion as if his soul were searching for roots in unfamiliar soil, making him feel lighter and more lost.

In the following days, Gregory's longing for his papal vestments intensified, stirring a deep need for reassurance. Before Marcus or Maria had awoken early one morning, he quietly rummaged through his belongings, uncovering the familiar garments. A sense of relief flooded him as he draped them over his shoulders. The fabric, weighted with years of tradition, brought a calm that grounded him, soothing the guilt that had simmered beneath the surface. Clad in the robes of his past life, he felt renewed, yet his resolve remained tinged with a quiet confusion.

With his robes billowing behind him, he returned to the shrine of Vesta, an odd mixture of reverence and defiance in his step. The sacred grove, with its flickering candles and silent offerings, had become a place of strange comfort, yet he was caught between two worlds standing there now, dressed in his papal vestments. As he knelt, honoring the recently adopted rituals, they seemed to take on a new understanding—a strange merging of his past beliefs with the reverence of this unfamiliar faith.

Without warning, a priest approached, his simple robes whispering against the earth. With a flicker of admiration and curiosity, his gaze fell on Gregory. His eyes trailed over the rich fabrics of his attire, noting the intricate details that hinted at a status uncommon in this world.

"Those are remarkable garments, my brother," the priest observed quietly, a note of wonder in his voice. "Not something I've seen before in our circles. Who, I wonder, would wear such a thing?"

Gregory hesitated, feeling the shadow of his past pressing against his tongue. "They… once held great meaning for me," he replied.

The priest nodded thoughtfully, his gaze softening with understanding as he studied Gregory's expression. "Ah," he murmured, "sometimes, what we wear carries the stories of who we once were— symbols woven with purpose and devotion." He paused, glancing at Gregory's attire with curiosity and respect. "And yet, here you are, carrying that meaning with you, even in a place far removed from where it was born. Perhaps it is not the garment alone that holds significance, but the heart of the one who wears it."

Gregory remained silent, his gaze drifting toward the altar dedicated to Vesta. The shrine's foreign, yet oddly comforting, presence stirred something deep within him. Its simplicity, its quiet devotion, reminded him of the sacred spaces he once cherished—places of prayer, reflection, and connection to the Divine. He felt a pang of longing for the world he had left behind, where his purpose had been clear.

The priest stood before him, his expression open and unassuming, his demeanor marked by a calm patience that invited trust. Gregory hesitated, wrestling with the depth of his story. Could this man—a servant of gods so different from his own—understand the magnitude of what he carried? And yet, there was something familiar in the priest's eyes: a shared sense of devotion to something greater than oneself.

Taking a steadying breath, Gregory made his choice. "I come from another world," he said softly, his voice steady but laden with emotion. He paused, watching the priest's reaction, searching for a sign of skepticism or disbelief. Instead, he found only quiet curiosity, a patient interest that urged him to continue.

Encouraged, Gregory pressed on, choosing his words with care. "A place where Christ and the Church guide the lives of millions. My faith… it was everything. I served as Pope, shepherding the faithful, dedicating my life to a God who shaped our world with His love and sacrifice."

The priest tilted his head slightly, his expression curious but not dismissive. "Christ?" he asked, the unfamiliar name rolling off his tongue. "Who is this… Christ, you speak of?"

Gregory hesitated, struck by the stark reality of his situation. To the priest, the name held no meaning—a thought that sent a ripple of sorrow through him. He steadied himself, meeting the man's gaze. "Christ is the Son of God, a teacher, a healer, the savior who gave His life so that humanity could know love, forgiveness, and grace," he explained, his voice tinged with reverence and melancholy. "He is the cornerstone of the faith I dedicated my life to."

The priest listened intently, his expression a mixture of intrigue and uncertainty. Gregory continued, his voice growing softer. "And now, I find myself here, where that faith has no name, no presence. I feel lost, adrift in a sea of beliefs and customs I do not know. But I still hold to the hope that there is purpose in my being here."

The priest nodded slowly. "You speak of things I do not understand," he said thoughtfully, "but I see they are sacred to you. Perhaps your journey here holds meaning you have yet to uncover."

Gregory felt relief, a small but vital confirmation that he had not been dismissed outright. He had taken a leap of faith, trusting this man who, like him, had devoted his purpose to serving something greater than himself.

Gregory looked off into the distance. "About a week ago, I encountered a glowing archway in the depths of the Vatican's hidden archives. Attracted by something I couldn't explain, I stepped through… and everything I knew disappeared when I emerged. My Church, my purpose… everything."

His voice softened, tinged with grief. "I am adrift here in a world where all I once held sacred has ceased to exist." He looked back at the priest, searching for understanding, hoping that even a glimmer of his predicament would be met with compassion.

The priest's brows furrowed though his gaze held only compassion and curiosity. "You're saying that this world is not your own?"

Gregory nodded, a hint of sorrow in his eyes. "Yes. Here, I am a stranger, adrift without the Church, without Christ—without the foundation of my life."

The priest remained silent, absorbing Gregory's words with quiet thoughtfulness. He adjusted the folds of his robe, his eyes narrowing slightly as he searched for understanding. "To be severed from one's world and beliefs… is no small wound. But perhaps you were brought here to find new truths or to see your faith through a different lens."

The priest studied Gregory, his gaze both curious and sympathetic. "And what is it you seek, then? Do you hope to return to your world, or is there something you are meant to learn here?"

Gregory sighed, looking up at the sky as if searching for answers. "I don't know. Part of me wishes to return, to find my place again. But perhaps… perhaps there's a reason I am here, in a place where faith takes such a different form. Maybe this is a test or an opportunity to see my beliefs through, as you say, a different lens. All I know is that I am lost—without my world or purpose."

The priest smiled. "Then perhaps, as we honor our gods, you may find a new path to your faith here. Faith, after all, is not just a place— it's a journey."

Gregory nodded, choosing his words carefully. "In my world, Christ is believed to be both God and man. He sacrificed Himself to redeem humanity, cleanse us of sin, and promise life beyond death. The Church I once led is the guiding hand toward this eternal life. Through Him, we find hope, forgiveness, and an end to suffering."

The priest considered this, his brows knitting in thought. "Our gods do not offer such a promise. They are powerful, but their concerns lie in guiding us through this life—war, love, the harvest. And we honor them for this guidance. But to promise forgiveness and eternal life? That is a burden they do not carry; hence, we do not offer."

Gregory felt a pang of longing as he spoke. "For us, Christ's love is boundless. Through faith in Him, we believe that our souls are lifted and we are loved despite our flaws. In the Church, we offer sacraments—rituals that bring people closer to this grace."

The priest's eyes softened, a flicker of understanding crossing his face. "It seems your faith provides comfort that ours does not. To be forgiven and redeemed… speaks to a deep human need."

Their conversation stretched on, with Gregory describing the role of the Church, the sacraments, and Christ's compassion. The priest listened intently, fascinated by this unfamiliar faith rooted in worship, love, and salvation. They began to see the delicate threads connecting their beliefs through their exchange, each reflecting humanity's search for meaning through vastly different paths.

As Gregory and the priest continued their conversation, they left the tranquil atmosphere of the shrine and began walking along the winding path toward the heart of the city. The priest's dignified yet unhurried steps led them past towering columns and statues that watched silently over their exchange. Gregory noticed the priest's quiet reverence, an almost sacred appreciation for the city and its architecture. As they approached the temple's grand entrance, he felt the echo of history in the stone underfoot, resonating with his memories of holy places.

The priest stopped beneath the towering figure of Jupiter, his eyes softening with curiosity. "My name is Lucius," he offered, extending a hand with a warmth that transcended their cultural divide. "And yours?"

"Gregory," he replied, clasping Lucius's hand. There was a moment of mutual respect, an understanding that they both walked paths devoted to guiding others, though in vastly different ways.

Lucius inclined his head, gesturing for Gregory to follow him further into the temple. "Tell me, Gregory, of your Christ. Who is he to you? Perhaps we may uncover truths that transcend our worlds in understanding each other's beliefs."

Seated in the shadow of Jupiter's statue, Gregory felt an unusual freedom to speak. As he began describing Christ—the Son of God, the Redeemer, the embodiment of mercy and sacrifice—he noticed Lucius listening intently, his expression contemplative. They spoke for hours, a conversation bridging worlds and beliefs, and both men found echoes of Divinity in each other's devotion.

CHAPTER EIGHT
A NEW PATH

As Gregory entered the temple, his breath caught. Vast columns soared upward, vanishing into shadowed arches, while the scent of frankincense clung to the cool air, mingling with a hint of aged stone. The flickering glow of candles cast dancing patterns along the marble floor, and each step echoed, a reverent hush filling the space around him. Memories stirred beneath the surface of his mind, each flicker of flame, each chanted whisper tugging at a place he'd almost forgotten, evoking the sacred halls of his other life. His pulse quickened, and he felt humbled and strangely at home as though he were walking through a memory brought vividly to life.

The high ceilings echoed with the soft murmur of prayers, and marble statues of gods loomed in every nook, each meticulously carved and full of reverence. The temple exuded an ancient grandeur, vibrant and full of life, unlike the solemnity of the Vatican. Gregory's eyes traced the delicate mosaics depicting myths and rituals, stories of valor and devotion, while Lucius guided him with a quiet reverence.

As they moved deeper into the temple, Lucius paused to let Gregory absorb the splendor, sensing his unspoken comparisons. "Each statue, each offering here, tells a story," Lucius said, his voice filled with quiet pride. "In honoring our gods, we keep our ancestors' values alive, connecting our past to our present."

As they walked through the temple's marble halls, Lucius glanced at Gregory, sensing the depth of his journey. "Tell me, Gregory, do you have somewhere to stay?"

Gregory nodded, describing the professor and his family. "They've shown me unexpected kindness, sheltering me since I… appeared here," he explained, the gratitude evident in his tone.

Lucius paused thoughtfully, then said, "I'm glad you've found warmth among us. But if you wish to immerse yourself fully, to seek answers and understanding, there is a place for you here, within the temple." He gestured around, the glow of torches casting gentle shadows on statues of the gods. "Stay with us. Let us learn together."

Lucius's offer hung in the air, the sincerity in his voice catching Gregory off guard. He hesitated, then turned to the young priest with a questioning look.

"Lucius," Gregory began, his tone cautious yet curious, "why do you believe me? Everyone else I've encountered here has looked at me as if I were mad—an old man raving about impossible worlds. But you… You've shown me grace and kindness, and now you invite me to stay. Why?"

Lucius stopped walking, his gaze steady as he studied Gregory's face. After a moment, he replied, his voice calm but filled with conviction. "You speak with a conviction that cannot be feigned. Your words and demeanor carry the force of truth, even if that truth seems impossible. And perhaps…" He paused, glancing at the statues that lined the hall as if drawing strength from them. "Perhaps it is the gods who have brought you here, Gregory. We are taught to listen and to look for signs beyond what the eyes can see. Something about you feels… significant, as though your journey is tied to something greater than can yet be comprehended."

Gregory's expression softened, and he exhaled slowly, the tension in his shoulders easing. "It's humbling," he said quietly. "To have someone see me as more than a lost soul."

Lucius offered a small smile. "Lost souls are often the ones who find the most important truths. Perhaps your arrival is no accident, Gregory. Perhaps you have something to teach us—just as we may teach you." He gestured down the hall once more. "Come. If you are willing, let's discover it together."

As Gregory looked up at Lucius, his voice softened, unexpectedly thick with emotion. "I would be honored," he managed, each word tinged with a vulnerability that surprised him. A warmth stirred within, unfamiliar yet grounding, as if he were grasping the faint outline of belonging. For a fleeting moment, the towering figures of ancient gods around them seemed less imposing, and Gregory's heart settled. This invitation was more than acceptance; it was an opportunity—a bridge to understanding and, perhaps, peace in this foreign world.

***

The next day, Gregory explained his decision to Marcus. Marcus's eyes softened with understanding. "It seems the path you're on is leading you deeper into this world," he replied, his voice filled with warmth. "I'm glad you've found a place where you can explore the mysteries of life more fully." Gregory was touched by Marcus's unwavering support and thanked him for his kindness and for being his first guide in this foreign land.

Settling into his new quarters, Gregory began a daily routine at the temple, participating in rituals and observing the priests' practices. Lucius became his mentor, guiding him through Roman traditions, philosophy, and the complex societal structure that had developed over the centuries. Lucius explained the city's devotion to the gods—not for salvation but for guidance in their mortal lives, with each god representing different forces in the human experience.

Lucius shared the pivotal events of the last two thousand years, a history devoid of Christ and the influence of the Catholic Church. Gregory listened, astonished, as he heard of Rome's uninterrupted dominance, its wars and expansions, and the evolution of its pantheon-based spirituality. He marveled at their advances in science, medicine, and philosophy. Yet, he also saw the darker consequences: a rigid society bound to hierarchy and civic duty without a theology emphasizing mercy and redemption.

"One cannot deny that we've achieved greatness," Lucius said, his voice filled with pride and resignation. "But I concede without the concept of universal forgiveness or the promise of salvation, justice here can be harsh. Honor and duty guide us, but some burdens are carried alone, with no hope of spiritual absolution."

Gregory absorbed these words, deeply moved by this world's resilience and solemnity. The Roman civilization had crafted its sense of purpose and morality but lacked the comfort and grace he had known in his faith. He began to see humanity's profound need to create meaning in any form it could—a theme that resonated across both worlds. It was a revelation that drew him closer to the people around him, fostering a deeper empathy as he confronted his beliefs in a world where salvation was not a given but a path to be carved through honor and remembrance.

Gregory's understanding grew as days turned to weeks, but so did his uncertainty. He was learning to appreciate the nuances of Roman faith, yet he continued to feel the loss of his own. Torn between two worlds, he wondered if his journey was one of discovery—or transformation.

As Gregory continued to absorb the ethos of this alternate world, he began sharing with Lucius the sweeping events that had shaped his own world—a world in which the Roman Empire fell, fragmented, and reformed under a new power: the Roman Catholic Church.

"In my world, the empire's collapse led to centuries of upheaval, what we called the Dark Ages," Gregory explained, his tone reverent as if recounting the rise and fall of a sacred legacy. "In the absence of centralized Roman rule, the Church stepped in, unifying Europe not through armies but through faith. Over time, it became the beacon of hope, the guardian of knowledge, and a source of comfort to a fractured people."

Lucius listened intently, his expression both thoughtful and inquisitive. "So the Church took Rome's place, not as a government but as a force that shaped society's soul?" he asked, leaning forward with a genuine fascination.

Gregory nodded, a mixture of pride and sorrow in his eyes. "Yes. The Church offered salvation, a guiding hand in the darkness. People looked to Christ, not to Caesar, for redemption. And through that devotion, we rebuilt from the ruins, establishing new realms of thought and learning, but always under the shadow of Divine purpose."

Lucius's gaze drifted toward the statues of Jupiter and Mars, figures of strength and worldly power. He murmured, "In our world, the empire never faltered. Rome's light remained constant, yet I wonder what our path would look like if we had been guided by such a deeply personal promise of salvation."

The two men sat in reflective silence, each glimpsing an alternative vision of humanity's eternal search for meaning in the other's world. At that moment, they were not divided by faith or culture but united by a shared curiosity—an exploration of what it means to believe, hope, and build a legacy in a world ever on the brink of transformation.

Gregory's expression grew somber as he continued, choosing his words carefully. "The Church did indeed step into the void left by Rome's collapse, offering unity and hope to a fractured world," he began, his voice low and reflective. "But there was a darkness within those centuries that we, the Church, must own. In our mission to preserve faith, we became gatekeepers, sometimes guarding the faithful too fiercely, even to the detriment of knowledge and progress."

Lucius watched him intently, the flickering torchlight casting shadows on his face as he absorbed Gregory's words.

"There was a fear," Gregory admitted, a hint of sorrow seeping into his tone. "A fear that scientific discovery and intellectual freedom might undermine the Church's authority. In an age where superstition often mingled with faith, anything that seemed to contradict scripture or challenge Divine mysteries was seen as a threat. And so, rather than nurture curiosity, the Church suppressed it. Scholars were silenced, discoveries were hidden, and questions were left unanswered. It was not just a battle against heresy, but a battle for control, denying humanity the chance to fully explore the wonders of God's creation."

Lucius's brow furrowed, his gaze unblinking. "So knowledge itself became a form of rebellion?"

Gregory nodded, a faint bitterness lacing his words. "Yes. The pursuit of knowledge was often seen as subversive, as though questioning the mysteries of the universe would unravel the very fabric of faith. Those who dared to explore realms that didn't conform to the

Church's teachings were branded heretics. Thinkers like Galileo and Copernicus—men whose work would later change the world—were scorned, threatened, and silenced. To protect the faith, the Church turned its back on science, condemning minds that could have lifted us out of ignorance."

He hesitated, glancing down at his hands. "The irony is painful, Lucius. By stifling these voices, the Church believed it was safeguarding the soul. But in truth, it stifled the human spirit, the very spark of curiosity that was, I believe, a gift from God. For centuries, we held back the progress of discovery and exploration. People lived in fear not only of God's wrath but of stepping outside the narrow boundaries of sanctioned belief. The faithful became afraid to see beyond the Church's teachings, to trust their own minds and seek answers beyond what was prescribed."

Lucius's gaze softened, a hint of compassion breaking through his stoic curiosity. "And yet, here you are, a servant of that very Church, reflecting on its missteps with such candor."

Gregory gave a faint, rueful smile. "Because I know that God's light shines as brightly on the curious as on the devout. But I speak as one who has seen history, who understands both the glory and the shadows of my Church. Faith should uplift, not confine. Knowledge and belief should walk together, not in opposition."

A silence fell between them, heavy with the weight of the Church's legacy—a legacy of light and shadow. Lucius broke it gently, his voice thoughtful. "In Rome, we honor reason and knowledge, yet we too have our blind spots, our fears that certain truths might disturb the order we cherish. Perhaps all great powers struggle with the balance between control and freedom."

Gregory looked at him with a sense of kinship, the barriers of faith and culture momentarily dissolving. "Perhaps. But the Church's fear of knowledge has left scars, Lucius. And while I am proud of the faith I have dedicated my life to, I cannot ignore that it has caused suffering by denying humanity the full wonder of God's creation."

Lucius leaned forward as if about to confide a secret of his own. "Perhaps there is a lesson for both of us here, Gregory. Building a legacy is to shape minds and souls and trust them. A world built on fear of knowledge can never fully flourish."

The conversation dwindled, leaving only the faint hum of the room and the heavy silence of unexpressed thoughts. Each man grappled with his inner turmoil. No words were exchanged, yet an invisible connection began to form—a delicate thread spun from shared struggles and the yearning for understanding. Gregory felt a flicker of something both foreign and profound: the realization that the barriers between beliefs and worlds might not be as insurmountable as they once seemed.

CHAPTER NINE
THE SENATOR

Lucius entered the dimly lit chamber where Gregory was seated. The lights cast uneasy shadows across the walls. Gregory glanced up, immediately noting the tension in Lucius's face. Something was wrong.

Lucius hesitated, his hand gripping the edge of his tunic, and he took a slow breath before speaking. "Gregory," he began cautiously, his tone heavy with the unwelcome news. "There is something I must tell you. Senator Quintus Varro is coming to see you."

Gregory's brow furrowed, his stomach tightening. "A senator?" he echoed, his voice laced with apprehension. "Why would a senator wish to meet me? And how does he even know of my existence?"

Lucius stepped closer, lowering his voice. "It is because of Magnus Decimus, the Archflamen of this temple. He is the head priest of Jupiter and a man of considerable influence. I… I was forced to share your story with him."

Gregory's expression darkened, his breath hitching as the words sank in. "You did what?" he demanded, his tone rising with shock and frustration.

"I know," Lucius said, raising a hand as if to calm him. "But, Gregory, you have drawn attention—more than you realize. One of the priests noticed your unusual behavior, attire, and how you speak and carry yourself. He began asking questions, and I feared his curiosity would turn into rumors. Magnus confronted me directly, and I thought it better to control the narrative than risk spreading unfounded speculation."

Gregory rose from his seat, pacing the room with a mix of anger and anxiety. "And what did Magnus do with this information? What does he think of me?"

Lucius sighed, his expression clouded. "Magnus is not a man of impulsive action. He is cautious and thoughtful, but your presence intrigued him. He believed it necessary to inform the senator, a man of great influence in Rome, who was also known for his intellect and curiosity. Quintus has agreed to meet with you—not as an accuser, but as someone who seeks understanding."

Gregory stopped pacing, turning to face Lucius. "And what if he doesn't find my story worth understanding? What if he sees me as a threat to your society?"

Lucius stepped forward, placing a firm hand on Gregory's shoulder. "Quintus is a patron of scholars and philosophers who value reason over fear. If you speak honestly and show him who you truly are, I believe he will see no threat in you."

Gregory shook his head. "This is a dangerous gamble, Lucius. You've brought the attention of powerful men upon me."

Lucius's grip on his shoulder tightened, his voice calm but resolute. "I understand your fears, Gregory, but I have faith in the truth of your words. Let them see the man I see—a man of conviction, of peace, and wisdom. That is the best chance we have."

Gregory exhaled slowly, the tension in the room pressing down on him. "Let us hope that your faith in them is justified, Lucius. For both our sakes."

A faint sound of footsteps echoed in the corridor beyond, signaling the senator's arrival. Gregory adjusted his robes. With a steadying breath, he turned to Lucius and said, "Let us face this together."

Lucius nodded, leading Gregory toward the doors where their fates would soon be decided.

The rhythmic clatter of boots on polished marble grew louder, bouncing off the chamber's towering columns. Gregory straightened, his hands clasping the folds of his papal robes as Lucius cast him a reassuring glance. The heavy oak doors creaked open, revealing a group of attendants who stepped aside to allow Quintus to enter.

Quintus was tall and broad-shouldered, his movements deliberate yet fluid. His finely woven toga, adorned with a deep purple stripe symbolizing his rank, shimmered faintly in the torchlight. His silver-gray hair was cropped neatly, and his chiseled face bore the lines of experience and contemplation. Gregory noted the intensity in his dark eyes—sharp, calculating, and brimming with intelligence. This was not a man easily swayed by rhetoric or deceit.

Quintus paused on the threshold, surveying the room with detached authority before his gaze settled on Gregory. His lips curled into a faint, almost amused smile as he took in the ornate vestments and Gregory's composed yet foreign demeanor.

"So," Quintus said, his voice smooth but edged with curiosity. "You are the mysterious stranger I've heard so much about." He stepped closer, his hands clasped behind his back as his eyes scrutinized Gregory. "They say you are not of this world. And yet, here you stand, flesh and blood like the rest of us. Tell me, are you mad, or is there truly something extraordinary about you?"

Gregory met the senator's gaze, his heartbeat steady. "Senator, I understand how strange my presence must seem. I assure you, I am not mad. What I say may defy logic, but I humbly speak the truth as I know it."

Quintus raised an eyebrow, his expression unreadable. "Truth," he echoed, the word laced with skepticism. "Truth is a fragile thing, subject to the perspective of the one who speaks it. Tell me, Gregory, what truth compels you to stand before me in these… unusual garments?"

Gregory straightened, his voice firm but calm. "In my world, I served as Pope, the leader of the Christian Church. My faith is centered on a single God, who manifested as a man—Christ—who sacrificed Himself for humanity. It is a faith rooted in forgiveness, compassion, and salvation. In our Church, we believe that each soul can find redemption through Christ's grace."

Quintus tilted his head slightly, his eyes narrowing as he absorbed Gregory's words. "Intriguing," he said, his tone measured. "A singular god. A man who is both mortal and Divine. And this faith of yours, this Church—how did it come to dominate your world?"

Gregory hesitated as centuries of history pressed against his tongue. "After the fall of Rome in my world, the Church rose to fill the void. It brought order to the chaos."

Quintus recoiled slightly, his expression shifting from curiosity to stunned disbelief. "The fall of Rome?" he repeated, his voice barely above a whisper, as though the very idea carried a weight too great to comprehend. His piercing gaze softened, not in kindness but in sheer bewilderment. "You speak madness. Rome is eternal. The empire is the foundation of civilization, the unyielding force that has shaped the world."

Gregory shrugged. "This is what happened."

Quintus's voice grew sharper, almost accusatory. "And this Church you speak of—this faith of yours—rose from Rome's ashes. A foreign belief replacing centuries of tradition and the will of the gods? You claim it brought order, but at what cost, Gregory? At what cost?"

His disbelief hung heavy in the air as though the mere suggestion of Rome's fall had shaken something deep within him, a certainty he had never thought to question. For the first time, Quintus looked at Gregory not as an enigma to be solved but as a man who carried a reality that was too alien and impossible to be true.

Quintus stepped closer, his gaze piercing. "And you believe this God of yours is superior to our gods? That this faith of yours is a remedy for what you see as a flawed world?"

"I do not seek to compare or to diminish your gods," Gregory replied carefully. "What I offer is a perspective shaped by my experiences and faith. I believe in the power of compassion, Senator. In the ability of humanity to find common ground through understanding and grace."

Quintus's eyes narrowed, a glimmer of curiosity and caution crossing his face. "Fascinating. But let me be clear, Gregory—Rome has no tolerance for zealots who disrupt our harmony. We have dealt with your kind in the past, and let's say we handle such matters decisively."

Forcing himself to swallow, he willed his face to remain composed. "I do not wish to disrupt the peace, Senator," he managed, his voice steadier than he felt. "I merely seek to understand the world where I find myself."

Quintus nodded slowly, the warning lingering in the air. "Good. Then let us keep it that way." He paused as if considering his next words carefully. "Perhaps you do not fully appreciate what keeps our empire so resilient. Rome is not held together by mere belief—it endures through governance, through a political structure that has safeguarded us for centuries."

Gregory tilted his head, intrigued. "I would be honored if you could share this structure with me, Senator. My world knew Rome, but it was a Rome of antiquity, not the enduring empire I see before me."

The senator's gaze softened slightly and he began with a measured tone, "Our empire is governed by the Emperor, a man of great power, but not absolute. He is tempered by the Senate, which represents the will of Rome's states and cities. While the ultimate authority, the Emperor is bound by tradition, duty, and virtues we hold dear—virtus, pietas, dignitas, and gravitas."

He paused for emphasis, his voice taking on a scholarly tone as he elaborated. "Virtus signifies courage and moral excellence, the foundation of all Roman values. It is the strength of character required to lead, defend Rome, and act with honor in all things. Pietas represents our devotion and duty—to the gods, our families, and the state. Through pietas, we balance Divine favor and earthly responsibility."

The senator leaned forward slightly, his expression intent. "Dignitas is the personal reputation and honor that one earns through virtuous deeds, a standing that reflects not only upon oneself but also one's family and lineage. Finally, gravitas is the seriousness and responsibility with which we conduct ourselves, embodying self-control and a sense of purpose. Together, these virtues are the pillars that uphold our society and guide our leaders."

He straightened, his eyes meeting Gregory's with a calm confidence. "We Romans do not separate personal character from governance. To rule is not merely to command but to embody these principles and ensure they thrive in all corners of the empire. In this way, our leaders are bound not only by laws but by the pull of tradition and the expectation of the people they serve."

Quintus allowed the words to settle before continuing. "An emperor must embody the virtues of Rome. Though he commands our legions and oversees vast territories, he is more than a ruler; he symbolizes Rome's ideals. And the Senate serves not as an obstacle but as his council. Together, they maintain the delicate balance that keeps the empire strong."

Gregory listened, absorbing the structure of power in this Rome. "So, the Emperor is both a leader and a servant to Rome, bound by its ideals."

"Precisely," Quintus affirmed. "The Emperor personifies Rome's strength and honor. His decisions must bring dignity to our people. But he is advised and, if need be, restrained by the Senate, ensuring he does not stray from the path of Rome's wisdom." Quintus leaned in slightly, his gaze unwavering. "We Romans believe that power without accountability leads to chaos. The Gods may provide guidance, but politics is our spine, the structure that sustains the empire."

Gregory hesitated, then ventured, "And yet, there is no forgiveness in this structure, is there? No Divine mercy, no absolution?"

Quintus's eyes glinted with a subtle intensity. "In Rome, we do not rely on forgiveness alone. Redemption is earned, not given freely. Each citizen carries the burden of their choices, seeking atonement through honorable deeds. Ours is not a world softened by mercy, but one strengthened by resilience and virtue."

The words struck Gregory deeply. He began to understand the strength and the cost of this Roman order—a strength built on discipline, a society sustained by tradition and duty.

Quintus allowed a slight smile to touch his lips. "Consider this, Gregory. Our leaders are chosen not by Divine right but by their wisdom and dedication to the empire. We do not place our fate in the hands of a singular god or prophet but in those who have proven their worth in service to Rome."

Gregory looked down, feeling both humbled and disoriented. This empire, so different from the one he had known, offered no effortless grace or promise of eternal salvation. Its strength was human, and its endurance was forged by centuries of rigorous governance and a commitment to ideals rather than a single creed.

Quintus's face darkened, his gaze piercing as he leaned closer to Gregory, his tone lowering to a whisper imbued with centuries of Roman authority. "Understand this, foreigner," he said, each word deliberate. "Rome is a city of laws, of traditions that bind us together in a web of order. We have endured because we root out disorder at its first sign. It is not forgiveness that has sustained us, but discipline, hierarchy, and the clarity of consequence."

He paused, letting his words settle over them like a shadow. "Many in the Senate view ideas like yours with suspicion and contempt. They would see it as a dangerous indulgence undermining our civilization's fabric. Mercy without merit, faith without discipline is seen as weakness here, Gregory, a threat to the unity we cherish."

Gregory's breath caught as he absorbed Quintus's words, feeling the sharp edge of the warning embedded within them. This was more than caution; it was a threat, a reminder of Rome's unforgiving stance toward anything that might disrupt its harmony.

"If you espouse these beliefs openly," Quintus continued, his eyes narrowing, "there are those who would silence you. And they would do so without hesitation, believing they were acting in the empire's best interest."

The chill that swept through Gregory was unmistakable. He struggled to maintain his composure, meeting Quintus's gaze with as much resolve as he could muster. "I have no desire to disrupt the peace, Senator," he said quietly. "I only seek to understand this world I find myself in, nothing more."

Quintus's gaze softened, but only slightly. "Then consider this a friendly caution. Rome may be where ideas converge, but not all ideas are accepted. Choose your words carefully, lest they bring you closer to an unpleasant fate. Here, we revere the gods, but we place our future in the hands of order and stability. Do not test the empire's tolerance."

A faint, almost paternal warmth flickered in Quintus's eyes as he added, "Take this to heart, Gregory of the Foreign Faith; Rome has endured precisely because we have learned when to listen and when to act. Perhaps, in time, you will find your place here. But for now, tread carefully. The walls of this city have ears, and not all who listen are as tolerant as I."

With that, Quintus straightened, his severe look melting back into a practiced neutrality as he inclined his head in a farewell and final warning gesture. Gregory managed a nod, watching as the senator turned to leave. His footsteps echoed in the vast atrium, each one a reminder of the empire's power.

With Lucius by his side, remaining silent, Gregory felt a mingling of awe and trepidation. The clarity he'd glimpsed—a purpose to bridge the divide between his faith and this ancient order—now seemed shadowed by a harsh reality. He would need conviction and caution to walk this path, a careful dance between his cherished ideals and the unyielding authority that ruled this strange world.

As he reached under his garment to clutch his cross, he felt its cold reassurance against his palm. Gregory understood that his journey here would be more dangerous than he had imagined and that his faith—his very identity—might become a perilous burden in the halls of Rome.

CHAPTER TEN
DANGEROUS TIMES

Lucius watched Gregory with a quiet, almost paternal concern. "I'm afraid your attire will only invite more questions," he said, his tone gentle but firm. "It would be wiser if you dressed like one of us. In this city, subtlety serves survival."

Later in his room, Gregory's hand lingered on the collar of his papal vestments, feeling the familiar fabric beneath his fingers. He hesitated, once again feeling like he was shedding a part of himself, a piece of the life he desperately clung to. But Lucius's words resonated, and he knew he could not afford the scrutiny his foreign attire would attract. With a reluctant nod, he agreed.

Gregory's hands fumbled awkwardly as he struggled into the plain white robe Lucius offered him. The rough texture of the homespun linen scratched against his skin, a stark contrast to the silk-lined opulence of his woolen papal vestments, now carefully set aside. Each hem and sleeve of his former attire bore symbols of his faith, meticulously embroidered with threads of gold and silver, and they seemed to gaze at him now, a silent testament to his sacrifice. Stripping himself of these garments felt like shedding his very identity, yet Lucius's warning echoed in his mind, grounding his resolve.

Lucius stood nearby, his face shadowed by concern. "Gregory," he said quietly, his voice firm yet tinged with unease, "the senator may appear cordial, but he is a man of Rome—a guardian of its traditions and order. Your way of speech and mannerisms… mark you as a foreigner, perhaps even a threat in the eyes of someone more zealous. Quintus is no fool or someone to be underestimated."

Gregory met Lucius's gaze, the significance of the moment settling over him. "You think he might see me as a danger?"

Lucius hesitated before answering, his tone measured. "I don't know. But Rome has endured centuries of enemies, both external and within. Its leaders are ever watchful for anything that might disrupt its balance. Your story and faith are unlike anything he will have encountered. It is safer if, for now, you appear as one of us. Let him see you as a man seeking understanding, not one who stands apart."

Gregory nodded slowly, his hands smoothing the unfamiliar fabric of the robe. "I will heed your counsel. The less I stand out, the more time we have to navigate this… precarious situation."

Lucius offered a faint smile, though his worry lingered in his eyes. "Good. Keep to the truth where you can, but tread carefully. The senator is a man of reason, but even the reasonable are bound by their loyalty to Rome."

As Gregory adjusted the plain priest's robe, he felt the strain of the compromise—not just his garments but his very identity. Yet he knew he must adapt to protect his little foothold in this foreign world. For now, the symbols of his faith would remain hidden, though they burned brightly within his heart.

Once he was dressed in the austere robes of a Roman priest, Lucius pulled him aside, his face serious. "There are things you must understand, Gregory, if you are to survive," he began, his voice low and guarded. "Quintus showed you Rome's strength, pride, structure, and stability. But beneath that surface lies a darkness that has persisted through centuries."

Gregory listened closely as Lucius spoke of Rome's foundations, built not only on the virtues of its citizens but on the backs of countless enslaved souls. "Slavery is as vital to Rome as its Senate and Emperor," Lucius explained, bitterness lacing his words. "Our vast empire's wealth and grandeur are built upon the labor of those treated as property, who toil in brutal conditions for the comfort of others. Laws exist to maintain order within this system, yes, but they exist for the benefit of the slaveholders, not for the protection of the slaves."

"I've been to the markets, walked these streets, even visited the university," Gregory began, his tone thoughtful. "And yet, I have not seen slavery on open display."

"That is because they blend in seamlessly, Gregory. The menial work you see—the porters hauling goods, the bath attendants, the scribes copying texts—all done by slaves. They are everywhere, though their presence is so ingrained into our society that most barely notice them."

Gregory frowned, his eyes darting to a young man stacking amphorae with mechanical precision near a wine merchant. "And these slaves," he said slowly. "Is there no hope for them? No path to freedom?"

Lucius exhaled sharply, a hint of bitterness creeping into his voice. "Hope? Rarely, though, exists in theory. Those clever or fortunate enough may earn their freedom, either through service, by purchase, or as a reward for loyalty. Once free, they may even become Roman citizens, though such cases are exceptions, not the rule. Most live and die as they are—chained not just by their masters but by the system itself."

Gregory's stomach tightened as Lucius's words settled over him. Slavery had scarred his own world, a dark chapter in human history, yet here, it thrived in modern times, woven seamlessly into the fabric of this empire. "And this… this institution," Gregory said, his voice thick with unease, "is it accepted without question?"

Lucius's expression darkened, his gaze fixed ahead. "For the most part, yes. The empire's wealth and grandeur are built upon their bones. The Senate, the Emperor, the temples—all stand because of the slaves who toil in their shadow. The laws, Gregory, were never made to protect the slaves. They exist solely to preserve order and reinforce the authority of the masters. This is the Roman way, a tradition rooted in the very origins of the city when the she-wolf nourished Romulus and Remus."

Gregory clenched his fists, his mind racing with the enormity of it all. "In my world," he said quietly, "slavery was a scar upon humanity. It left wounds that took centuries to even begin to heal. Seeing it thriving here, accepted as natural, makes my heart ache."

Lucius regarded him for a moment, a flicker of something unreadable crossing his face. "You see what many Romans do not—or choose not to. Perhaps that is why your presence here is so… unsettling. You bring a perspective that challenges the very foundation of what we have always known."

Gregory nodded, though Lucius's words only deepened his unease. Slavery, invisible yet omnipresent, cast a shadow over the grandeur of this empire, and Gregory could not help but feel the magnitude of the human cost buried beneath its glory.

Lucius continued, his tone growing colder as he spoke of the spectacles that occupied Roman minds. Gladiatorial games, he explained, had not faded with time but had evolved, their brutality preserved as a testament to Rome's unyielding strength. "The Coliseum stands as a monument to our endurance, and the blood that stains its sands serves as a reminder of the consequences of defying Rome," Lucius said grimly. "Advanced weaponry may have enhanced these brutish displays, but the message remains the same—Rome's power is absolute, and those who oppose it will be crushed publicly and without mercy."

Lucius continued, his tone growing colder as he described the gladiatorial games that still captivated the populace, a grim legacy that Rome carried forward even after centuries of supposed advancement. "The games have become even more elaborate," he said, his voice tinged with disgust. "There are orchestrated spectacles where whole teams of gladiators, each representing different countries, clash in carefully staged skirmishes meant to evoke the empire's ancient victories."

He paused, looking darkly toward the towering Coliseum visible through the temple's arches. "Picture it, Gregory—a hundred men against a hundred others, each side adorned in the traditional armor, weapons, and colors of defeated tribes. They are made to fight in formations, reenacting the battles Rome won long ago, reminding the people that our strength is not equal. The crowd cheers as the ground grows slick with blood, and the Emperor stands to give his verdict when the last man falls. Mercy is rare; it is given not out of compassion but as a calculated gesture to keep the populace entertained, to show that even in violence, Rome decides who lives and dies."

Gregory felt a chill as Lucius continued. "Then there are the beast hunts," he said, his lips curling in distaste. "Exotic animals from across the empire—lions, elephants, tigers—are brought into the arena, their captors pitting them against condemned prisoners or desperate gladiators. These men are forced to fight without armor or weapons in what the crowd calls 'the Trial of the Gods'—a display of man versus nature, where Rome's mastery over both is demonstrated in the most savage way possible. The screams of these unfortunate souls mingle with the roars of the beasts, and the crowd cheers louder as if Rome's strength itself feeds on this spectacle of death."

Gregory shuddered at the thought, his mind reeling as he tried to comprehend such cold, ritualized violence. Lucius's face was grave as he went on. "And then, there are the executions," he said. "Criminals, prisoners of war, and political dissidents are given the cruelest fate of all. They are often brought into the arena unarmed, set upon by trained killers, as the crowd jeers. In some cases, they are forced to act out famous legends from Roman mythology, their deaths mirroring the gruesome fates of the characters they portray. Imagine a man reenacting the tale of Prometheus, bound to a stone while birds of prey descend upon him, tearing him apart piece by piece as the crowd watches, enthralled."

Gregory's face had gone pale, his hands trembling as he clutched the cross beneath his robe. The very fabric of Rome's entertainment seemed to be woven from the suffering of those deemed unworthy, a machine of cruelty that ground down its victims for sport. He could scarcely believe that such brutality could be normalized, that a people so advanced could find pleasure in spectacles of death. Lucius's voice dropped to a near whisper as he finished, his expression haunted. "This is what they call the glory of Rome, Gregory. Strength, power, and dominance are the values instilled in every citizen from birth. And in the Coliseum, they see that power made flesh, a reminder that Rome fears nothing, that all who oppose her will meet the same fate."

Gregory swallowed hard, his soul recoiling at the image Lucius had painted. He understood now that he was dealing with a society that prized power over compassion, spectacle over humanity. The games were more than entertainment—they were a warning to anyone who might dare to challenge the empire's might, a testament to a legacy of fear that had endured for centuries.

The image of roaring crowds, baying for blood, flashed through Gregory's mind, and he felt a deep revulsion. How could a civilization so advanced still indulge in such primal violence? How could human life be treated as mere entertainment?

Gregory's thoughts drifted to the teachings of Christ, which preached compassion, equality, and the value of every soul. In his world, there had been a movement to uplift the marginalized and offer grace where there was only suffering. However, Rome's rigid structure allowed little room for such ideals, and he felt the harshness of that rigidity settle heavily on his heart.

As Lucius spoke of Roman justice, Gregory's sense of dread deepened. Justice here was swift and unyielding, punishments brutal and often public. Crucifixions, public floggings, and exiles were common, not as instruments of reform but as deterrents against rebellion. "Mercy is seen as weakness," Lucius murmured, his eyes dark with an emotion Gregory couldn't place. "Rome does not forgive; it punishes. It expects its citizens to carry the weight of their actions alone, without the comfort of redemption."

Here, mercy was a luxury Rome could not afford, an indulgence viewed with disdain. Justice was an iron fist, not an open hand, and Gregory realized what that meant for those who stood against the empire.

Lucius spoke of the militaristic culture that pervaded Rome, a society that glorified conquest and saw expansion as a Divine mandate. "Rome's legions are its pride, its honor," Lucius said. "Our empire stretches across all the continents, fueled by a belief in Roman superiority. But each victory brings resentment; each conquered people bears the scars of subjugation." Gregory sensed the exhaustion in Lucius's voice, the weariness of a man who had seen the toll of these endless conquests. The promise of civilization came at the cost of freedom and autonomy for those who fell under Roman rule.

Finally, Lucius spoke of the deep-seated arrogance underpinning Roman culture—a belief in their exceptionalism, a certainty that they were the pinnacle of human achievement. This self-assuredness justified the subjugation of others, the enslavement of foreign peoples, and the enforcement of Roman laws across all territories. "Rome's unity, its strength, relies on this belief," Lucius concluded. "It keeps us together, yes, but it also breeds resentment, rebellion. Those who are not Roman may live within the empire's borders but are never truly seen as equals."

A profound sorrow welled within him as he realized what he faced. In a world where compassion was seen as weakness, mercy as folly, and obedience as the currency of survival, Rome's grandeur and cruelty bore down on him, casting a shadow over everything he had once believed was immutable.

Lucius placed a hand on his shoulder, his gaze solemn but steady. "You must be cautious, Gregory," he warned. "This empire tolerates only what it can control. Speak carefully, act carefully, for even the smallest misstep can bring about ruin. Rome does not forgive, and it does not forget."

Gregory met his gaze with Lucius's words pressing down on him like an iron shroud. This world was dangerous, and he would need more than faith to navigate its treacherous paths.

CHAPTER ELEVEN
CONFESSION

Several days later, as Lucius's words faded into the temple's stillness, Gregory stared out a window at a lush garden. His circumstances pressed heavily, and each moment in this foreign world reminded him how far he was from home. The vibrant and meticulously maintained grounds seemed an ironic contrast to the turmoil within.

Footsteps echoed softly behind him. Lucius approached, his stride slower than usual, as though he carried his own burden of thoughts. His face held an unusual, contemplative expression, the lines of his brow deeper, his gaze distant. He stood beside Gregory in silence for a moment, the unspoken tension between them hanging in the air.

"I have served Rome all my life," Lucius said at last, his voice low and deliberate. "I have seen its strength… and its darkness. Your words, Gregory—" He hesitated, the admission catching in his throat. "They have lingered with me, unsettling what I thought was certain. I find myself questioning things I once accepted without thought."

Gregory turned to him, surprised by the raw vulnerability in Lucius's voice. "What is it you question?" he asked gently, sensing the man's inner conflict.

Lucius's gaze dropped to the marble floor. "Your talk of mercy and compassion," he said slowly. "They are foreign concepts here. I was raised to see compassion as weakness and mercy as folly. To show mercy in Rome is to invite ruin; to act with compassion is to risk being consumed by it. Yet, when you speak of these things, Gregory…" He looked up, his eyes searching, almost pleading. "They seem like something… necessary. A part of me wonders if there is more to life than duty to the state, more than Rome's endless pursuit of power."

He paused, his hands tightening into fists at his sides. "You must understand, I was taught that our empire endures because we are relentless. We conquer, we build, we dominate. But for all its greatness, Rome is… hollow. It demands so much yet offers no comfort to those who serve it. Your words have made me see this in a way I never allowed myself to."

Gregory placed a hand on Lucius's shoulder, the gesture gentle but firm. "Mercy and compassion are not weaknesses," he said. "They are strengths of a different kind. They require courage—the courage to see another's pain, to recognize their humanity, and to act, even when it costs us something."

Lucius shook his head slightly, his skepticism mingling with curiosity. "But what is the purpose of such sacrifice? What does it achieve in a world where power is everything?"

Gregory smiled faintly, his voice steady and filled with conviction. "It achieves connection, Lucius. It binds us together, not as masters and subjects, but as brothers and sisters. Mercy allows us to break the cycle of violence and retribution; compassion reminds us that we are more than the sum of our ambitions. Through these virtues, we find not just peace with others, but peace within ourselves."

Lucius fell silent, the vulnerability in his words and questions hanging between them. He seemed almost afraid to admit the change stirring within him. "Tell me, Gregory," he whispered, his voice barely audible, "what is this mercy you speak of? This compassion that seems so vital to you?"

Gregory met his gaze, his own eyes filled with quiet determination. "Mercy is the hand that lifts, not strikes. It is the choice to forgive when vengeance would be easier. And compassion… compassion is the bridge between hearts, the willingness to suffer with another so they do not suffer alone. These are not ideals meant to weaken us, Lucius. They are what make us truly human."

Lucius turned back toward the garden, his expression contemplative. "Perhaps," he murmured, almost to himself. "Perhaps there is something greater than Rome's might. Something worth seeking beyond power and conquest."

Gregory said nothing, sensing that Lucius needed space for his thoughts. Together, they stood silently, the garden's soft hum blending with the city's distant sounds. For the first time, Gregory saw in Lucius not just a servant of Rome but a man yearning for something more—a spark of humanity waiting to be kindled.

Gregory looked at him, a faint smile of understanding crossing his face. He recognized the stirrings of a shift within Lucius—a seed of light taking root in the heart of one who had known only Rome's shadowed strength.

Gregory recognized a glimmer of hope. Here was an opening, a chance to speak of the values that defined his faith—not as doctrines or creeds, but as living truths. He shared with Lucius his belief in kindness, forgiveness, and the quiet strength of humility. "To me, true power does not lie in conquest or bending others to one's will," Gregory said softly. "It lies in lifting others up, in seeing the Divine spark within each soul."

Lucius's brow furrowed as he absorbed these ideas, so foreign to Roman ideals. "Rome was built on strength and dominance," he murmured. "To be compassionate, to show mercy… these are things we were taught to view as weaknesses."

"Or perhaps," Gregory replied, "they are the ultimate strength. Is it not more powerful to love than to control? More enduring to inspire than to command?"

Lucius fell silent, the impact of Gregory's question stirring something deep within him. His face softened, his eyes shadowed with regret. "I have seen things… done things… that weigh on me," he murmured. "Sometimes, I wonder if there could be another way."

Gregory studied him, sensing that beneath Lucius's hardened exterior lay a man burdened by choices he could no longer justify. He leaned forward, his voice gentle but firm. "Lucius, there is another way. If you carry these burdens, perhaps it is time to let them go."

Lucius looked at him, confusion mingling with a flicker of hope. "What do you mean?"

"As a priest and later as a Cardinal, I devoted myself to listening to the confessions of those in need," Gregory began, his voice steady and filled with quiet authority. "The act of confession is not simply a recitation of sins or wrongs. It is a sacred moment, a bridge between the soul and its better self. When someone confesses, they unburden their heart of guilt and shame, bringing into the light that which festers in the darkness. It is an act of humility, yes, but also of courage."

Lucius's brow furrowed as he listened, his arms crossed tightly across his chest. Gregory continued, undeterred by the silence. "Through confession, the soul can face its failings honestly, without fear of condemnation. And when forgiveness is offered, it is not mere words—it is a cleansing, a renewal. It allows the penitent to begin again, to strive for something higher, free of the chains of the past."

Gregory stepped closer, his gaze steady but gentle. "In my time as Pope, I have seen the act of confession transform lives. I have witnessed the proud brought to humility, the despairing lifted to hope, and the hardened moved to tears. It is not easy, Lucius, to confront one's failings. But it is necessary if we are to grow into something better."

Lucius's eyes darted away. He seemed lost in thought for a moment, his fingers tightening around his upper arms as though bracing himself. Gregory saw the hesitation, the fear, and the deeply buried pain etched into the man's face.

He softened his tone, speaking with quiet compassion. "Would you allow me to hear your confession, Lucius? To help you release whatever burdens your soul carries? You may find it is not weakness to admit what weighs upon you—but the first step toward true freedom."

Lucius's breath caught, his jaw tightening as he stared at the ground. The silence stretched between them, tense and unyielding. At last, he exhaled sharply, his voice barely above a whisper. "Confession is not a thing we do in Rome. To admit fault is to show weakness, to lower one's standing. But…" He hesitated, his voice trembling slightly. "I cannot deny that there are things I carry. Things that weigh heavily on my mind and heart."

Gregory said nothing, allowing Lucius the space to process his thoughts. Finally, Lucius raised his eyes, meeting Gregory's gaze with fear and determination. "Yes," he said, his voice firmer now. "Yes, I would."

Gregory inclined his head, his expression one of quiet understanding. "Then let us begin," he said softly, gesturing for Lucius to sit. "Speak freely, Lucius, and know that nothing you say will be met with judgment."

Lucius lowered himself onto the bench, his posture stiff and uncertain. The vulnerability in his eyes was raw, unguarded, as though he were preparing to step into unfamiliar and treacherous terrain. Gregory sat across from him, his hands folded calmly in his lap, waiting with patient silence. Then he pulled the golden cross from the folds of his robe, its polished surface gleaming faintly in the flickering lamplight. He had hidden it away for so long, worried how it would be perceived here. As he held it in his palm, its significance felt heavier than ever.

Lucius's breath caught audibly. His body stiffened as his eyes locked onto the cross. A shadow of fear and revulsion swept over his face. He recoiled, nearly rising from his seat, as though the symbol radiated something vile and dangerous. His voice, when it came, was jagged with disbelief and anger. "Gregory," he hissed, leaning forward but keeping his distance, "do you even understand what you're holding? A cross? It's an instrument of humiliation. Death. Reserved for the lowest—traitors, criminals, slaves. To carry it openly is not just madness—it's a provocation."

He glanced nervously toward the door, his hands tightening into fists as though bracing for an unseen threat. "Put it away," he growled, his voice trembling with something primal—fear, disgust, anger all mingling. His gaze flitted toward the object and back again, unable to fully look at it, yet unable to ignore it. "That thing—it doesn't belong here. Take it out of my sight."

Gregory met Lucius's wide-eyed stare with calm resolve, though he could see the fear and revulsion in the man's reaction. "I know what it means here," he said quietly, his voice steady. "But in my world, this symbol has a far deeper meaning—a meaning that has transformed countless lives."

Lucius narrowed his eyes, glancing at the cross as though it might lash out at him. "How could that be? It's a device of cruelty, of execution. What deeper meaning could such an object hold?"

Gregory shifted the cross in his hand, holding it up so the light danced across its surface. "Because Christ died on the cross," he explained, his tone reverent. "In my world, this instrument of suffering became a symbol of hope and redemption. It's not a mark of disgrace, but of love—the love of God for humanity."

Lucius stared at him, disbelief etched into his features. "You carry this as though it were sacred," he murmured, shaking his head. "But it represents agony, humiliation. It's… it's a warning, a reminder of Rome's absolute power."

Gregory nodded, understanding the depth of Lucius's reaction. "I know it seems impossible to you, but the cross was reclaimed in my world. Christ's sacrifice on it transformed its meaning. It's no longer about Rome's power or the finality of death—it's about triumph over despair. It's a reminder that even in our darkest moments, there is light."

Lucius's eyes flicked back to the cross, his expression softening though confusion and discomfort lingered. "You say it represents love," he said slowly, "but how can such a thing inspire anything but fear?"

"Because Christ's death was not the end," Gregory said, his voice gaining strength. "Through His sacrifice, He offered forgiveness, redemption, and the promise of eternal life. What was once a tool of execution became a beacon of hope, a symbol of the Church, and a testament to the power of love over hatred."

Lucius's shoulders sagged, the tension draining from his body. He looked at Gregory, his expression raw and uncertain. "You truly believe that? That even here, in this world, such a thing could hold meaning?"

"I do," Gregory said firmly. "Because the cross is not about where we are, but who we are. It's about the courage to confront our fears, to face our flaws, and to embrace the possibility of change. It's about finding light, even in the darkest places."

Lucius exhaled slowly, his eyes lingering on the cross. He did not recoil from it. Instead, he regarded it with a tentative curiosity as though he were beginning to see it through Gregory's eyes. "Perhaps," he said softly, "there is something I have yet to understand."

Gregory nodded, his grip tightening around the cross. He held it aloft, the soft glow of the golden emblem catching the dim light. "Perhaps there is something we both have yet to discover," he said quietly, his voice steady. He kept the cross in his hands, its presence anchoring him as he prepared to listen to what Lucius had carried silently for so long. It symbolized his faith and a bridge between worlds, a tangible reminder of the Divine grace that could transform even the heaviest burdens into light.

Gregory's gaze softened as he turned back to Lucius, his voice gentle but steady. "Lucius, I know this is not a custom of your world, but I must ask—are you ready to unburden yourself? To speak of the things that weigh on your soul?" He paused, studying the conflicted expression on Lucius's face. "Confession is not a sign of weakness. It is a courageous act, a step toward clarity and release. You do not need to carry these burdens alone."

For a long moment, Lucius breathed, his chest rising and falling as he wrestled with the words that would not come. Then, slowly, haltingly, he began to speak. "There are things I have done… things I regret. Not openly, perhaps, but in the quiet hours of the night, they haunt me." He paused, his voice faltering. "I have betrayed trust, Gregory. I have been cruel when I could have been kind. And there are lives…" He swallowed hard, the words catching in his throat. "Lives that might have been better had I acted differently."

He looked toward Lucius, his voice soft yet firm. "Speak freely, my son. There is no judgment here, only the hope of release."

Lucius closed his eyes as if willing himself to face the memories long buried in the recesses of his mind. "I have served Rome's authority, and in doing so, I have sanctioned punishments… cruel punishments," he began, his voice hoarse. "I've watched men broken under the weight of 'justice,' condemned for minor infractions. I believed I was upholding order for the good of Rome… but I knew, deep down, it was wrong."

His voice trembled as he continued, his confession pouring forth in fragments. Tales of public beatings, of innocents caught in the gears of Rome's merciless system, of friends turned away for their dissension—

all because he had once believed that obedience to the empire's ways was paramount.

"There was a man," Lucius said, his voice breaking. "A scholar who questioned the gods, who dared to think differently. I was ordered to silence him, to make an example of him. I carried out the command without question… I watched as he was flogged before the crowd, his voice silenced forever." Lucius paused, a tear slipping down his cheek. "I can still see his face, even now. His eyes held not fear, but… sadness, as if he mourned for my soul instead of his own suffering."

Gregory's heart ached as he listened, bearing witness to Lucius's sorrow with compassion. He reached out, placing a hand on his shoulder. "Your heart is troubled because you know the consequences of these actions. But acknowledging them, seeking forgiveness—this is the beginning of redemption."

Lucius's shoulders slumped, the weight of his confession almost unbearable. "Can someone like me ever be forgiven? My sins are not small—they are vast, and the suffering I've caused is immeasurable."

Gregory met his gaze, unflinching. "Lucius, forgiveness is not reserved for small sins but for all who seek it sincerely. Your remorse shows that the darkness has not consumed you. You stand at the edge of a new path."

"But how can I be forgiven for what I've done?" Lucius's voice trembled. "The blood on my hands cannot be washed away."

"No, it cannot," Gregory said, his voice heavy with sorrow and resolve. "The past cannot be undone, and the pain you caused will not disappear. But forgiveness is not about erasing the past—it is about transforming the future. I offer you forgiveness, not to diminish your sins, but to free you from being defined by them. Redemption is not forgetting but choosing a better way forward."

Lucius swallowed hard, tears welling in his eyes. "What can I do now?"

"You can choose," Gregory said, his voice steady. "Choose love where you once chose hate. Choose compassion where there was once cruelty. Rome's power may be built on fear and domination, but we will build ours on love and redemption. Walk with me, Lucius, and show the world that even the greatest sins can give way to the greatest acts of grace."

The words lingered, resonating like a distant bell, their echo stirring something deep within Lucius. Gregory observed him in the stillness that followed, the silence heavy yet charged with possibility. In Lucius's eyes, he saw something shift—a spark of hope flickering amidst the shadows of his past. Gregory felt a deep sense of purpose stirring within him, knowing this was a pivotal moment. When Lucius finally spoke, his voice carried the resolve Gregory had hoped for. "I will walk this path with you, Gregory. Whatever it takes." Gregory nodded solemnly, a steady calm in his gaze, silently vowing to guide Lucius toward the peace he had glimpsed.

Gregory suddenly felt a profound sense of purpose settle over him, a reassurance that perhaps his journey was not in vain. Lucius's confession had laid bare the deep cracks within Rome's seemingly impenetrable walls, where its strength could not reach, where light might seep in if only someone dared to open the way. Yet the realization came slowly, a hesitant dawning in his mind: perhaps this land, so steeped in ambition and power, was more ripe for the gospel than he had first understood.

Rome was ruled by discipline and fear, but beneath the iron grasp of its laws, Gregory sensed a yearning—a hunger among its people for something gentler, something that called to the quiet places of the heart. And perhaps, in Lucius, he had found an ally and the first spark of a greater purpose. He wondered if Lucius could find the courage to step beyond his role and stand beside him as more than a confidant. Could Lucius become a fellow seeker of souls who might even gather others who shared this vision of compassion and light?

The thought stirred something within him, echoing his Savior's calling. This was not simply about speaking truths in the dark corners of Rome; it was about igniting a movement of the spirit, planting seeds of hope in a land that had long forgotten the gentle power of love. Gregory imagined how each quiet act of kindness, each heart touched by mercy, might ripple outward, spreading not through defiance or rebellion but through a peaceful, undeniable transformation.

As he looked upon Lucius, he felt an unspoken question rising: would this man, so burdened by Rome's harsh demands, find the courage to reach out to others, to invite them into the light? Or would he retreat into the comfort of familiarity, the rigid safety of Roman law? Gregory felt the significance of this question, realizing that for this vision to grow, he would need Lucius as a fellow shepherd seeking out others who yearned for something more.

At that moment, a quiet hope blossomed within Gregory. Lucius could be the first to carry this light forward, to spread the word with courage born not of might but of compassion. And through him, others might join—not as rebels against Rome, but as souls bound to a gentler, more profound truth. Gregory felt himself standing at the edge of a path that stretched far beyond what he could see, a journey requiring faith, resilience, and a willingness to trust in the quiet power of love to break the strongest chains.

In that silent resolve, he wondered if he had gained an ally and a disciple—a soul willing to turn from the darkness of Rome's power toward the light of a new path grounded in peace. That realization stirred Gregory, and he imagined his Savior must have known it: a calling to gather, nurture, and inspire a quiet revolution of the heart. In this vision, he saw a movement that could, in time, transform not only Rome but perhaps the entire world.

***

The next day, Lucius took Gregory through the bustling streets of a city of majesty built on the backs of its subjects and slaves. They passed grand statues, marble buildings, and fountains, symbols of a mighty empire with little space for compassion. In the crowded marketplace, they saw a man, most likely a slave, being dragged through the streets accused of theft. A gathering crowd watched as he was beaten, the spectacle framed as justice in the eyes of Rome.

Gregory's hand twitched, his instinct to cry out, to plead for mercy, but Lucius gripped his arm firmly, warning him with a look. Gregory understood. This was Rome. He forced himself to remain silent, feeling a sense of helplessness but also a simmering resolve. He could not change Rome through a single act of defiance, but he could plant seeds.

***

Under the glow of the moonlight, its silvery beams spilling through the open colonnades, Lucius and Gregory sat in the quiet seclusion of an alcove. The stillness of the night wrapped around them, broken only by the distant rustling of leaves and the faint murmur of water from the temple's sacred fountain.

The air was heavy with the faint scent of incense, a reminder of the gods who watched silently over their world. For a long moment, neither man spoke, the stillness between them filled only by the distant murmur of voices echoing through the colonnades.

Finally, Lucius broke the silence, leaning closer, his voice barely more than a whisper. "There are others," he began, his eyes darting cautiously toward the empty doorway. "Friends of mine—merchants, scholars, soldiers—who have grown weary of Rome's iron hand. They see what I see: the weight of its cruelty, the suffering it demands. They wonder if power must always come at such a cost."

Gregory straightened, the words sparking a faint light of hope within him. "Others? Do they share your doubts about Rome's path?"

Lucius nodded but hesitated, his face clouding with unease. "They do. But their doubts are whispered, hidden in the shadows. To speak openly is unthinkable. You must understand, Gregory—this is not just defiance. To question Rome's authority is to risk everything. If the wrong ears hear our words, the punishment would be… unspeakable."

Gregory watched him before asking, "What would they do?"

Lucius's voice dropped lower, his gaze fixed on the stone floor as if it might shield him from what he was about to say. "For priests like me, there would be no mercy. The sentence is crucifixion—public, brutal, and final. It warns others who might dare to question their authority."

A chill ran through Gregory as the magnitude of Lucius's words settled over him. The image of the cross loomed larger now, no longer a sacred reminder of salvation but a grim shadow of what might await them. "And yet," Gregory said, his voice steady but filled with conviction, "is this not the very reason to act? The cruelty and suffering thrive because no one dares to challenge it. Perhaps the danger is what unites us in purpose."

Lucius looked up sharply, his eyes searching Gregory's face. "And if that purpose leads to your death? Or to the death of those who might follow you? Do you believe the risk is worth the cost?"

Gregory paused, his hands resting on his knees as he considered the question. "I cannot speak for others, Lucius. But I know this: to stay silent is to allow fear to triumph. If we do nothing, the cruelty continues unchallenged. And if we act, if even one soul finds hope or strength in what we stand for, then perhaps the cost is not in vain."

Lucius leaned back, his expression torn between admiration and doubt. "You speak as though your faith shields you from fear, Gregory. But I see its toll in your eyes. You don't know what the empire is capable of. How can you hold such resolve in the face of it?"

Gregory smiled faintly, the lines of his face softening. "Because fear is a test, Lucius—a shadow that only grows if we flee from it. To face it is not to deny its power but to refuse to let it rule us. I believe I am here, in this moment, not by chance but by purpose. And I believe that purpose is worth the risk."

Lucius exhaled slowly, the tension in his posture easing just slightly. "If we proceed, we do so carefully. The empire watches everything, Gregory. One misstep, one word too loud in the wrong place…"

"I understand," Gregory interrupted gently, his gaze steady. "But silence cannot be our answer."

Lucius studied him for a moment longer, then nodded. "Then we must prepare. If we are to move forward, it will be with caution—and with faith."

CHAPTER TWELVE
FIRST MEETING

A few nights later, with a mixture of caution and determination, Lucius led Gregory to a secluded courtyard where a small group had gathered—Romans who, like Lucius, had grown uneasy with the harshness of their society. Nestled between towering marble columns and weathered stone walls, the courtyard was softly illuminated by the glow of nearby street lamps.

Shadows danced across the intricate mosaic floor, which depicted scenes of Roman victories and Divine blessings, a stark contrast to the unease etched on the faces of those gathered. The air was tinged with the faint scent of the earthy aroma of the surrounding gardens, where cypress trees swayed gently under a pale moonlight.

Julia stood near the edge of the gathering, her simple tunic of muted linen contrasting sharply with the vibrant, ornate fabrics often worn by Roman elites. Her dark hair was pulled back into a loose braid, and her arms were crossed defensively, though her eyes betrayed a flicker of hope as they darted toward Gregory. Her posture was guarded, but her fingers tapped lightly against her arm as if wrestling with the tension between caution and curiosity.

Caius, broad-shouldered and clad in a plain woolen cloak, bore the weathered features of a man who had seen too much. A jagged scar ran from his temple to his cheek, a testament to the battles he had fought in the name of the empire. His hands, calloused and rough, gripped the hilt of a sheathed gladius at his side—a habit he had not yet shed, even in moments of peace. Yet, his gaze was fixed on Gregory, not with hostility, but with a glimmer of quiet desperation, as though seeking absolution for the shadow of his past.

Decimus, older and more deliberate in his movements, adjusted the hem of his dark green tunic, its fabric worn but carefully maintained. His silver-streaked hair was combed back, and his hands, adorned with faint ink stains from years of trade records, were clasped tightly together. He leaned slightly forward, his expression a mixture of skepticism and intrigue. His eyes, shadowed by years of witnessing human suffering, lingered on Gregory as if searching for some sign of truth amidst the uncertainty.

Lucius stood slightly apart, his posture betraying a mixture of protectiveness and anxiety. His gestures were measured, his voice calm yet urgent as he introduced Gregory to the group. He carried himself with the bearing of a man accustomed to leadership, yet his unease was palpable as his eyes darted between his friends.

The group moved with a restrained tension, their movements subtle yet deliberate. Julia shifted from foot to foot, occasionally glancing at Caius as if seeking reassurance. Caius, in turn, adjusted the position of his gladius repeatedly, his fingers brushing the hilt in small, nervous motions. Decimus's hands tightened and loosened around each other as he nodded thoughtfully, his gaze never straying far from Gregory.

Standing at the heart of the gathering, Gregory felt the depth of their collective yearning. Each face bore the marks of a life lived under Rome's unyielding grasp, yet in their expressions, he saw a shared hunger—for something kinder, something brighter. The moment was heavy with unspoken words, their gestures and stolen glances speaking of a fragile hope that this meeting might offer a path beyond the harshness of the world they had known.

Speaking carefully, Gregory shared his vision of a world bound by compassion, where true strength lies in love rather than fear. He spoke of forgiveness, unity, and the profound power of serving others. His words were simple, but they had a depth that resonated in the hearts of his listeners. As he described a richer, more meaningful life than any earthly power could offer, they leaned in, captivated, as though he were unveiling a truth they had always longed to hear.

To these Romans, bound by the unyielding structures of law and power, Gregory's words fell upon them like a miracle, like the gift of sudden sight granted to the blind. It was as if scales were lifting from their eyes, revealing a world they had always longed for but had never dared to imagine. His message was foreign yet deeply familiar, resonating with a truth that seemed to echo from within their souls like a half-remembered melody.

It was more than instruction; it was an awakening, a Divine revelation that stirred the very core of their beings. They felt as if a long-forgotten light had been reignited within them, calling them to something higher, something holy.

Julia's face softened, her guarded expression melting into one of wonder. "Why do you believe in these things, Gregory? Why do you care about strangers in a world that offers no such kindness?"

Gregory held her gaze, his expression steady, his conviction unwavering. "Because I believe every soul has a Divine spark within, a light that connects us all. When we act with love, we strengthen that light in each other. And I believe…" His voice dropped to a reverent whisper as if sharing a sacred truth. "I believe that light can transform even the darkest places."

A profound stillness settled over the group as if the very air had thickened, holding them in place. Eyes softened, breaths stilled; each face reflected a flicker of awe, an expression so vulnerable and unguarded that it seemed they had, for a moment, glimpsed something beyond themselves. Gregory's words lingered in the silence, weaving through them like a quiet flame, warm and persistent. He could almost feel this invisible thread binding them together, filling a hollow space that had perhaps always been there, unnoticed, like an ache they'd learned to ignore.

In their eyes, Gregory saw a shift, a softening. Julia's gaze held a light he hadn't seen before as if some long-locked door had opened within her. Caius, the soldier, swallowed hard, a faint tremor betraying the disciplined mask he wore. Even Decimus, the hardened merchant, seemed caught off guard, his usual skepticism dulled, replaced by something softer, almost childlike. With a thrill of quiet awe, Gregory realized that his words had touched a place in them that Rome could neither conquer nor command—a part that yearned for connection, meaning, and love that no empire could offer.

For the first time, they glimpsed a vision of themselves as part of something larger, bound together by a light that could heal and redeem. They saw, if only dimly, a way of being that defied the cruelty of their world, a truth that offered not domination but salvation.

In that sacred moment, Gregory felt their hearts open, and each one received the message as if from Divine hands. He wondered if he had planted seeds of faith that might one day grow into something Rome could neither contain nor understand.

The group fell silent, Lucius's steady gaze meeting Gregory's as the significance of his words filled the night air. Breaking the quiet, Lucius leaned forward, his voice calm but firm. "This is not about rebellion for rebellion's sake," he began, addressing the group with the measured tone of a man who had thought deeply about his convictions. "It is about honoring something greater than ourselves—a truth that calls for action not out of anger, but out of courage."

He paused, letting the moonlight catch the subtle lines of his face as he scanned the gathering. "Rome teaches us that loyalty is the highest virtue, but I ask you this—what if our loyalty is misplaced? Should it not lie with something beyond power and conquest? Honor comes from standing for what is just, not merely following the strongest voice."

Lucius's words landed heavily, each syllable drawn with care, and the tension in the courtyard softened. "Strength does not always shout," he continued, "and it does not always wield the sword. True strength lies in quiet resolve, the ability to endure, and sacrifice for what is right, even when it is not easy or certain. That is the kind of loyalty Rome has forgotten."

The group nodded slowly, the first flickers of belief sparking in their eyes as Lucius's words connected with something deeper, something they had perhaps forgotten. In their faces, Gregory saw it now—a readiness, fragile but growing—the soul of a movement taking its first breath.

As the gathering ended, Julia approached Gregory. "Your words remind me of my dreams," she said softly. "A world where people are more than instruments of power." She paused, her gaze intense. "If you truly believe this, then… I would hear more."

Gregory's heart swelled. Here was the beginning, a gathering of souls willing to listen, question, and perhaps even follow. It would not be easy, and it would be dangerous, but he sensed a quiet power building—a movement that could ripple outward.

Walking back to the temple, Lucius and Gregory spoke in low voices, their conversation filled with quiet determination. Lucius warned him of the risks, of Rome's intolerance for any form of dissent, but Gregory met his gaze with unwavering resolve. "Rome is strong," he said, "but love is stronger. We may start as a whisper, but in time, even a whisper can grow to fill the world."

Lucius extended his hand, and Gregory took it, sealing a pact not only between two men but between their shared purpose—a movement grounded in compassion and humility, something deeper than Rome's iron grip could understand.

As Gregory lay in the quiet darkness of the room that night, he knew he would not walk alone. With Lucius by his side and the first stirrings of belief in the hearts of those they'd spoken to, he could feel a gathering strength. He was not here to overthrow an empire but to kindle a flame in the hearts of its people; a flame that would spread slowly and quietly, reaching those willing to open their eyes and see the light.

CHAPTER THIRTEEN
MESSIAH

Night after night, Gregory and Lucius found themselves drawn back to the courtyard, a space that began as a secluded refuge but quickly transformed into a focal point of whispered hope. It started with only a few—the disillusioned merchant Decimus, the weary soldier Caius, and the introspective Julia. Their cautious exchanges under the moonlight painted a portrait of yearning—a quiet rebellion seeking meaning amidst Rome's iron rule.

Word of their gatherings spread like whispers in the market, reaching ears eager for something beyond conquest and power. Each evening, the crowd grew. New faces emerged from the bustling streets: merchants with the scent of spices clinging to their clothes, craftsmen with hands worn from shaping stone and metal, and servants who slipped away from their duties, seeking a moment of solace. Among them were philosophers, their robes flowing as they leaned in to listen and curious children clutching their parents' hands, eyes wide with wonder at the strangers who spoke passionately about love and forgiveness.

Lucius remained tense, his sharp eyes constantly scanning the perimeter, watching for signs of betrayal or spies sent to sniff out insubordination. Yet, even he couldn't deny the shift in the air and how people listened to Gregory's words, as if they were drinking water after days lost in the desert.

By the third night, the courtyard was alive with a hum of quiet anticipation, the soft murmur of voices weaving a symphony of longing and cautious hope. The street lamps cast light and shadow across the faces of those who had gathered, their expressions a mixture of apprehension and determination. The smell of earth mingled with the faint perfume of crushed herbs carried by an apothecary who had overheard the message at the market that day.

Gregory spoke with measured resolve, his voice steady and rising above the crowd but never forceful. "Love is not weakness," he would say, his hands extended to embrace them all. "It is the power that endures beyond empires, beyond armies. It does not break under the weight of fear; it transforms."

Standing slightly behind Gregory, Lucius watched the crowd as their faces softened, their postures leaning forward to catch every word. He glanced at Gregory, a flicker of doubt shadowing his features. Later that night, when they returned to the temple's safety, Lucius finally voiced his concern.

"This cannot continue unchecked, Gregory," he said, pacing with restless energy. "The more they come, the harder it will be to avoid attention. Rome's silence now is not complacency—it's patience. Trust me, they are waiting to strike."

"And what would you have me do, Lucius?" Gregory asked, his voice calm yet tinged with weariness. "Turn them away? These people seek something beyond fear, beyond power. Would you deny them their only chance to hear that there is another way?"

Lucius stopped pacing, his gaze intense. "I'm not asking you to stop, but understand the stakes. Every night you speak, the shadow of the cross looms larger. They will not allow you to preach love and compassion without consequence. They will seek to break you—to exemplify you."

Gregory held his gaze, the fire in his eyes burning brighter. "Then let them come, Lucius. So be it if my words can spark even the faintest light in their darkness. Let Rome show its power. We will show them something greater."

***

As Gregory and Lucius stepped into the courtyard the following evening, they were met with a sight that stole their breath. The space, once intimate and shadowed, now thrummed with energy. What had begun as a handful of curious onlookers had grown into a dense crowd. The hum of murmured conversations rippled like a restless tide, silencing as Gregory emerged. The towering columns of Rome framed the scene, their imposing presence a stark reminder of the risks they all faced. Yet in the eyes of the gathered, there was something undeniable— an unyielding spark of hope, fragile but alive, flickering against the vast, unrelenting darkness.

Gregory took a deep breath, steadying himself. Before him stretched a sea of faces, eyes wide with expectation. Behind them loomed the towering structures of Rome, symbols of power and conquest. Yet here, in this gathering, was something different—a stirring, like the anticipation before a storm.

He raised his voice, calm yet commanding. "I come to you not with promises of wealth or power," he called out. "No gold, no rank, no titles. I speak of something greater—a strength that comes not from domination but compassion."

The crowd stilled, leaning in, captivated by words that defied everything Rome had taught them. He could see it in their faces—a flicker of recognition as if his words were unlocking something buried deep within.

A woman in the front row raised her hand, her voice edged with both doubt and hope. "Why should we care about those who would see us suffer? Why forgive those who do us harm?"

Gregory's gaze softened, his voice carrying a quiet conviction. "Because when we forgive, we break free from the chains of hate. When we love, even those who despise us, we find a strength that no empire, ruler, or weapon can destroy. We do not forgive for their sake but for ours. To carry love within us, even in the face of cruelty, is the truest power."

A murmur ran through the crowd. Gregory watched as hardened faces softened and brows relaxed. He saw their eyes glisten with the faintest touch of wonder as if they were glimpsing something they hadn't realized they needed—a gentleness, a kindness that defied their world.

"Tell us more!" a voice called from the back, the words carrying a fervor that rippled through the crowd.

Gregory's heart surged as he felt the crowd shift, leaning closer, each person hungry for his wisdom. He spoke of the Divine spark within every soul, a light connecting them all and transcending the brutality of Rome's rule.

"Imagine," he urged, his voice growing stronger, "a world where we lift each other up, where power is measured not by conquest but by compassion, where we are bound not by fear but by love."

The crowd surged closer, eyes shining with awe and longing. He had touched something sacred within them that defied Rome's ambitions. They didn't just hear his words; they felt them, each syllable a quiet revolution igniting within their hearts.

A voice from within the crowd, quivering with reverence, called out, "Are you… are you an oracle?"

Gregory hesitated, feeling the question settle over him. "I am but a servant," he replied softly. But he could see the veneration in their eyes, the unspoken hope that they had found a guide, a shepherd. They looked at him as if he were more than a man, and in their eyes, he saw the glimmer of belief, of faith.

At that moment, Lucius stepped forward, gently taking Gregory by the arm. "Enough," he whispered, his voice urgent. "You've given them what they need. Any more, and it could become a frenzy."

As Gregory turned to follow Lucius back into the temple, hands reached out, brushing against him, seeking his touch, his blessing. He looked back at the crowd one last time, feeling the pull of their yearning.

As the doors closed, sealing Gregory from the fervent crowd outside, he found himself lost in a torrent of emotions. The memory of those reaching hands lingered—a longing for something deeper, something beyond the iron discipline of Rome, beyond the stoic resolve they had always known. He could still feel the warmth of their touch, the unspoken plea in their eyes, and a profound sense of responsibility settled upon him.

In that quiet moment, Gregory closed his eyes, and his thoughts drifted back to the story of Christ, as he had always understood it—a humble man, wandering through towns and villages, gathering followers drawn not by riches or power but by the simple, radical promise of love.

Christ had not sought a kingdom of wealth or territory but of hearts. Gregory had preached these stories for decades, but until now, he had only understood them as words. Now, he was living them. He could feel the raw, transformative power of belief surging through the crowd, binding them to him, almost as if he were not Gregory, the Pope of his world, but a vessel for something far greater than himself.

In his mind's eye, he saw the images of Christ walking barefoot along dusty roads, surrounded by the poor, the sick, the desperate—people who clung to him with the same hunger Gregory had seen in this crowd. He remembered the accounts of Christ's eyes, warm and steady, meeting each person's gaze with unwavering compassion. And he understood that this was not mere history; this was a journey of the soul, a path that transcended time, one he was now called to walk in this strange new Rome.

Christ's journey had been filled with danger, too. The power of his message threatened the authorities of his time, just as Gregory's words now unsettled the Roman order. But Christ had pressed on, even though the cross awaited him. Gregory felt a chill run through him. Was he prepared for such a fate? Could he continue to speak these words, knowing where they might lead him?

And yet, how could he do otherwise? How could he deny the yearning he had just witnessed, the cries of those seeking a new way, a different life, a light in the darkness? A familiar warmth filled his heart—a mixture of courage and purpose that silenced his doubts. This was why he had been brought here; he felt it in every fiber of his being. The Divine purpose he had always sought in his world had crossed with his path here, in this ancient Rome.

Gregory felt the enormity of his mission settle over him. In that instant, he was no longer just a visitor from another world but a bridge between two realms, bearing a message that had once defied death and now sought to take root again. The risks were great, but his purpose was clear.

Standing in the dim glow of the temple's flickering candles, he realized he was prepared and had been called for this moment. In the eyes of the crowd outside, he had seen the first spark of transformation, the same spark that had once ignited a revolution of the soul. He knew he was not alone on this journey. The spirit of the one he had followed all his life was with him, guiding his steps, and in that knowledge, Gregory found a strength that nothing in Rome could extinguish.

CHAPTER FOURTEEN
THE RISING TIDE

Marcus paced the length of his study, casting anxious glances toward the door as if expecting someone to burst in unannounced. Maria's disapproval lingered in the room like a storm cloud, her unspoken warnings weighing on him with each step he took. She had tried to steer him away from Gregory to quell his interest, but he couldn't longer ignore the pull. Gregory was becoming something more than an enigmatic outsider; he was becoming a presence, a force stirring people's hearts in ways Marcus had never seen.

"Marcus." Maria's voice broke the silence, sharp with worry. "Why must you involve yourself with that foreigner? Bringing him here… What if someone sees him? What if we're reported?"

He stopped his pacing, turning to face her. "Maria, can't you see what's happening? He's touching something in people. They're beginning to believe there's more to life than Rome's iron hand."

"And that terrifies me," she replied, her arms folded tightly across her chest. "Belief can be dangerous. Rome has crushed men for far less. If they even suspect that we're associating with someone like him—"

"Rome," Marcus interrupted, his voice thick with frustration, "is precisely the problem. They've instilled fear in everyone and smothered any hope of change. And yet here is this man, speaking of love, compassion, and forgiveness. Can't you feel it, Maria? He's… different."

Maria's face softened slightly, but her worry didn't fade. "I feel it, yes. But that's what makes him dangerous. People are talking about him like he's more than just a man. The wrong person hears these whispers, and suddenly, it's not just Gregory in danger—it's us, Marcus. Our family."

He sighed, running a hand through his hair. "I understand your fear. But what if this talk about him is right?"

She looked at him, her expression both weary and imploring. "I don't doubt his words may hold a truth. But can't you see the risk? We are Romans, bound by duty and law. Such beliefs as forgiveness are punishable. If they find out we're supporting him, even quietly… Do you really want to put everything we've built on the line?"

Marcus hesitated, Maria's warnings echoing in his mind, but his conviction held. "I can't turn my back on this, Maria. Not when something this important is unfolding before us. I feel… compelled."

Maria's shoulders slumped, her gaze filled with both love and frustration. "Just promise me you'll be careful, Marcus. Rome does not tolerate defiance, and the price for even a whisper of dissent is steep."

Marcus nodded, feeling the fire in his chest that wouldn't be doused. His path was dangerous, but turning away felt even more impossible. As he resumed his pacing, her warnings stayed with him, yet so did the quiet, persistent belief that perhaps this was a risk worth taking.

When Gregory arrived, he appeared serene. He looked at his friend with calm eyes, a faint smile playing on his lips as if he sensed the urgency in Marcus's summons. Maria, as always, avoided Gregory's gaze. Her face tightened with worry as she moved briskly about, setting out cups of wine before retreating without a word.

As they settled in, Marcus studied Gregory with admiration and wariness. "There's talk at the university," he began, voice low despite the privacy of their surroundings. "Your gatherings… the way people speak of you… It's spreading, Gregory. The students whisper of you in the halls, the philosophers debate your teachings, and even the professors… Some of them have started attending. It's no longer a few quiet meetings behind closed doors; it's becoming a groundswell."

Gregory's expression brightened, and he took a sip of wine, seemingly unconcerned. "That is the nature of truth, Marcus. Once revealed, it cannot remain hidden. It seeks the light, finds a way into every heart willing to receive it."

"Perhaps," Marcus replied, frowning. "But truth has consequences, especially here, in Rome. Do you not realize that this… following could bring ruin upon you? Rome is not a place that tolerates divergence, let alone reverence for ideas that could disrupt its power."

Gregory shrugged, the faintest hint of amusement in his eyes. "I am well aware of Rome's might. But do you see what I see, Marcus? They come to me not with fear but with open hearts. They ask questions they were once afraid to speak aloud, and I answer them. And they leave with a new understanding that Rome's force cannot shatter."

Marcus ran a hand through his hair, unsettled by Gregory's confidence. "You say this as if it were a glorious thing. As if you were destined to be received as some… some savior." He hesitated, studying Gregory intently. "You call yourself Pope in your strange story, this tale of a parallel world. But tell me, Gregory—what's greater than being Pope? What's grander than leading the faithful in your world?"

Gregory tilted his head as though bemused by the question. "What do you mean?"

"Perhaps," Marcus pressed, leaning forward, "you're being pulled into something more than you realize. Perhaps you're beginning to play a role you don't fully see yet. If this world has no Christ, what stops you from filling that void? A Pope, you say? What if you're becoming more than that—a Messiah in your own right?"

Gregory fell silent, a flicker of something unreadable crossing his face. For a moment, he looked uncertain, as though Marcus's words had reached a place within him that he hadn't considered. Then he chuckled softly, shaking his head. "You mistake admiration for devotion, Marcus. The people are drawn to me not because I am Divine but because I offer them an idea they have longed for—a life beyond fear and strict obedience."

"Perhaps," Marcus replied, unconvinced. "But have you not felt the way they look at you? They do not see a mere man, Gregory. They see something larger. I have watched them—the reverence, the awe in their eyes. They look to you with the same fervor, and I imagine they would look to a god if one stood before them. Apollo's light is not meant for mortals to wield—it can illuminate, but it can also burn. Those who follow you see something Divine in you, something that transcends their lives, but are you sure you understand the fire you're playing with?"

Gregory's smile faded, his gaze turning thoughtful. "I won't deny," he murmured, almost to himself, "that I have never been received in my own world as I am here. In my Rome, there are expectations, traditions… boundaries that keep the Church contained and its power… tempered. But here, I am untethered, and it seems my words strike deeper."

"And does that not concern you?" Marcus asked, his voice rising slightly. "Does it not worry you that this could become more than you intended?"

Gregory met his gaze, and for the first time, his expression showed a hint of vulnerability. "It does… but I cannot turn away now. They are yearning for something, Marcus. You see it too, don't you? These people need hope and compassion. And if I can give that to them and offer a path, then perhaps… perhaps that is my reason for being here."

Marcus looked down, a shadow of doubt still lingering within him, yet he could not deny the quiet conviction he felt growing. "I don't know what I believe, Gregory. I don't know if I can accept that you come from another world or were once what you call a Pope. But I see your effect and that… it troubles me, even as it intrigues me."

Gregory placed a gentle hand on his friend's shoulder. "I ask nothing more than your willingness to listen, Marcus. The journey we are on, it's not one I can take alone. I need you and those like you who are willing to seek the truth, even if it disrupts the life you have known."

"You may be willing to risk all, Gregory," he said, "but remember that those who follow you—they will face that same danger. They look to you, perhaps not as a leader but as something more. Do not let that lead you down a path you cannot control."

Gregory's gaze hardened, his voice soft yet resolute. "I understand, Marcus. But I believe that what we are doing… is necessary. Rome's rule is powerful, but it is not eternal. It does not touch the spirit, the soul. And if I must stand in defiance of that power, so be it."

Marcus nodded slowly, recognizing a resolve he could not shake in his friend's words, a purpose beyond mere rhetoric. "Then let us hope, Gregory," he murmured, "that the path you walk will not end in ruin."

They sat in silence, each man contemplating the dangerous road ahead, each aware that the seeds of something profound—and perilous—had been planted within Rome's mighty walls.

Gregory looked at Marcus thoughtfully, sensing the lingering doubt that clouded his friend's face. "Tell me, Marcus," he asked quietly, "why do you still not believe my story? After everything we've discussed, after all you've seen… why do you hesitate?"

Marcus paused, searching for the right words. "It's not that I don't want to believe, Gregory," he admitted, his tone softened by an inner conflict. "A part of me… a part of me does. I see what you inspire in people and how your words touch something deep within them. But your claim—coming from another world, a place where the gods I know are mere myths, and where you carry this title of 'Pope'… It's beyond comprehension. How can I accept such a thing without proof?"

Gregory stopped pacing and turned toward Marcus with an air of resignation. He spread his hands helplessly, his voice calm but tinged with weariness. "I have no proof to offer you, Marcus; nothing tangible would satisfy logic or reason. All I have is my word, the truth as I know it. Whether you accept it or not is entirely up to you." His gaze held steady, and a quiet challenge lingered in his tone.

Marcus remained silent, studying Gregory intently. For a moment, the room was filled only with the faint crackle of the fire and the occasional creak of the wooden floor. Then, as if coming to a decision, Marcus straightened and crossed the room to a small table near the window. He picked up an object, hesitated briefly, and turned back toward Gregory. The expression on his face was unreadable as he stepped closer and extended the item—a small, weathered manuscript— with deliberate care.

"Is this proof?" Marcus asked, his voice low and measured.

Gregory's jaw dropped. "Where did you find this?"

"Maria found this beneath the bed you slept in," Marcus said, calm but tinged with curiosity. "I believe it belongs to you."

He couldn't speak for a moment; seeing it again made him mute. Slowly, almost reverently, he reached out and took the book, his fingers brushing against the frayed edges of its leather-bound cover.

"I had forgotten…" Gregory murmured, his voice barely audible. "I had forgotten I even brought it with me."

He traced the faded lettering on the cover, his touch as light as if he were handling a relic from a sacred altar. The ancient Latin script whispered of secrets long buried, a language Gregory understood only in fragments but which still felt alive under his fingertips. He held the book to his chest as though the very act of reclaiming it was a reunion with a piece of himself.

"What is it?" Marcus asked, his tone carrying a mix of curiosity and apprehension.

Gregory took a deep breath, holding the book out so Marcus could see it. "This… this is an ancient manuscript. I took it from the Vatican before I passed through the portal. I don't know what compelled me to bring it, but something told me it was important. Something… or someone."

Marcus's eyes narrowed as he leaned closer, the table lamp illuminating the faded ink on the brittle pages. He didn't recognize the language, but the intricate symbols and patterns suggested a depth of meaning transcending mere words.

"It's written in ancient Latin," Gregory continued, his voice tinged with awe. "I know the language, but much of this remains incomprehensible. The style is archaic. I think it's older than the Vatican itself—perhaps a relic from the early days of the Church, or maybe even before."

Marcus carefully removed the manuscript from Gregory's trembling hands, his fingers grazing the delicate parchment. He turned a page gingerly, the faint scent of aged paper rising to meet him.

Gregory's breath hitched as he reached for the manuscript again, his eyes bright with a mixture of wonder and anxiety. "If this book was with me when I arrived, could it be connected to why I'm here?" His voice was quiet but carried an urgent undertone. "It might hold answers, Marcus. Answers about this world, my purpose, perhaps even how our realities intersect."

Marcus glanced at him, intrigued but cautious. "Do you believe it's a map, then? A guide of some kind?" he asked, flipping another delicate page, his gaze scanning the faded script.

Gregory hesitated, his fingers brushing over the frayed edges of the manuscript as though it might crumble under his touch. "I don't know what this means yet," he admitted, his voice low and uncertain. "But it's not just an old book. It's… something. I can feel it, Marcus, though I can't say why. Maybe it's connected to why I'm here. Maybe it isn't. I don't know."

"Then you must find out," Marcus said, his voice measured but firm. "But, Gregory, don't let speculation become certainty too quickly. If this book holds answers, let them reveal themselves in time."

Gregory accepted the manuscript with both hands, cradling it like a fragile museum piece. The weight of the parchment felt heavier now, though not in a physical sense. "I'll take it back to the temple tonight," he murmured. "There's too much I don't understand. I need quiet. Space to think."

The flicker of the light from the fireplace offered wavering shadows around the room, the quiet punctuated by the soft crackle of the dry wood. Marcus stepped forward, placing a hand on Gregory's shoulder. "If you feel its pull, follow it. But let caution guide you as much as curiosity. There's no telling what truths lie within or what consequences they might bring."

Gregory met his gaze, the words both grounding and unsettling. "I don't know where this will lead," he said, almost to himself. "But whatever it is, I can't ignore it."

With that, he tucked the manuscript into a pocket of his robe. The cool night air greeted him as Marcus opened the door, a whisper of wind carrying the faint sounds of the city beyond.

Gregory's thoughts swirled with uncertainty and fragile hope as he stepped into the darkness. The manuscript might be an ancient curiosity, a relic of another time. Or it might hold secrets he couldn't yet fathom—answers to questions he hadn't even known to ask.

CHAPTER FIFTEEN
THE SEER

The night wrapped around Gregory like a shroud, the cold air brushing against his face as he stepped deeper into the city's labyrinthine streets. Tucked securely within his robe, the manuscript felt heavier with each passing moment. Distant lamps flickered faintly, casting erratic shadows on the ancient stone walls looming on either side, their surfaces slick with moisture from the evening fog.

The streets were eerily quiet, the usual hum of the city absent. It was as if this corner of Rome existed in a pocket of suspended time, untouched by the modern chaos beyond its borders. The occasional echo of his footsteps felt intrusive, disrupting the heavy stillness that clung to the air. Gregory's thoughts churned with questions, his mind returning repeatedly to the manuscript and the secrets it might hold. Was this relic from his world a key to understanding the impossible journey that had brought him here? Or was it simply just another ancient book from the archive, its significance magnified only by his desperation for answers?

As he rounded a corner, the atmosphere shifted subtly, almost imperceptibly. The air grew colder, tinged with a strange, electric stillness that prickled the back of his neck. Gregory slowed his pace, his senses alert. The narrow alley opened into a small, dimly lit square, its cobblestones uneven and glistening under the faint glow of a single, flickering streetlamp. At its center stood a figure cloaked in shadow, their presence at once foreboding and magnetic.

The figure turned as Gregory approached, revealing a face partially hidden by the hood of a weathered cloak. Their luminous and otherworldly eyes locked onto his, and Gregory felt an unexplainable pull as though they had been waiting for him. It was a woman, and without a word, she gestured with a crooked finger for him to follow, turning and slipping into the narrow, twisting passages.

Gregory moved cautiously, glancing over his shoulder as he neared a darkened entrance of a shrine hidden in Rome's narrow, winding alleyways. Inside, the air was cool and carried the faint, earthy scent of herbs mingled with the sharper tang of incense. The shrine had an ethereal beauty, simple yet profound, its walls draped in faded tapestries adorned with symbols that seemed to stir something deep within Gregory. They were not entirely unknown to him; their patterns felt oddly familiar, like fragments of a dream he had once grasped but could not fully recall.

In the dim light, she stood at the center, cloaked in deep indigo. Her presence was commanding and enigmatic, as though the shadows bent to her will. The hood of her cloak obscured most of her face, but her piercing eyes shone from the darkness, luminous and searching as if they saw straight into his heart.

"Come closer, Gregory," the woman intoned, her voice smooth and ageless, reverberating softly within the stone chamber.

Startled, Gregory froze mid-step, his heart jolting as the woman addressed him by name. Her smooth, layered voice, with an almost musical resonance, felt like it had been waiting for this moment.

"You… you know me?" he managed, his words strained and uncertain.

"Names," she said, her tone dismissive, carrying an air of timeless wisdom, "are fleeting echoes, fragments of identity. What I know is your essence, the vibration of your being. It is out of place here—a thread pulled from a tapestry where it belongs, stitched instead into this one, where it was never meant to be."

Her words pressed on Gregory's chest, each syllable rippling with an authority that left no room for doubt. His unease deepened, mingling with awe and an insistent, gnawing apprehension. "Who are you?" he asked, his voice a whisper against the heavy stillness of the shrine.

Her head tilted slightly, the hood obscuring most of her face, though her eyes glimmered faintly beneath the shadow. "My name is Maia, though that question matters less than why I am here, Gregory. I am a witness. A guide for those who need direction when the fabric of their existence begins to fray."

His breath hitched. Her presence felt as though it clarified and deepened the mystery surrounding him. "A guide for what? For me?"

Maia took a measured step forward, her movements as deliberate as her words. "You do not understand your situation. This world trembles under your presence, an anomaly that strains its foundations. The air, the light, and even time whisper of your misplacement."

Gregory felt the chill return, creeping along his spine. "Misplacement," he repeated, the word strange on his tongue. "Why am I here, then? If I don't belong… why was I brought?"

She lifted her hand, her fingers delicately brushing the air, and gestured toward him, her eyes glinting with an unsettling clarity. "The answer is not far, Gregory. You carry it with you."

Gregory frowned, his brow furrowed as he searched her face for meaning. "Carry it with me?" he echoed.

Maia tilted her head, her tone softening. "You have held it close all this time, unaware of its significance. It is your guide, your key, though you do not yet know how to decipher its meaning."

Gregory hesitated, her words tugging at the edges of his awareness. Slowly, his hand moved to his side. His fingers grazed the fabric before he paused, a flicker of realization blooming in his eyes. "The manuscript?" he murmured, his voice wavering between disbelief and dawning comprehension.

Maia nodded, her expression grave. "Yes, the volume you hid so carefully, not even fully understanding why you brought it with you. This is no ordinary relic. It holds the threads of your journey, the map to your return."

Gregory reached into the hidden inner pocket, his hand trembling as it closed around the fragile, ancient text. The parchment felt alive beneath his touch, humming faintly as if responding to the charged air between them.

Gregory held the manuscript under the dim light, the flickering shadows playing across its worn surface. The symbols came alive, shifting subtly, teasing him with meanings just out of reach. His voice was quiet, almost reverent. "I've tried to make sense of it."

Maia's steady gaze didn't waver, her voice soft yet firm, weaving through the tension in the room. "That message within was forged for this moment, for you, Gregory. Its purpose is not simply to foretell but to guide. Those symbols carry the knowledge to mend what has been torn, to lead you back—not just to where you belong, but to what you are meant to become."

Gregory opened the leather-bound cover and stared at its weathered parchment, the ancient script blurring before his eyes as a rush of emotions gripped him. Doubt, hope, and an uneasy sense of destiny churned within him. "I've tried to read it," he confessed, his voice tinged with frustration. "Most of the language is unfamiliar. The symbols… they evade me."

"Absorb it," Maia said, her tone now soft but insistent. "This is a text meant for the soul. Its secrets will not reveal themselves through reason alone. It would be best if you looked beyond, Gregory. Feel the truth it holds. Allow it to guide you."

His grip on the manuscript tightened as her words sank in. The book seemed heavier now, as though it carried not just his answers but the fates of two worlds. He looked up at her, his voice breaking. "And if I can't understand it?"

Her faint smile flickered like the shadows cast by the flickering candles. "You see it as ink on parchment, but it is far more. That text is a key meant to guide you back to where you came from. But only if you are willing to see beyond the physical, beyond the limits of the mind."

Gregory looked up from the manuscript, his voice trembling. "And if I fail? If I can't leave?"

Her gaze, unyielding yet not unkind, locked with his. "The failure would not be yours alone. The fracture you've caused will widen. This Rome and the Rome you left behind will begin to unravel, colliding until both are lost. To fail here is to risk unmaking both realities."

Her words crushed him; the enormity of his presence in this world was no longer abstract. He had become something far greater—and far more dangerous—than he'd ever imagined. "What must I do?"

The seer's gaze did not waver, her eyes unblinking and sharp, pierced through layers of his being. "Your presence in this world is like a jagged tear in the fabric of reality. You do not belong here, Gregory. This place, this Rome, was not meant for you."

Gregory swallowed, her words sinking into him with a weight he hadn't anticipated. "I know I am different here and have tried to make sense of it. But why do you call my being here a… a tear? What does that mean?"

The seer extended her hand, her fingers pale and delicate yet exuding an undeniable strength. "Come," she urged, her voice a soft yet commanding whisper that seemed to ripple through the air. "Let me show you."

Gregory hesitated, his instincts screaming to retreat, but something in her tone pulled him forward. As their hands met, a jolt of energy surged through him. It wasn't warmth or cold—it was something else entirely, a raw, electric force that coursed through his veins, igniting sensations he didn't have words to describe.

And then the images came.

They exploded in his mind like shattered glass, fragments of two distinct worlds colliding, twisting, and merging into a kaleidoscope of impossible visions. He saw his Rome first, vivid and familiar—the Vatican's grand domes glowing under a golden sky, the narrow streets bustling with pilgrims, the comforting hum of prayers echoing through ancient stone corridors. Faces flashed before him—figures he knew, loved, and trusted—blurred and distorted as if they were slipping away.

Then came the other Rome—this Rome. Stark, cold, and unyielding, its streets sprawled out like veins across a hardened landscape. The Colosseum loomed in shadow, not as a ruin but as a thriving centerpiece of power and fear. The air was heavy and dense, with an almost suffocating tension, as if the city itself was holding its breath, bracing for something cataclysmic.

The two Romes clashed in his mind, one overlaying the other like mismatched transparencies. Buildings fractured and bled into one another. Crowds mingled and split apart. The sky rippled and tore, the very fabric of reality buckling under the weight of their convergence. He could feel the chaos—the pressure of two worlds trying to occupy the same space, fighting against an inevitable collapse.

The visions grew brighter and sharper, and then, as suddenly as they came, they vanished. Gregory staggered backward, releasing the seer's hand as though it burned him. His breaths came in ragged gasps, and his heart hammered in his chest.

"What…" His voice broke, the words caught in his throat. He swallowed hard and tried again. "What was that?"

The seer's expression softened, but her eyes held the wisdom of centuries. "You've seen it now," she said quietly. "The fracture. Two Romes, two realities, colliding. They were never meant to coexist, Gregory. And yet, they are drawn together by forces that defy understanding. The longer they remain entangled, the closer they come to annihilation. You… you are the thread between them. And the thread must choose which fabric to mend."

Gregory's mind reeled, her words spiraling through him. "Are you saying that I must leave? That my purpose here, the message I've been spreading… it's wrong?"

Maia's gaze softened. "It is not a matter of right or wrong, but of necessity. If you were to fail in this world, Gregory, the consequences would ripple across the boundaries of existence and send tremors through the veil, weakening it beyond repair. Not only would this world suffer, but so would the one you call home."

A chill crawled up Gregory's spine as her words took root. He felt the pull of truth he couldn't escape—a truth that went beyond his understanding into realms he hadn't dared to consider. "But… my mission. The people here need guidance and hope. How can I turn my back on them?"

Maia's face softened, a faint glimmer of empathy in her eyes. "You are not the first to walk between worlds, Gregory, nor will you be the last. But each journey carries its own burden, and yours is to maintain the balance. Perhaps you were brought here to share what you know, to plant seeds of change. But the roots of that change must grow without you. To stay beyond your purpose is to invite chaos into both realms."

He took a shuddering breath, feeling as though the ground beneath him was crumbling. "How… how do I leave? If I must return, how do I find my way back?"

The seer studied him for a moment, her gaze contemplative. "The path to return is not one of the body, but of the spirit. You must sever the ties that anchor you here—ties of pride, ambition, and the intoxicating allure of power. I see it within you, Gregory. This world tempts you and draws you with promises of influence and adoration. But you must let these urges go."

Her words struck a chord he could not ignore, stirring something uncomfortably familiar within him. He had felt it too—the allure of being revered, the intoxicating pull of seeing his words ignite hope and devotion in a way that went beyond his duties in his own Rome. Here, he wasn't just a Pope; he was a beacon, a guide, and, dare he admit it—a messiah.

"What must I do?" he asked, his voice quiet, laced with both resignation and determination. The question wasn't only for the seer but for himself as he grappled with the delicate balance between purpose and pride.

Her piercing gaze settled on him, unyielding yet tinged with a faint glimmer of empathy. "The pathway lies in what you already possess," she said, her voice soft but resonant. "The answers are etched within the volume you carry. Its words will guide you back, but only if you learn to see beyond what is written."

Gregory's fingers brushed the edges of the ancient leather binding, worn smooth from time and care. "This book," he murmured, disbelief mingling with dawning comprehension. "It's filled with symbols and words I barely understand. How can it help me?"

The seer stepped closer, the dim light casting flickering shadows across her veiled face. "It is more than ink and parchment," she replied. "It is a bridge—a map hidden in plain sight, waiting for its bearer to awaken to its truth. But the path it reveals is not one of logic alone. You must surrender your doubts, pride, and longing for power to follow it. Only then will its secrets unfold."

"And if I fail?" he asked, his voice trembling with the enormity of the moment. "What happens if I can't find my way back?"

The seer's expression softened, though her eyes remained unwavering. "As I said, if you fail, the rift between worlds will grow, and both will suffer. The balance must be restored, Gregory. This is no longer just your journey—the thread upon which countless lives hang. Whether you accept it or not, the power you wield has consequences far beyond yourself."

Gregory felt a chill as her words settled over him. His destiny was no longer guiding others, spreading hope, or defying Rome's grip. It was instead about survival—not just his own but the survival of two realities teetering on the edge of chaos.

The seer's voice broke through his thoughts, low and commanding. "Do not squander the time you have left. Study the volume. Let it guide you. The answers will not come easily, but they are there, waiting for you to see."

She stepped back, her form fading into the shadows surrounding the shrine. Her final words echoed softly, carrying with them a sense of foreboding and resolve: "Remember, Gregory. Your path is not to be forged by ambition but by humility. Only then will the way home reveal itself."

And with that, she was gone, leaving Gregory alone in the flickering torchlight. The book felt heavier now, its presence more profound than ever before. As he held it close, fear and determination surged within him. The path forward was fraught with peril, but it was a path he could no longer avoid. The answers were within his grasp, but the journey to uncover them would demand everything he had—and more.

CHAPTER SIXTEEN
HELENA VORENUS

Gregory sat in solitude; the wood blinds tilted to block out the harsh glare of the Roman sun. The room was silent except for the faint rustle of the manuscript's brittle pages as he carefully turned them, his eyes scanning the cryptic symbols under the soft glow of a desk lamp. The faint hum of the city outside barely registered in his consciousness; his entire focus was consumed by the ancient text before him. Each page vibrated with quiet energy as though the intricate symbols and faint Latin phrases carried their own pulse, weaving into a hypnotic rhythm.

Gregory wrestled with the text for hours, straining his mind to grasp its meaning. The symbols were unlike anything he had encountered in his years of theological study, yet they stirred something deep within him—an elusive familiarity that refused to surface fully. Some phrases in Latin were precise enough to provide fragments of meaning. Compassion, wisdom, and sacrifice were repeated enough to form a tenuous thread of understanding.

He leaned back, exhaustion settling over him. The flickering light of the desk lamp cast long shadows across the walls, their shapes shifting like silent echoes of his thoughts. The seer's voice reverberated in his mind, her ominous warning clear: *You must not die here*. His thoughts strayed to the crucifixion. The image loomed unbidden, vivid and terrible—the echoes of Christ's fate mingling with his fear that this world would see him meet the same end.

The book lay open before him, its cryptic symbols and fragmented Latin phrases taunting him with their indecipherable secrets. Gregory's fingers brushed the worn parchment, his mind racing with half-formed theories. He needed help—someone with the knowledge and clarity to make sense of this ancient text. The thought of Marcus surfaced naturally; the philosopher had already proven to be both an anchor and a bridge in this bewildering world. Perhaps within the university's walls, among the scholars and experts of this Rome, lay the key to deciphering the manuscript's mysteries. With a deep breath, Gregory closed the volume and resolved to seek Marcus's insight.

Gregory spotted Marcus hunched over his desk through the office door's glass pane. Late afternoon light streaming through the window cast a golden glow over the room. Shelves crammed with books stretched to the ceiling, the spines worn and faded from years of use. The desk was a controlled chaos of papers, journals, and coffee-stained notes. Marcus's expression was one of deep focus as he pored over a student's paper, occasionally scribbling a note in the margins.

Gregory paused, his hand hovering near the doorframe. The hum of campus life filtered faintly through the corridor, a distant reminder of the world outside. But inside, in this moment, Gregory felt the sharp pull of his purpose. The seer's warning echoed his thoughts. Steeling himself, he gently pushed the door open.

"Marcus," he began, his voice cutting through the stillness of the room.

Marcus looked up, startled by the unannounced visitor but quickly masking it with a warm, if slightly curious, smile. "Gregory. To what do I owe this surprise?"

Gregory sat across from him, setting the manuscript on the desk. "I've been struggling with this," he admitted, gesturing to the worn volume. "And after last night, I'm certain I can't do it alone."

Marcus's brow furrowed as he leaned forward, eyeing the manuscript with interest. "Last night? Why, what happened?"

Gregory hesitated, the gravity of his encounter with the seer making his confession feel urgent and surreal. "After leaving your home, I met someone. An elderly woman—a seer."

Marcus's curiosity deepened, though he remained silent, encouraging Gregory to continue.

"She told me that my presence here—my very existence in this Rome—is a disruption, a tear in the fabric of reality. If I don't find my way back, this world and the one I came from could be damaged beyond repair."

The room fell silent except for the faint rustle of papers, which was stirred by the breeze wisping through the open window. Marcus leaned back in his chair, his expression unreadable, but his eyes were sharp with thought.

"This seer," Marcus began carefully, his fingers resting on the edge of his desk, "you showed her the manuscript?"

"I did," Gregory said with a nod.

"What did she say about it?"

"She said it's both a guide and a key, holding the answers I need to return to my world. But, Marcus, I've been trying to make sense of it, and I… I can't. The symbols and the structure are as though they were written to evade understanding. I need your help, your connections."

Marcus's fingers drummed lightly on the desk, his brow furrowed in contemplation. "A guide and a key, you say? That sounds more than symbolic—it's intentional."

"I thought so, too," Gregory said, his eyes narrowing. "But without help, I can't make any progress. This book could hold answers; not just for me, but for all of us."

Marcus sighed, his lips tightening into a thoughtful line. "I don't know, Gregory. My expertise lies in philosophy, not in deciphering ancient scripts. However…" He hesitated as if weighing the risks. "I do know someone. A colleague here at the university. She's a linguistics scholar with a reputation for uncovering the meanings behind the most obscure and esoteric texts."

Gregory straightened. "Who?"

"Dr. Helena Vorenus," Marcus said, carefully closing the manuscript. "She specializes in ancient languages and symbology, but more than that, she has a way of uncovering the meaning beneath layers of obfuscation. If anyone can help you, it's her."

Gregory's heart surged with fragile hope. "And you think she'll believe me? That she'll help?"

Marcus leaned back in his chair, rubbing his chin thoughtfully. "Gregory," he began, "Helena doesn't need to believe your story. She doesn't need to understand the seer, alternate worlds, or why you're here."

Gregory frowned. "Then why would she agree to help?"

Marcus gestured toward the manuscript, its frayed edges illuminated by the afternoon light spilling through the window. "Helena thrives on challenges like uncovering what's hidden in ancient texts. She doesn't need to believe where it came from or what it means to you. She will focus on interpreting the symbols, the language, and the drawings. If there's a way to make sense of it, she'll find it."

Gregory sat back, the tension in his shoulders easing slightly. "You think she'll see it that way?"

Marcus leaned forward, his expression intent. "Gregory, you've shown me enough to know this manuscript is extraordinary. If anyone can make sense of it, it's Dr. Vorenus. She's one of the brightest minds at the university, with a passion for unraveling ancient mysteries. I'll contact her today and arrange a meeting."

Gregory hesitated, clutching the manuscript as though it might slip from his grasp. "And you think she'll take it seriously? This… this isn't just an academic text. It's something much more."

Marcus gave him a reassuring smile. "Helena's curiosity far outweighs her skepticism. If there's even a hint of truth to what you've told me, she'll want to see this through."

Gregory nodded, though the idea of parting with the manuscript, even temporarily, unsettled him. "Thank you, Marcus. I don't think I could face this alone."

Marcus waved off the sentiment with a smirk. "You'd manage somehow. You always do. But fortunately, you don't have to this time. Let's see what Helena can uncover."

***

Later that afternoon, Marcus led Gregory through the university's labyrinthine corridors until they reached Dr. Vorenus's office. The door was slightly ajar, revealing a room teeming with energy and intellect. Stacks of books teetered precariously on every surface, their spines worn, and titles faded. Maps of ancient civilizations adorned the walls, interspersed with meticulously detailed sketches of cryptic symbols. The scent of old parchment mingled with faint traces of ink and something metallic, like the tools of a forgotten trade.

Helena was seated at her desk, her sharp features illuminated by the soft glow of a desk lamp. Her graying hair was pulled back, and her eyes, piercing and precise, darted across a fragment of aged parchment she held with steady fingers. She looked up as they entered.

"Marcus," she said curtly, her tone brisk but not unkind. Her gaze shifted briefly to Gregory, and he felt the full intensity of her scrutiny, as though she were instantly cataloging every detail about him. "And you must be the one with the mysterious manuscript."

Marcus shifted uncomfortably, his hands clasped behind his back, as Gregory shot him a skeptical glare. "You told her about it? About me?" Gregory's voice was tense, and his frustration was barely contained.

Still seated at her desk, Helena looked up with calm curiosity. "Marcus shared some details, yes," she admitted plainly, her piercing gaze fixed on Gregory. "I understand your concerns about your privacy, but let me assure you, I have no interest in revealing your story. My focus is on the manuscript itself."

Gregory turned back to Marcus, his expression mixed with disbelief and anger. "Keeping this secret isn't a petty request—it's survival."

Marcus raised his hands slightly in a gesture of apology. "I understand, Gregory. Truly. But Helena is someone we need. Her expertise could be the key to making sense of this. I wouldn't have told her if I didn't trust her completely."

Helena leaned forward slightly, her tone softening. "Gregory, I get it. You don't know me and have every right to be cautious. But I promise you, your secrets are safe with me."

Gregory hesitated, the impact of her words hanging in the air. He studied her for a moment, searching for any sign of doubt. Finally, he let out a slow breath, some of the tension easing from his shoulders. "Fine," he said reluctantly. "But no one else. Not a single word."

Helena nodded firmly. "Understood. Now"—she gestured to Gregory—"why don't you show me what we're working with? Let's see if we can uncover the answers you're looking for."

Marcus offered Gregory a small, reassuring smile. "We'll figure this out. Together."

Gregory sighed, rubbing the back of his neck. He reached into his pocket, withdrew the volume, and placed it on the desk. Helena's expression shifted from curiosity to deep focus. Her fingers hovered above the cover as though sensing its significance in more than a physical sense.

"Fascinating," she murmured, carefully flipping through the pages. "This isn't just old—it's ancient. The symbols here draw from a blend of traditions and the Latin… it's poetic, almost ritualistic. Where did you come by this?"

Gregory exchanged a glance with Marcus before answering. "That's… part of the complication. Let's say it's not from here. And I need your help to decipher it."

Helena's brow arched as she closed the manuscript gently and regarded Gregory with renewed interest. "Not from here?" she echoed, her tone laced with intrigue rather than skepticism. "Marcus mentioned your story was unconventional, but he didn't elaborate. No matter—it's the text that interests me. I'll need time, of course, but if your words are true, this manuscript must be extraordinary."

"Do you think you can translate it?" Gregory asked, his voice tight with anticipation.

Helena tilted her head, her expression thoughtful. "Translation is only part of the task. Texts like this are often layered with meaning—symbols, metaphors, riddles. Deciphering it will require more than just linguistic skills. But yes, I believe I can help."

Relief washed over Gregory, and he nodded. "Thank you. I'll tell you everything I can to help, but the truth is… I'm relying on you."

Helena's gaze softened slightly, and she gave a slight nod. "Then let's begin. Leave the manuscript with me, and I'll contact you as soon as I have something to share."

As they left the office, Gregory felt a glimmer of hope take root. Whatever secrets the manuscript held, he prayed Helena was the key to unlocking them.

CHAPTER SEVENTEEN
THE SEVEN SEEDS

Several days had passed since Gregory left the manuscript with Helena, but the cloud of uncertainty lingered heavily on his shoulders. Each hour stretched into eternity, the silence amplifying his restless thoughts. He had tried to distract himself, diving into mundane tasks, yet the enigmatic script haunted his mind, each symbol a taunt in its indecipherable complexity.

Finally, the summons came—a note from Helena delivered by one of Marcus's students. She had requested his immediate presence. Gregory's pulse quickened as he and Marcus made their way through the university's crowded corridors, the quiet determination between them unspoken but palpable.

The door was slightly ajar when they arrived at Helena's office and a faint hum of scholarly energy radiated from within. Helena sat at her desk, leaning intently over the manuscript. The soft glow of a desk lamp illuminated her sharp features, and her graying braid trailed over one shoulder. She didn't look up as they entered, her fingers poised over the parchment like a pianist preparing for the first note of a sonata.

Gregory felt his breath catch as he stepped inside, the tension of the past days pressing in on him. Marcus gave him a brief nod of encouragement before speaking. "Helena," Marcus began, his voice breaking the stillness, "we came as soon as we received your message."

Helena glanced up, her piercing gaze meeting theirs. "Good," she said, her tone brisk but laced with the faintest trace of excitement. "I've made progress."

Helena gestured for them to sit, her sharp eyes scanning Gregory as though trying to gauge his readiness. Without waiting for their response, she turned to the leather-bound volume and began. "This," she said, her voice deliberate, "is unlike anything I've ever studied. The title, as best as I can decipher, is written in a proto-Italic script—predating classical Latin by centuries."

Gregory leaned forward, frowning. "And what does it say?"

Helena hesitated, her fingers lightly tracing the etched lines of the ancient symbols as though their meaning might seep into her skin. "Septem Seminae," she murmured, the words rolling off her tongue. "Seven Seeds."

Gregory leaned forward, his brow furrowed. "Septem Seminae," he repeated, each syllable foreign and heavy in his mouth. "Seven Seeds. But why would such a straightforward phrase require such an ancient and intricate script?"

Helena's gaze sharpened, her voice carrying a subtle intensity. "It's not straightforward at all, Gregory. The words are veiled in layers of meaning. 'Septem' does not simply signify 'seeds.' It speaks of origins, potential, and even sacrifices tied to creation itself. And 'Seminae'—

while it may represent the number seven—suggests far more than a numerical value. It evokes cycles, Divine harmony, and a sense of inevitable completion."

She paused, her fingers lingering over the glyphs. "And this isn't just a text. It's a key to something larger that cannot be understood by words alone." Her voice dropped lower, almost a whisper. "These symbols… they resist us, Gregory. They are meant to withhold their secrets until the ready one truly sees them."

Gregory shook his head slightly, frustration flickering in his expression. "This is written in a script that should mean nothing to me. But the name… it stirs something. It feels familiar, somehow."

Helena leaned back in her chair, studying him closely. "Perhaps it's the manuscript itself. The text seems… alive, almost. It doesn't communicate in a straightforward manner—it's meant to evoke something deeper in its reader. Like a mirror reflecting more than just your outward self."

Gregory's lips tightened, his unease clear. "And these Seven Seeds? What do they mean?"

Helena flipped the page, revealing an intricate diagram surrounded by a more enigmatic script. "The text describes them as acts—symbolic, deeply spiritual gestures. These aren't literal seeds to be planted in soil. Their actions are to be carried out in places of significance. Each represents a virtue—compassion, forgiveness, sacrifice—and must resonate with the people who witness it."

Gregory frowned, leaning closer to the diagram. "And the purpose of these acts? What do they lead to?"

Helena pointed to a recurring phrase in the text, underlined by the interlocking spirals etched into the manuscript. "The text refers to them as opening a 'threshold.' A gate between this world and another."

Gregory's pulse quickened. "A gate? And you're certain this is what the text says?"

"As certain as I can be," Helena admitted. "But, Gregory, this isn't a set of instructions written for someone fluent in ancient languages. It's encoded, layered with meaning meant to evolve as the reader engages. These Seven Seeds are as much a journey inward as they are outward."

He took a deep breath, his hands resting on the edge of her desk. "What are these acts, Helena?"

Helena met his gaze, her expression both severe and cautious. "Each act corresponds to a virtue, and each must be performed in a specific location that amplifies its meaning. For instance," she said, flipping to another page, her fingers tracing the faded outline of a detailed sketch, "compassion might manifest by feeding the hungry in the heart of the city. Forgiveness could require reconciliation in a place marred by betrayal or conflict—somewhere the act carries the weight of history."

Gregory leaned closer, his brow furrowed. "And you're certain these actions aren't just symbolic gestures?"

Helena's lips pressed into a thin line as she considered the question. "The text is explicit—these acts carry an inherent power. They're not symbolic for the sake of ritual; they're designed to resonate. Each seed leaves an imprint that endures and ripples through the people and places touched by them. They're… transformative." She paused, her eyes narrowing. "But the manuscript also warns of the toll they exact."

Gregory's expression hardened. "You said these acts grow more dangerous. How so?"

Helena nodded grimly, flipping further into the manuscript. She gestured toward an intricate diagram, an array of circles and intersecting lines. "The text suggests each step draws more heavily on the person performing them. The final acts…" She hesitated, her gaze flickering to Gregory before settling on the manuscript. "They imply sacrifice— something deeply personal. The phrasing is vague, but there's a sense of loss. A surrender of something… essential."

Gregory's chest tightened, his fingers curling instinctively against the edge of her desk. "And what happens if the acts fail?"

Helena sighed, the burden of the question drawing her shoulders downward. She glanced back at the manuscript, her finger brushing lightly over the delicate script. "Failure," she said slowly, "suggests something is left broken—not just within the person, but within the world. It's unclear how or why, but the implication is profound." She hesitated, her voice softening. "It speaks of 'unraveling'—a harm beyond the one who attempts the acts."

Gregory's jaw tightened as he processed her words. He leaned back, his gaze falling on the manuscript. The ancient symbols pulsed faintly in the lamplight, their meaning now heavier with Helena's interpretation. He could feel the enormity of the task before him, an almost tangible pressure settling in his chest.

But beneath that pressure, a fear gnawed at him. The seer's warning echoed in his mind, her voice as haunting as the night she delivered it—*You must not die here.*

Helena's voice broke through his spiraling thoughts. "Gregory, are you all right?"

"And this gate," Gregory said after a long pause. "You said the acts would open it. What exactly is on the other side?"

Helena's gaze flickered, her uncertainty evident. "That, the text doesn't say. It simply calls it a 'threshold'—a passage that bridges what is and what could be. What lies beyond it… I don't know. But the acts are the key to reaching it. That much is clear."

Helena's sharp eyes glinted in the lamplight as she leaned over the manuscript, her voice steady with her interpretation. "This text is far more than it seems," she began, meeting Gregory's gaze. "These acts aren't symbolic gestures—they're transformative steps designed to resonate deeply with those who witness them. Each one is meant to heal fractures."

Gregory clenched his hands, his pulse quickening. To Helena, this was an ancient philosophical roadmap. But to him, it felt like a Divine compass—a path back to his world or perhaps a way to redeem the chaos his presence had caused in this one.

He exhaled slowly. "Can you outline these acts? What does each one require?"

Helena leaned closer, her expression contemplative as her finger traced the unfamiliar symbols etched into the ancient page. "The text," she began, her voice soft but certain, "outlines seven acts—each one a seed, as the manuscript calls them. Together, they seem to forge a path toward something transformative."

Gregory exchanged a glance with Marcus, his mind already bracing for what was to come. "What do these acts require?" he asked, his tone quiet but firm.

Helena hesitated, her brow furrowing. "The first seed is compassion. The symbols suggest a place of suffering—a sanctuary for the broken. The actor must deliver healing, not figuratively, but something real that leaves an enduring impact."

Gregory frowned. "A hospital, perhaps? Or a place where the forgotten gather?"

Helena nodded. "The manuscript is clear: comfort the afflicted, mend the broken. It's not enough to sympathize; the act must endure beyond the moment."

Her hand moved to another page, her gaze sharpening. "Forgiveness is the second seed," she said, her finger tracing a symbol of two hands reaching toward each other, their edges blurred as though dissolving into one. "The text speaks of reconciling with those who have caused harm. It's not just an act of personal liberation but one that ripples outward, transforming even the hardest hearts."

Marcus's jaw tightened. "Forgiveness in Rome is forbidden."

"It is," Helena agreed. "But this act must heal a wound that feels beyond repair."

She turned to another section, her tone resolute. "The third seed is humility. The manuscript calls for kneeling before those society deems unworthy—serving them without question."

Gregory tilted his head. "You mean the outcasts? The condemned?"

"Yes," Helena confirmed. "It's a gesture transcending charity—it must demonstrate grace."

Her finger brushed a flowing spiral on the next page. "The fourth seed is justice," she said. "The text describes standing against corruption and confronting oppression. Justice demands bold action that will draw resistance, even danger."

Gregory's expression darkened. "Resistance is inevitable."

Helena nodded. "The manuscript is clear: true justice doesn't come without conflict. It must challenge power and uplift the powerless."

Her voice softened as she reached the fifth symbol. "Wisdom," she said. "It calls for a revelation—a truth that disrupts and enlightens. Gregory, the wisdom you seek must bridge divides, shifting perspectives and uniting those who witness it."

Gregory's brow furrowed. "A universal truth, then? One that transcends differences?"

"Exactly," Helena replied. "But it must resonate deeply—it cannot be forced."

The sixth seed was next, a jagged emblem of a lion's open maw catching the light. "Courage," she said, her tone steady. "It speaks of stepping into danger, of standing firm where fear reigns."

Gregory's pulse quickened. "What kind of place?"

Helena met his gaze. "A tribunal, perhaps. Or an arena. Courage must manifest in the face of overwhelming odds."

Finally, her hand hovered over the last page, her tone reverent. "The seventh seed is sacrifice. The manuscript doesn't detail its meaning but implies something profound—giving everything for the greater good."

Gregory felt his breath hitch. "A martyr, then?"

Helena's gaze lingered on the jagged script. "Or it could mean something more—a transformation that endures beyond death itself."

Gregory exhaled. Each seed was not just a step but a test, a challenge to embody the virtues that could reshape a fractured world. And yet, he knew that the path ahead would demand nothing less than everything he had to give.

The room fell silent, the manuscript's cryptic symbols glinting faintly in the lamplight. Gregory's thoughts churned, and the enormity of the Seven Seeds settled on his shoulders. To Helena, these acts were enigmatic rituals shrouded in mystery. They were a map to Gregory—a fragile path back to his world or something far more significant.

Helena leaned back, closing the manuscript gently as though it might crumble under the weight of its secrets. "Each act grows more dangerous, Gregory. Each demands more than the last. But if the actor succeeds, the manuscript speaks of a 'gate' opening—a threshold to somewhere beyond."

Helena's piercing gaze lingered on Gregory as she finally spoke, her voice low but resolute. "Gregory, this manuscript… it's not just a guide. Every line and symbol was meant for the one who carries it. And that person appears to be you."

Gregory froze, her words sinking into him like stones. "You… you think so?" he asked, his voice barely above a whisper.

Helena exhaled deeply, her hands resting on the closed book. "I've seen the stirrings of something remarkable. People speak of you in the streets, Gregory. They gather when you pass, drawn as if to a force they cannot name. Your urgency, your knowledge, and the way you speak of compassion, forgiveness, and sacrifice as if they're etched into your soul—it's inspired something here: hope, defiance, faith. This manuscript… it's a guide, but you're the one it's waiting for. The fractures you spoke of, your origins—they're tied to you."

Gregory's shoulders sagged under the weight of her words, the enormity of his task pressing down on him. "And you still believe I can carry it?" he asked, his voice barely above a whisper.

Helena leaned forward, her gaze steady and unyielding. "It's not about whether I believe you can. This isn't just a burden, Gregory—it's a calling. You've awakened something in this city, something it hasn't known in centuries. People are listening to you, following you. The seeds of change are already being sown, and this manuscript… it's part of that. But whether you're ready to carry it—that's a question only you can answer."

Gregory hesitated, his hand hovering over the ancient book. "What if I fail?" he asked, his voice cracking under the strain of the question.

Helena's expression softened, and for the first time, her intensity gave way to something gentler. "Then you'll leave behind whatever you've already given."

Marcus stepped closer, placing a steadying hand on Gregory's shoulder. "You won't face this alone," he said firmly. "Whatever this journey requires, I'll walk beside you."

Gregory finally grasped the manuscript, the worn leather warm under his fingers. As he stood, the heft of the book seemed to anchor him while simultaneously urging him forward. The Seven Seeds weren't just acts—they were a crucible, a way to forge something greater than himself—a way to heal not just the fractures between worlds but the fractures within humanity.

As he stepped into the cool night air, the stars above seemed brighter and clearer, guiding him toward his destiny. The path ahead was steep, treacherous, and fraught with unknown dangers. But for the first time, Gregory felt ready—not just to walk it but to leave something behind that would echo long after he was gone.

CHAPTER EIGHTEEN
CATCHING UP

Gregory climbed the final steps to the Temple of Jupiter, his heart heavy with anticipation. The fading sunlight cast long shadows across the stone, and the cool evening air carried the distant murmurs of the city below. He hesitated at the threshold; the weight of the manuscript tucked away somehow felt lighter than the weight of his thoughts. For days, he had been immersed in deciphering the secrets of the Seven Seeds, but as he returned, he realized he had left someone behind in his silence.

The overhead lights buzzed faintly, casting a sterile, fluorescent glow across the hollow interior of the Temple of Jupiter. The stark brightness drained the space of warmth, leaving behind an imposing and clinical atmosphere. Gregory's eyes adjusted as he stepped inside, the hum of the city outside replaced by the eerie quiet of the temple's vast emptiness.

As he ascended the final steps to the priest's quarters and Lucius's room, he paused outside the door, slipping his hand into his deep pocket and gripping the manuscript tightly. His heart raced, not from exertion but from the importance of what he carried and the silence he had imposed on Lucius. The thought of how his absence might have been perceived unsettled him.

He rapped softly on the heavy wooden door, barely audible in the stillness. A muffled shuffle came from within, followed by the creak of floorboards. Moments later, the door opened just enough to reveal Lucius's face, his expression shifting from guarded to surprised relief.

"Glory to the gods," Lucius said, his voice laden with tension. He opened the door wider and gestured for his friend to enter. As Gregory stepped inside and before closing the door behind him, Lucius glanced down the hall to ensure they hadn't been noticed.

The room was sparsely lit, a desk lamp casting a faint pool of warm light across the cluttered surface of Lucius's desk. Piles of papers, old books, and a few stray pieces of clothing lay scattered, the only signs of life in the otherwise austere quarters. Lucius leaned back against the door, his arms crossed tightly over his chest.

"You've been gone for days," Lucius said in a low voice, his tone sharper now that the initial relief had passed. "I thought…" He hesitated, his words catching. "Perhaps you'd found your way back to your world—or the authorities had caught you."

Gregory met his gaze, the raw concern in Lucius's voice cutting through him. "I wouldn't leave without telling you," Gregory replied quietly. He set the manuscript on a nearby table, deliberate, almost reverent. "But I needed to disappear for a while. The work I've been doing—it's bigger than I imagined."

Lucius pushed off the door, his expression tightening with frustration. "You might have thought to let me know, Gregory. Do you have any idea what's been happening here? I asked around, but no one knew where you were."

"I'm sorry," Gregory said earnestly, his voice soft but firm. "I didn't mean to leave you in the dark. But what I've found could be the key to everything I've been searching for."

Lucius's eyes dropped to the manuscript, his skepticism warring with curiosity. "And this?" he asked, nodding toward it. "What is it?"

Gregory moved closer to the table, his hand hovering over the manuscript as though speaking about it might awaken its ancient power. His finger traced the faded title at the top, *Septem Seminae*, the archaic Latin words etched with an almost mystical precision. "Seven Seeds," he interpreted, his voice hushed, as though the very phrase bore a significance beyond language. "It's a guide," he continued, his tone deliberate. "An ancient text, older than anything I've ever encountered. It speaks of seven transformative acts tied to virtues: compassion, humility, forgiveness, justice, wisdom, courage, and sacrifice. Each seed, when sown, has the potential to alter not just a person, but the world itself."

Lucius's brow furrowed, his skepticism sharpened by the cryptic explanation. "And where did you get this? A book like this doesn't just appear out of nowhere."

Gregory hesitated, his hand resting lightly on the worn leather cover. He glanced at Lucius, his expression unreadable for a moment before he spoke. "I brought it with me," he said quietly.

Lucius blinked, confusion flickering in his eyes. "Brought it? From where?"

Gregory took a breath, steeling himself. "From the Vatican. From the archives in my other world."

For a moment, Lucius didn't respond. He first studied Gregory, but his expression was unreadable. "You're saying this manuscript came from your world? From the Vatican?" His tone was a careful mix of disbelief and curiosity.

"Yes," Gregory confirmed, his voice steady. "It was one of the few things I had with me when I crossed over: this manuscript, my cross, and my vestments. I didn't know what it was at first. I'd never seen it before that day I crossed over. It was just… there, hidden among countless relics and forgotten texts. It caught my eye, and something about it called to me, though I couldn't have explained why at the time."

Lucius leaned forward, his eyes narrowing as he studied the manuscript. "And now you think you've figured it out?"

Gregory nodded, his hand brushing the worn leather cover, his fingers tracing its edges as if drawing strength from it. "Not on my own," he admitted. "When I first opened it, I couldn't understand it. The text was written in a language I couldn't identify—proto-Italic or even older. Most of it was incomprehensible, but I could pick out phrases and fragments that seemed to echo in my mind. And now, everything has changed."

Lucius tilted his head, his curiosity sharpening. "Changed how?"

Gregory exhaled, his thoughts briefly drifting back to those early days of confusion and desperation. "Marcus insisted I show it to someone who might help. He introduced me to Dr. Helena Vorenus, a scholar at the university with an unmatched knowledge of ancient languages and cultural history. She examined the manuscript and said it was unlike anything she had ever studied—older than even the most ancient scripts she'd encountered."

Lucius's expression hardened slightly, his skepticism flickering. "You trusted her with this? With something so important?"

"I'm glad I had," Gregory replied firmly. "If I hadn't shown her, the manuscript would've remained an enigma. Helena discovered it wasn't just a book but a guide."

Lucius glanced at the manuscript, his fingers tapping against the edge of the table. "And what exactly did she uncover?"

Gregory opened the manuscript carefully, revealing the intricate drawings and ancient script that filled its pages. "She found references to what the text calls 'seeds.' Seven acts tied to virtues—compassion, humility, forgiveness, justice, wisdom, courage, and sacrifice.

"They're transformative, meant to be performed in this world, in specific places of significance. And together, they open what the manuscript calls a 'threshold.'"

Lucius frowned, leaning closer to the manuscript. "A threshold? To what?"

Gregory hesitated, the question pressing on him. "I believe it's a portal," he said, his voice steady but quiet. "A connection between this world and the one I came from."

Lucius's brow furrowed deeper, confusion and disbelief flickering across his face. "Your world? You're saying this threshold could send you back home?"

"Yes," Gregory admitted. "At least, that's what I hope. The manuscript describes it as a bridge to reconnect what has been severed. Helena said it's transformative, which could restore me to my proper place and time."

Lucius leaned back, his arms crossed, his sharp gaze fixed on Gregory. "So, this book of yours is a way back," he said, his voice steady. "Your way back to the world you left. Back to being Pope."

Gregory nodded, his hand resting on the manuscript as if drawing strength from it. "I do, yes," he said quietly but firmly. "This world, as much as I've tried to make sense of it, isn't where I'm meant to be. My place is in my world, where I served as Pope. My role wasn't about power or status, Lucius—it was about purpose. A responsibility to guide, to protect, to lead. That responsibility didn't vanish just because I was brought here."

Lucius frowned, his brow furrowing in thought. "And you believe this manuscript, these acts, will take you back? That by completing them, you'll reopen this threshold?"

"I do," Gregory said, his voice unwavering. "The manuscript is my bridge, my connection between worlds. The acts are the key to building it—restoring what's been severed. If I can complete them, I can return to where I belong."

Lucius studied him for a long moment, his expression inscrutable. "You must understand, Gregory, these acts are not just about you. If the manuscript is right, these seven acts will also mark this world. Are you prepared for what that might mean?"

Gregory met his gaze without hesitation. "I am," he said. "These acts aren't just a means to an end. They're meant to heal, to mend fractures in this world and, I suppose, in mine as well. I don't see that as a burden—it is part of my purpose."

Lucius's frown deepened as he leaned forward, his elbows resting on his knees. "And what happens if you fail? If the threshold doesn't open?"

Gregory's expression shifted, the resoluteness in his gaze flickering with a shadow of something deeper—fear, perhaps, or the depth of a truth he had yet to share. He took a slow, deliberate breath before speaking. "If I fail, Lucius… it's not just about being stuck here. It's about the consequences for both worlds. The seer warned me what would happen if I died here."

Lucius froze, his eyes widening in surprise. "The seer? What seer? You never mentioned anything about meeting a seer," he said, his voice laced with astonishment and suspicion. "Why am I only hearing about this now?"

Gregory looked down at the manuscript, his fingers brushing the worn cover as though grounding himself. "She said if I die in this world, it would spell doom—not just for me, but for both worlds. Whatever fractures already exist between them would grow wider and deeper. They'd spiral out of control, tearing apart the balance that holds them together." He hesitated, his voice dropping lower, adding, "I'm sorry I haven't had a chance until now to tell you about her, Lucius—the seer knew the second she met me that I wasn't from this world. She saw through me, saw everything I was hiding, and she made it clear: my survival isn't just about me. It's about preserving the fragile threads tying these worlds together."

Lucius sat back slowly, his expression darkening. "And you believe this?"

"I wasn't ready to believe it then," Gregory admitted, his voice quieter but no less steady. "I didn't understand what she meant—not fully. But as I've learned the manuscript's meaning and pieced together what these acts mean, I've realized she was right. My presence here isn't just a mistake or a coincidence—it's a fracture, a disruption to the natural order. If I die here, I don't just fail to return to my world. The consequences ripple outward, destabilizing everything."

Lucius's lips pressed into a thin line, as Gregory's words weighed heavily in the room. "And you're sure about this? That your death here would be… catastrophic?"

"I have no reason to doubt her," Gregory replied, his voice firm despite the tension in his expression. "The seer knew things about me she couldn't have guessed. And her warning was clear: I must not die here. This manuscript states that these acts are not just a way back. They're a way to restore the balance. To mend what's been broken."

Lucius was silent for a long moment, his sharp gaze locked on Gregory. Then he exhaled sharply, sitting back in his chair as his arms unfolded. "Then we'd better make sure you don't fail," he said, his voice tinged with reluctant acceptance. "So, Gregory—what does your guide say is the first step?"

Gregory opened the manuscript, his fingers carefully turning the pages until he found the intricate symbols surrounding the image of a cracked vessel. "The first seed," he said, his voice steady, "is compassion. The text describes a place of suffering where brokenness and despair are palpable. The act must bring healing, not just a gesture but something real that endures. That's where we begin."

Lucius was silent for a long moment, his gaze flickering to the manuscript and then back to Gregory. "And these acts," he said finally, his voice measured. "They're the price for crossing this threshold? The way to open this portal of yours?"

Gregory nodded. "That's what the Seven Seeds suggests. As I said, each act is tied to a virtue. They're not just tasks; they're transformative actions. Each one leaves an imprint, something that endures. And only when all seven are completed can the threshold be opened."

Lucius leaned back, his expression unreadable but his eyes glinting with interest. "Compassion," he repeated, the word foreign on his tongue as though testing its weight. "You've spoken of this before, Gregory. In your world, you claim it is a virtue, a foundation for strength. Here… it's seen as weakness, a flaw."

Gregory met his gaze steadily. "And yet, it is the first seed," he said, tapping the open manuscript. "The text describes it as the root of all others—a virtue that transcends personal gain and binds humanity together in its purest form."

Lucius crossed his arms, his brow furrowed. "How does one prove compassion? Is it a word? A feeling? In Rome, to show mercy is to surrender power. To show kindness is to invite betrayal."

"It is neither word nor mere feeling," Gregory replied, his voice firm but gentle. "It is action. A deed that mends something fractured. It must be tangible and enduring, a salve to the wound of another."

For a moment, silence hung between them, heavy and expectant. Lucius's jaw tightened, and he averted his gaze. "I've seen suffering," he admitted at last. "I've caused it. If this seed demands action, tell me—what would you consider an act of compassion worthy enough to fulfill its meaning?"

Gregory's lips curved into a faint, hopeful smile. "That is for you to decide, Lucius. But the seed is clear: it must be done where suffering cries the loudest, where the act of compassion can offer true healing."

CHAPTER NINETEEN
THE FIRST SEED

Tucked into the heart of Rome and flanked by the grander districts, the Subura was a labyrinth of narrow, winding alleyways and crumbling tenements. It is where Rome's forgotten masses lived and struggled, a place of sharp contrasts and unrelenting poverty. The looming shadows of temples and imperial buildings on the horizon only underscored the neglect and desperation below. Faintly visible through the haze of smoke and dim light, laundry lines crisscrossed the alleyways like sagging veins, connecting one dilapidated structure to the next.

The streets glistened with the remnants of the day—a chaotic tapestry of spilled wine streaking crimson trails, greasy scraps of discarded food scattered like forgotten offerings, sharp tangs of urine mingling with the damp air, and stagnant puddles shimmering in the dim, flickering glow of barrel fires, their light dancing like restless spirits against the shadows of the alley.

A growing cacophony marked Gregory's approach, each sound layering upon the other: a mother's frantic shouts for a lost child, the wheezing gasp of an elder struggling for breath, and the occasional clatter of pots as a street vendor packed up for the night. The group slowed as they entered, their eyes adjusting to the dim, uneven light. The Subura's presence was overwhelming, assaulting the senses and spirit. Yet Gregory felt no hesitation. As they stepped deeper into the district, its raw, aching humanity laid bare before them, he drew a steadying breath.

This was where Rome hid its scars, and Gregory knew Lucius had been right—suffering was carved into the very stones of these streets. If compassion could take root anywhere, it was here.

Behind Gregory, his small group gathered in tense silence. Julia stood closest, clutching a woven basket of bread so tightly her knuckles whitened. Her sharp eyes darted over the crowd, scanning faces with wariness and longing as though seeking a kindred spirit in the sea of desperation. Her guarded demeanor belied the flicker of hope she carried—a spark she barely acknowledged but couldn't extinguish. She had grown up not far from here, her childhood a blend of hardship and defiance. This place reflected where she had been and reminded her of where she refused to return.

Caius stood a step behind, his broad frame rigid as if ready to spring into action at the first sign of danger. His scarred hands, calloused from years of wielding a soldier's sword, now gripped a bundle of blankets with surprising gentleness. His eyes, sharp and calculating, swept the alleyways, scanning for threats as though he were back on the battlefield. Yet there was something else in his gaze—something softer, hidden beneath the layers of a soldier's instinct. Caius was a man at war, not with others but with himself, his past battles weighing heavily on his soul.

Decimus lingered at the edge of the group, his stance casual but his eyes sharp with curiosity. Though plain enough to avoid drawing undue attention, the merchant's fine tunic still hinted at a life far removed from the poverty surrounding them. He carried vials of medicine in a satchel slung over his shoulder, the strap cutting across his well-fed frame. Decimus's skepticism was etched into every line of his face, but so was his intrigue. He hadn't yet committed to Gregory's vision but couldn't bring himself to leave. Something about this man had stirred a question in his pragmatic heart—one he wasn't ready to answer.

Beyond them, a handful of students and citizens stood clutching their modest supplies. Their faces were a mix of apprehension and determination, drawn to Gregory not by understanding but by the whispers of his growing reputation. Together, they represented a fragile alliance, bound by little more than hope and the desire to be part of something greater. Gregory glanced at them, his heart heavy with what they were about to attempt. This wasn't just about food or blankets. It was about planting a seed that could grow into something far more powerful—a force that might transform not only this broken neighborhood but the hearts of those who witnessed it.

"This is where we begin," Gregory said softly, his voice barely carrying over the murmurs of the group. "But remember, this isn't just about giving. It's about showing them they're seen, and they matter. Compassion has to reach their hearts—not just their stomachs."

Julia stepped forward, her gaze scanning the crowded square. "There are children here," she whispered, her voice tinged with sorrow. "Orphans. Everyone has forgotten them."

Gregory placed a hand on her shoulder. "Then let's remind them they're not forgotten," he said. "Start with the youngest, Julia. Show them kindness first. That's how the seed grows."

The group dispersed, moving among the people with careful steps. Julia knelt beside a small boy clutching a frayed blanket, offering him bread and speaking in hushed tones. Caius approached a cluster of men, some with injuries from labor or battle, sharing his soldier's stoic empathy. Decimus handed out blankets and spoke to those willing to listen, his merchant's charm turning into quiet reassurance.

Gregory remained at the center, observing as the acts of compassion unfolded. Then he knelt on the cobblestones, the cold, damp stone pressing through his robes. A group of children hesitated near him, their faces smeared with dirt, their eyes wide with both fear and fascination. He beckoned gently, his voice low and soothing. Slowly, they approached.

He pulled a water jug from their supplies, its surface rippling as it reflected the streetlights. Gregory poured into a basin, dipped a cloth into the water, and washed the grime from a young boy's feet. The boy flinched at first, but Gregory's touch was gentle and reverent, as though this simple act was a sacred ritual. He dried them with his robe and kissed them, murmuring a prayer: "Lord, let these hands be your hands, bringing comfort where there is pain, hope where there is despair, and light where darkness dwells." Gasps rippled through the gathering, the crowd thickening as others moved closer to witness. Word spread like wildfire, and soon dozens surrounded Gregory, their expressions a mixture of awe and disbelief.

He moved from one person to another—an elderly woman with gnarled hands, a laborer with cracked, calloused feet—washing, drying, and anointing each as though they were royalty. His actions were deliberate, each motion imbued with reverence. Caius and Julia exchanged uneasy glances, unsure of how the crowd would react, but neither interfered. Even Decimus, ever the skeptic, seemed caught in the gravity of the moment, his usual remarks swallowed by the sheer intensity of Gregory's servitude.

As he worked, Gregory spoke, his voice steady yet imbued with profound conviction. "True strength is not found in dominion over others but in the courage to kneel and serve. Real power resides in touching the untouchable and lifting those who have fallen. Compassion is not a sign of weakness; it is the foundation of a heart willing to heal and restore." His hands moved tenderly, rinsing the feet of a frail man as he continued, "We are not here to tower above one another but to stand together, bound by the shared trials of our humanity. When we choose to serve, we mend the fractures dividing us. Love, given freely, is the bond that holds us all."

The crowd leaned closer, fascinated not only by his actions but by the simple truth of his words. Mothers wiped tears from their cheeks. Men hardened by years of toil and loss softened, their shoulders relaxing as their despair momentarily lifted. Gregory's voice resonated through the Subura like a balm, healing the body and the spirit of those gathered.

"When we wash the feet of another, we cleanse the wounds of their soul. When we kneel, we rise together. This is what we must show each other."

For a brief moment, the Subura seemed transformed. Suspicion softened into curiosity, fear yielded to gratitude, and despair gave way to something fragile but unmistakable—hope. Barrel fires glowed in the alleys, but now the shadows seemed less oppressive, the air lighter with the collective breath of lives touched by compassion.

At the height of this miraculous moment, as Gregory finished washing the feet of an elderly man who wept openly, Lucius appeared at his side, his face pale. "They're here," he whispered, nodding toward the edge of the crowd.

Gregory stood, his knees stiff from kneeling, and turned to see a line of armored figures pushing through the onlookers. Their uniforms gleamed coldly under the flickering fires, a stark contrast to the soot and grime of the Subura. The polished chest plates bore the insignia of the Custodes Urbis—a golden eagle with outstretched wings—and their black leather boots struck the ground in a synchronized march. Each carried a short baton and a gladius holstered at their side, their expressions as unyielding as the iron discipline they exuded.

One of them stepped forward, a towering man whose presence seemed to draw the very air from the plaza. His face was like carved granite, with deep-set eyes glinted with authority and lips pressed into a severe line. A jagged scar traced his cheekbone, a permanent reminder of his years of enforcing the city's harsh order. His sharp, commanding voice cut through the crowd's murmurs like a blade. "What is this?" he demanded, his hand resting lightly on the pommel of his gladius. "A gathering of this size is forbidden without sanction. Who leads this?"

Before anyone could stop him, Gregory stepped forward, his expression calm but resolute. "I do, sir," he said, his voice steady despite the growing tension. "We are here to serve, to aid those who need it most. Is that a crime in this city?"

The officer's eyes narrowed, his grip tightening on the hilt of his sword. "Charity is a mask for defiance," he said coldly. "It stirs rebellion in the hearts of those who should know their place. Disperse, or you will regret the consequences."

The Custodes began closing in, their batons pounding against their shields like old war drums. The crowd shrank back in fear, pressing into the adjacent alleys, but Caius, the ex-soldier, stepped forward, his face dark with rage. In one swift motion, his hand moved to his belt, drawing his gladius. Its steel glinted menacingly as the Custodes hesitated, momentarily caught off guard by the sight of the weapon.

"Back off!" Caius roared, holding the blade low but ready. "You've abandoned these people, left them to rot, and now you attack the only ones offering them hope?" His voice, rich with the authority of his military past, echoed off the stone walls, and for a moment, even the Custodes faltered. The officer leading them narrowed his eyes and gestured for his men to close in.

"Caius, no!" Gregory's sharp and commanding voice rang out, cutting through the tension like a blade. He moved swiftly, stepping between Caius and the advancing Custodes, his arms raised, urging peace. "Sheath it," he said, his tone firm and imploring, as if willing the weapon and its wielder to surrender to reason.

Caius's knuckles whitened on the hilt of the gladius, his breathing heavy, his eyes burning with the instinct to fight. "They will kill us, Gregory," he growled, his voice trembling with fury and frustration. "They will kill us all."

"Stand down, Caius," Gregory said, his voice soft but unyielding. "This is not how we fight. We are not here to spill blood but to heal it."

For a moment, the world paused. The crowd, the Custodes, and even the flickering fires in the sawed-off barrels held their collective breaths. Then, with a growl of frustration and anguish, Caius sheathed his gladius.

The officer sneered and stepped forward. "A noble speech," he said coldly, "but it changes nothing. Your gathering is illegal. Disperse now, or face the consequences."

Two Custodes moved to grab Caius, roughly shoving him against the wall. One raised his baton, ready to strike, but Gregory stepped forward again, his hands outstretched. "Enough!" he cried, his voice filled with both authority and desperation. "If you seek justice, then show it now. Be the protectors you claim to be, not the oppressors."

The officer hesitated, his gaze narrowing as he assessed the unarmed man standing before him with reckless courage. With a curt wave of his hand, he ordered his men to stand down. "Take your people and leave," he barked. "And take that fool's sword with you. If I see you here again, there will be a price to pay."

Lucius grabbed Gregory's arm, pulling him back. "We need to go," he whispered urgently, his eyes darting toward the retreating Custodes.

Gregory nodded, turning to Caius and placing a firm hand on his shoulder. "You must understand," he said, his voice low but steady. "Violence would have destroyed everything we've built tonight. The first seed is compassion, not rebellion."

Caius, still shaking, retrieved his fallen gladius and sheathed it. "I… I wasn't thinking," he muttered, his voice ashamed.

Gregory offered him a small, reassuring smile. "You were thinking as a soldier. Now, think as a healer."

As the group slipped into the shadows, the crowd's murmurs followed them like an undercurrent of hope. Behind them, the poor and broken whispered what they had witnessed—not just the confrontation but Gregory's unyielding stand for peace. The first seed had been planted, marked by the choice to lay down a weapon and raise a people.

CHAPTER TWENTY
IT BEGINS

The colonnade behind the temple stood bathed in the moon's silver light, its towering columns casting long shadows on the stone floor. Gregory leaned against one of the pillars, his chest still heaving from the night's events. Around him, Lucius, Caius, Julia, and Decimus gathered, their faces illuminated by street lamps. Each of them carried the impact of the confrontation with the warden of Rome differently—Caius still clutching his gladius with knuckles white from tension, Julia staring into the distance as if unraveling the implications of their actions, Decimus pacing, his skepticism tempered by a newfound sense of urgency.

"I didn't think we'd make it out of there," Lucius muttered, breaking the heavy silence. He rubbed his temples, glancing toward Gregory. "You realize what you've done, don't you? The Subura will be talking about this for days. The full force of the Custodes will come looking for us."

"That's the point," Gregory replied calmly, standing upright and brushing the dust from his robe. "We don't hide from this. We've planted the first seed, and it's already beginning to grow. The people need to see that compassion infused with courage is stronger than fear."

A stir echoed in the night air, and faint footsteps grew louder as figures emerged from the shadows. Three more approached cautiously: a young stonemason named Felix, a former temple scribe Octavia, and an aging healer Severus. They bowed their heads, their expressions humble yet resolute.

"We heard about what you did in the Subura," Felix began, his voice trembling with awe. "Word is spreading. People say you stood up to the Custodes."

"We want to join you," Octavia added, her eyes shining with conviction. "Whatever this cause is, we believe in it."

Gregory's brow furrowed as he absorbed their words. Surprise flickered across his face, a mixture of disbelief and concern. "Already?" he murmured, more to himself than to the group. He glanced at Lucius, whose expression mirrored his unease.

"It seems what happened in the Subura has taken on a life of its own," Lucius said quietly. "Rome isn't as vast as it appears when news like this travels."

Gregory exhaled slowly, his thoughts racing. The confrontation with the Custodes had been perilous enough without drawing this much attention this quickly. Yet, before him stood Felix, Octavia, and others, their faces alight with belief. The magnitude of what they carried—the potential, the risk—pressed against him with renewed force.

His gaze softened as he took in the group, sensing the sincerity and determination emanating from their gathered forms. "Before we continue, you must understand what you are committing to," he began, lifting the manuscript from his satchel. Its intricate script on its spine seemed almost alive in the shadows. "This is no ordinary mission," Gregory continued, holding the book like a shield and banner. "It is a Divine calling."

He took a breath, his words settling over the group. "The Seven Seeds," Gregory began, his voice steady and deliberate. "Each seed represents an act, a virtue, a flame that must be ignited to heal this fractured world. Compassion, humility, forgiveness, justice, wisdom, courage, and sacrifice. These are not mere ideals—they are transformative actions. Each seed we plant must take root not only in the soil but in the hearts of all who witness it. Tonight, in the Subura, we sowed the first seed of compassion. In doing so, we've awakened something greater than ourselves. But this is only the beginning."

A murmur rippled through the gathering, a mixture of awe and apprehension. Gregory continued, his voice rising in quiet intensity. "The manuscript speaks of a threshold that can only be unlocked through these seven acts. If we succeed, it will open a path to renewal, hope, and balance that this world desperately craves. But each step will test us. Each act will demand more than the last. It will require us to set aside fear and embrace a faith that goes beyond what we see before us."

Gregory's gaze swept over the gathering, the firelight casting shifting shadows across the determined faces of his followers. "Tonight's work is done," he said, his voice steady but firm. "Disperse into the city. We must not attract further attention. When the time comes for the next seed, we will send word."

A young man, one of the newer recruits, hesitated before speaking, his voice tentative. "But how will we know, Gregory? Where to go, when to gather? Rome is vast, and the watch sees everything."

The question caused a ripple of murmurs among the group, others nodding in agreement, their concern evident. Gregory's eyes softened as he considered their worry. He turned to Caius, silently seeking the soldier's wisdom, and said, "We cannot afford to falter. Humility will be our next seed, but every move must be precise. All will be lost if the wrong ears catch wind of us."

Caius stepped forward, his voice steady and confident. "We'll use the Tabularium network. It's secure, and its features are built for this. Private channels allow us to share messages directly with our followers without prying eyes, and with the self-destructing messages—they'll vanish once read, leaving no trace behind."

Lucius, standing nearby, nodded in agreement. "That could work."

The followers nodded solemnly, their resolve unshaken. As they melted into the labyrinthine streets of Rome, Gregory watched them disappear one by one, his heart heavy with their shared mission. Lucius lingered at Gregory's side as the last of the followers departed. "You've given them hope," Lucius said, his voice low. "Let's pray they can hold onto it."

Gregory nodded. "Hope is fragile, but tonight we've planted something deeper—conviction. Now, let's rest. Tomorrow will bring new challenges."

The two retreated to the quiet sanctuary of the temple's inner quarters. The silence of the night wrapped around them like a cloak, but neither truly slept. Gregory remained deep in thought, the manuscript resting beside him as if it might whisper its secrets in the stillness.

***

Several hours later, their uneasy peace was shattered by the echo of boots against stone. Lucius was on his feet in an instant, peering through the narrow slit of the window. "It's Quintus," he hissed, his tone urgent. "And he's not alone this time."

Gregory joined Lucius at the edge of the colonnade, watching as the Custodes, led by the senator, approached with methodical precision. Their flashlights pierced the darkness. "They move swiftly," Gregory murmured, his voice steady despite the peril. "We cannot stay."

Lucius was already leading Gregory toward the temple's interior. "There's a passage beneath the altar," he said urgently. "It leads to the Via Antiqua. From there, we can disappear into the city."

With Quintus's commands echoing through the hallowed halls, they slipped behind the grand altar and lifted the ancient trapdoor. The hidden passage below was narrow and damp, the air thick with the scent of earth and decay. Gregory glanced back one last time, seeing the faint flickers of light as the Custodes entered the temple. "Hurry," Lucius urged, his voice low but firm.

The narrow tunnel carried them into the night, the muffled sounds of pursuit echoing like a distant threat. Gregory and Lucius emerged into the open air, the city's cool nocturnal breeze brushing against their faces. They paused briefly, catching their breaths, before Lucius motioned for them to move. The streets were quiet, save for the faint clatter of far-off voices, and the two men slipped through the shadowed alleys of Rome. Lucius led with purpose, his familiarity with the city's secretive routes serving as their lifeline.

As they turned a corner and found a reprieve, Lucius glanced at Gregory. "We can't wander the streets all night," he said, his tone urgent. "We need a safe place, somewhere they won't think to look."

Gregory hesitated, weighing their options. "Marcus," he said finally. "His home is unassuming, but we must tread carefully. His wife might not take kindly to our arrival."

Lucius raised an eyebrow. "Might not take kindly? I thought she told you never to come back after last time."

"She did," Gregory admitted, his expression resolute. "But Marcus has always been supportive, and I trust him. We have no other choices right now."

The two quickened their pace, navigating through the backstreets until they reached Marcus's home. Lucius rapped softly on the wooden door. After a tense moment, it creaked open to reveal Marcus, his face pale and taut with worry. "Gregory," he said, stepping aside quickly to let them in. "You shouldn't be here. The Subura incident is already on the news. You've been labeled as an agitator by the authorities."

Inside, the modest home was an oasis of calm amid the city's chaos. Marcus motioned them to sit, his gaze flickering nervously toward the door. "My wife and son will be back in the morning. They're visiting her mother," he added, his voice low. "You can stay the night, but you must leave before she returns."

Gregory nodded, gratitude etched into his features. "Thank you, Marcus. That's all we need. Just one night to regroup and plan our next step."

Marcus sighed heavily, rubbing the bridge of his nose. "You've started something big, Gregory. I hope you're ready for the storm that's coming."

Gregory entered, reverently setting the manuscript on the table and emphasizing its importance. "It begins, Marcus," he said, his voice calm but firm. "We knew this path would be perilous. What's done cannot be undone."

"Whatever you're doing, Gregory, it's bigger than all of us now," Marcus said gravely. "But you're playing with fire. Rome will burn before it lets you succeed."

Gregory looked up, his eyes steady and unwavering. "Then we will quench its flames with compassion," he said. "The first seed has been planted. We must prepare for the next, no matter the cost."

The room fell into a tense silence, their shared purpose settling heavily over them. Outside, the city buzzed with restless energy, unaware of the revolution within its shadows. Gregory reached into his pocket and tightened his grip on the manuscript, ready for the tempest ahead.

CHAPTER TWENTY-ONE
BY THE TIBER

The morning was young when Gregory and Lucius slipped out of Marcus's home, the faint light of dawn casting long shadows down the boulevards. The city stirred to life around them—bakers stoking their ovens, merchants unloading their wares, and the occasional wailing of a patrol car siren. Gregory kept his hood low, and Lucius stayed close, his eyes darting for any sign of danger. They moved with purpose, disappearing into the maze of alleys and side streets that shielded them from prying eyes.

"We need somewhere safe," Lucius muttered as they ducked into the shadow of a narrow alleyway. His sharp eyes swept the crowded streets, watching for any flicker of a Custode's uniform or the familiar robed figure of an informant. "They'll be sweeping the markets, the temples, the slums—everywhere they think we might hide. It's only a matter of time before they close in."

Gregory leaned against a stone wall, his expression calm, his voice steady despite the tension in the air. "Then we won't hide."

Lucius turned to him, his brow furrowing. "You're not serious. We're barely staying ahead of them as it is. Hiding buys us time. It's what we need right now."

"Hiding delays the inevitable," Gregory replied evenly. "If we're to plant the second seed, it must be bold. It must challenge everything this city stands for."

Lucius's voice dropped, low and sharp. "Boldness gets us killed, Gregory. Do you think Quintus will let you waltz into another district and preach humility? You saw what happened in the Subura. They're waiting for us to slip."

Gregory stepped closer, his eyes unwavering as they met Lucius's. "Where is arrogance celebrated the most in this city? Where does Rome's pride tower above its people, casting them in its shadow?"

Lucius hesitated, trying to read Gregory's intent. "Everywhere. The temples, the palaces—Rome thrives on its pride."

"Yes," Gregory said, his voice softening, "but where is that pride concentrated, displayed for all to see? Where does arrogance reach for the heavens?"

Lucius frowned, realization dawning in his eyes. "The Pantheon."

Gregory nodded, his calm demeanor masking the gravity of the decision. "Exactly. If the second seed is humility, it must take root in the very heart of arrogance. The Pantheon isn't just a temple—it's a monument to human pride and power. That's where we'll go."

Lucius let out a long breath, his skepticism tempered by grudging respect. "You're not serious?"

"I am," Gregory said. "We will reach out to the others. By the time the sun rises tomorrow and the doors to the Pantheon open, we'll be there, ready to plant the second seed."

Lucius shook his head, a faint smile tugging at his lips despite himself. "You have a way of making the impossible sound inevitable."

Gregory's voice carried a quiet conviction. "It is. Humility isn't just a virtue, Lucius—it's a force. One that can reshape even the mightiest of empires."

The two men moved through the winding alleys with practiced caution, their footsteps barely audible against the sidewalk. The city felt alive but restless, its usual hum tainted with unease. Gregory and Lucius kept to the shadows, their movements deliberate and silent as they navigated the maze of streets.

At last, they reached the modest workshop tucked at the edge of a quiet courtyard. The heavy wooden door stood before them, its surface weathered by time. Gregory stepped forward and knocked twice, his hand firm but restrained.

Lucius shifted his weight, glancing nervously at the empty alley behind them. After a tense moment, faint footsteps sounded from within. A narrow slit in the door creaked open, and Caius's sharp, cautious eyes appeared, scanning Gregory and Lucius before flicking to the shadows behind them.

Satisfied, Caius unlatched the bolt with a metallic scrape and eased the door open just enough for them to slip inside. As soon as they entered, he secured the door again, the bolt sliding back into place with a decisive clunk.

"Why are you here," Caius said, his voice low but steady.

Gregory pulled back his hood, his face set with determination. "We need to talk."

Caius bolted the door behind them and crossed his arms, leaning against a worktable cluttered with tools and scraps of metal. "The Custodes are crawling all over the city."

Gregory stepped forward, his gaze steady, though the tension in his shoulders betrayed the gravity of the situation. "We need you, Caius. Tomorrow morning, at the Pantheon."

Caius raised an eyebrow, his expression a mix of curiosity and skepticism. "The Pantheon? Bold move. What are you planning?"

Lucius cut in; his tone edged with urgency. "The second seed—humility. We're planting it where it will strike at the heart of Rome's pride."

Gregory nodded, his voice calm but resolute. "At nine, as the doors open, we'll gather there to demonstrate humility in its purest form. The steps of the Pantheon will become a stage—not for rebellion, but for reflection. We'll confront the arrogance and excess that defines this empire and offer a different path. A path of service, not domination."

Caius narrowed his eyes, leaning forward slightly. "And you think that'll go unnoticed? The Pantheon is at the heart of everything—their power, their gods, and their pride. The Custodes won't let you turn it into your pulpit."

"We're not going to shout," Gregory explained. "This is about action, not words. We'll kneel on the steps, offer bread and water as symbols of true offerings, and wash the steps clean. It's a gesture to show that humility doesn't weaken us—it strengthens us."

Lucius added, "But we need you to reach the others. Julia, Decimus, Felix, Octavia—they'll help spread the word. If we're careful, they can bring those who believe in the cause without tipping off the Custodes."

Caius groaned, running a hand through his hair. "And how, exactly, do you plan to make this happen? Stand in the middle of the temple and declare war on their gods?"

"No," Gregory said with a faint smile. "Not war—Transformation. The Pantheon represents all gods, all power, and all pride. We will not destroy it, but we will redefine it. The second seed is not about defiance but showing Rome a better way."

"You must spread the word to the others," Lucius explained. "We need the support of our followers."

"What do I tell them?" he asked, glancing up at Gregory.

"Tell them the seed of humility will be planted in the shadow of pride," Gregory said. "The Pantheon. In the morning as the doors open. We will need their voices, their actions."

Lucius smirked faintly. "Subtle as ever."

"And remind them," Gregory added, his tone sharpening, "that humility begins with us. How can we ask others to follow if we do not act with the courage to kneel?"

Caius scratched at his stubble. "But, Gregory, are you sure about this? If this fails—"

"It will not fail," Gregory interrupted, his voice firm. "Even if we are silenced, the act itself will speak. Humility cannot be snuffed out like a flame. It spreads quietly but powerfully."

Caius sighed, rising to his feet. "Let's hope you're right."

Gregory glanced toward the door before nodding reluctantly. "Then we'd best get some rest. Tomorrow will demand every ounce of strength we have."

***

The night passed in uneasy quiet, the group taking turns keeping watch while the others dozed in the dim confines of Caius's home. The faint flicker of an oil lamp cast long shadows on the walls, and the air was thick with unspoken tension. Gregory spent much of the night with his hands clasped in silent prayer, his thoughts alternating between determination and doubt. Caius occasionally stirred, pacing as though the weight of what lay ahead kept him from finding peace.

As dawn broke, they prepared themselves in the sparse light of the early morning. Caius handed out bits of bread and dried fruit, his movements brisk and businesslike, though his eyes betrayed his concern. "Eat while you can," he muttered. "Once we step outside, there's no turning back."

After leaving Caius's home, they melted into the crowd, blending in among slaves and merchants. Each step brought them closer to the Pantheon, its towering dome visible even from a distance. When they reached the bustling square surrounding it, the morning sun emerged, its light reflecting off the monument's majestic facade.

The streets were beginning to awaken, the faint hum of activity growing steadily. Hawkers unpacked their wares, arranging trinkets and goods with practiced precision, while a few early risers exchanged quiet words about the latest decrees. Priests moved purposefully, overseeing the preparations for another elaborate ritual. Gregory paused at the edge of the square, his gaze fixed on the imposing structure that loomed above the emerging bustle.

The Pantheon stood as a testament to Roman engineering and imperial power, its massive columns and perfect dome proclaiming the dominance of the empire over all aspects of life, even the Divine. Gregory's expression hardened as he took in the spectacle.

"This," he murmured, "is where we plant the second seed."

Lucius gave him a skeptical look. "And what exactly is our plan, Gregory? Walk in, denounce the gods, and hope the Custodes feel merciful?"

Gregory turned to him, a faint smile tugging at the corner of his lips. "Not denounce, Lucius. Transform. Humility is not about tearing down but showing a better way. The Pantheon will not fall, but its meaning will change."

Lucius sighed, shaking his head. "You have a dangerous gift for optimism. Let's hope it's enough to keep us alive."

As they approached the temple, Gregory's mind churned with possibilities. With all its grandeur and pride, the Pantheon was the perfect stage for their next act—a public gesture that would challenge the empire's obsession with power and excess and instead offer a vision of humility as strength. The second seed would be planted here, beneath Rome's watchful eyes.

Lucius shook his head, his voice low and urgent. "You risk everything. The Custodes, the Senate—they won't tolerate this."

Gregory turned to him, his expression calm but resolute. "Humility is not without risk, Lucius. It is the courage to kneel before truth, no matter the cost."

CHAPTER TWENTY-TWO
THE PANTHEON

The morning sun cast a golden glow over Rome as the towering doors of the Pantheon creaked open, unveiling its vast and majestic interior. Worshippers and dignitaries streamed in, their footsteps echoing beneath the grand dome that reached the heavens. Gregory and Lucius crept among the crowd, their hooded cloaks drawn tightly. The air was thick with the scent of burning incense, mingling with murmured prayers.

The Pantheon stood as the pinnacle of Roman achievement—a sacred nexus where human ingenuity and Divine favor converged. Its towering columns and majestic dome embodied the empire's pride, a testament to its unyielding dominance. Yet, for Gregory, it symbolized something far different. This was not merely a temple but a monument to human arrogance cloaked in reverence. Here, amidst the opulence and pride, he saw an opportunity—a stage to sow the next seed, where humility would challenge the very heart of Roman excess.

As the morning crowd swelled, worshippers and onlookers mingled beneath the dome, their eyes upon the glimmering altars and the imposing presence of the priests. Julia, Decimus, Felix, Octavia, and others carefully positioned themselves among the gathering, blending into the sea of faces. Caius's message had reached them, and now they mingled quietly, their shared purpose concealed beneath the guise of ordinary citizens. Gregory and Lucius moved to the edge of the steps, their hearts pounding in unison as the priests began their elaborate preparations.

A hush fell over the crowd as the head priest stepped forward, his arms raised to signal silence. His voice rose with the cadence of practiced authority. "Behold the blessings of the gods, bestowed upon this great empire. We ascend above all others through the might of Rome and the favor of Jupiter. Today, we honor their power with offerings worthy of their glory—gold and jewels, the fruits of our labor and conquest."

He gestured toward the gleaming altar, its surface laden with ornate chalices and gilded bowls overflowing with offerings. "It is through such tributes that we uphold the bond between Rome and the heavens. For the gods smile upon those who display their devotion with splendor."

As the priest continued, his voice swelling with pride, a quiet movement in the crowd drew attention. Gregory stepped forward, his hood hung low, his stride deliberate. The murmurs of the onlookers grew as he ascended the steps, the stark contrast of his presence disrupting the grandeur of the ritual.

The priest faltered mid-sentence, his gaze narrowing as Gregory knelt before the altar. "What is the meaning of this?" he demanded, his voice tinged with outrage.

Gregory, undeterred, placed a loaf of bread and a pitcher of water with reverent care.

The head priest's face flushed with indignation. "Who dares interrupt this sacred ceremony with such… trivial offerings?" he demanded, his voice thunderous.

Gregory rose slowly, his calm voice cutting through the tension. "No god worthy of worship desires gifts born of vanity and excess. Bread to sustain the body and water to quench the spirit are the only offerings that matter. Humility, not gold, is what binds us to the Divine."

Gregory's voice carried through the chamber, steady and firm, drawing the attention of all. He gestured toward the soaring dome above them, its oculus a perfect circle framing the sky. "Look at this dome," he began. "A marvel of human achievement, a testament to Rome's ambition. It is a monument to power, to pride. What makes it sacred is not the stones or the craftsmanship—but the light streaming through, a gift from the heavens that no man can command."

He turned his gaze to the crowd, his eyes filled with quiet conviction. "Humility is the seed we must plant. It is not submission or weakness but the wisdom to understand our place in the vastness of creation. It is the courage to see that no matter how high we build, we remain dependent on something greater—on the light that fills this space, on the earth that sustains us, and on one another."

Gregory's tone grew softer but no less powerful. "This oculus reminds us of what we lack and cannot control. Yet, it also offers us hope that we can open ourselves to a greater purpose through humility. Pride builds walls, but humility opens windows to the infinite. Through humility, we find the strength to serve, build, and heal."

He spread his arms wide, addressing the assembly with heartfelt passion. "Rome's pride has brought grandeur, but it has also brought division and suffering. Today, we cleanse these steps not to dishonor the gods but to remind ourselves that true greatness is not found in domination but in service. Humility teaches us that only by kneeling can we truly rise."

Gregory's words rippled through the crowd, silencing their murmurs as the high priest, his composure shaken, signaled for Gregory to leave. Instead, Gregory stood firm. Lucius stepped forward from the crowd, his face calm but his eyes resolute. With deliberate reverence, he handed Gregory a small basin and cloth as though passing sacred tools. Gregory accepted them without hesitation, descended the steps, and knelt on the lowest one. He began to wash the step in slow, purposeful movements, each action a quiet defiance that resonated through the onlookers.

Lucius joined Gregory, pulling a cloth from his belt. Together, they scrubbed the marble, their actions imbued with quiet purpose. The crowd watched in confusion, murmurs building among them. A young woman tentatively stepped forward, accepting a cloth from Gregory. An elderly man followed, then others, until a small group formed, kneeling in an act of cleansing and solidarity.

"This is a desecration!" the high priest cried, his voice echoing off the walls of the Pantheon. "You mock the gods with this display."

Gregory paused, looking up calmly. "I do not mock the gods. I cleanse this place of the pride that defiles it."

When the steps glistened under the morning light, Gregory stood and turned to the crowd. His voice rose, steady and resonant, carrying over the murmurs of the gathered citizens. "Too long have these steps borne the weight of vanity," he declared. "Today, they will bear the weight of humility. Let this temple serve not as a monument to pride but as a symbol of service."

He stepped forward, his gaze sweeping over the assembly. "Humility is not a sign of weakness, nor is it the lowering of oneself to be trampled underfoot. True humility is recognizing who we are—fallible, finite, and interwoven with one another. It is the acknowledgment that none among us is self-sufficient, that we all depend on forces beyond ourselves: on the kindness of others, on the vast mystery of existence, and yes, on the Divine, however we understand it."

Gregory gestured to the towering columns and the gleaming dome of the Pantheon. "This place," he said, "is a marvel of human ingenuity and ambition. But what is ambition without purpose? What is pride without compassion? These walls and this dome cannot shield the human heart from its deepest need—connecting, serving, and finding meaning beyond one's desires."

He knelt once more, his hands tracing the polished stone of the steps. "In a world driven by power, humility teaches us to kneel—not in submission, but in reverence. Reverence for the dignity of all life. Reverence for the shared struggles and joys that make us human. Reverence for the truth that our greatest strength lies not in dominion, but in service."

Gregory's voice softened, yet its clarity pierced the air. "Imagine a world where leaders chose humility over hubris, where greatness was measured not by what one takes but by what one gives. Imagine a world where we lift one another up, not for gain, but because it is right. That is the power of humility. It does not diminish—it transforms. It takes pride, strips it of its arrogance, and reveals its truest form: a quiet, steady strength that builds rather than destroys."

The crowd stood in silence, his words settling over them like a gentle but unshakable truth. Gregory rose to his feet, his expression resolute. "This temple need not fall to be reborn. Let its steps no longer serve as a pedestal for pride but as a foundation for unity, humility, and the Divine within each of us."

The crowd shifted, an almost imperceptible tremor passing through them like wind rustling through leaves. Some clenched their fists at their sides, their knuckles pale, while others lowered their heads, Gregory's words pressing heavily on their shoulders. A woman in the front wiped her eyes with the corner of her shawl, her breath catching as though she'd been holding it too long. Beside her, a man reached out, his hand trembling, to clasp hers in quiet solidarity.

Gregory's steady and calm voice hung in the air as he took a deliberate step forward. His fierce yet tender eyes swept over the gathered faces, catching the flicker of hope and the simmering embers of change in their expressions.

No one moved. It was not silence but the stillness that blooms before a storm—the air charged, his message sinking deep into the soil of their hearts. In that quiet, something unseen began to grow.

His words lingered in the air as he stepped back, the simple basin and cloth in his hands. The crowd stirred and watched as Gregory knelt again to wash the steps, his quiet actions speaking as profoundly as his words.

As murmurs of agreement rippled through the crowd, the sharp rhythm of armored boots echoed through the Pantheon's grand hall. The gathering shifted uneasily, parting to make way as Quintus strode in, his presence commanding and deliberate. Flanking him, the Custodes moved in lockstep, their polished armor glinting in the shafts of sunlight streaming through the oculus above, starkly contrasting with the humble attire of those gathered.

Quintus's senatorial garb proclaimed his rank with unapologetic grandeur. A deep crimson toga edged with broad bands of purple draped over his shoulder, the fine Merino wool fabric catching the light with subtle elegance. A golden fibula, intricately carved with symbols of

Rome's might, secured the folds at his shoulder. Beneath the toga, his tunic bore the crisp white of Roman authority, unmarred and pristine. His heavy bronze belt, engraved with laurels, swayed slightly as he came to a halt, and his leather boots, dyed the deep red reserved for senators, gleamed with meticulous care.

His sharp gaze swept over the scene—the gleaming marble steps damp from the offerings of the kneeling citizens, their heads bowed in solemn unity. Finally, Gregory stood resolutely, his hand still clutching the cloth. Quintus's expression hardened, his lips thinning into a scowl.

"What is the meaning of this?" the senator demanded, his voice cold and cutting, reverberating through the sacred space. "You defile this hall with your insolence, staining it with these… theatrics." His tone carried the weight of disdain and his station's unyielding authority.

Gregory met his gaze without flinching. "I have defiled nothing, Senator. I have sought only to restore the sanctity of this place—not with gold or power, but with humility."

Quintus stepped forward, his expression darkening. "You presume to teach Rome humility? Your arrogance is as dangerous as it is absurd."

The Custodes moved forward at his signal, seizing Gregory by the arms. Lucius tensed beside him. "Gregory…" he offered.

"It's okay," Gregory said softly. "The seed is planted. That is what matters."

Quintus turned to the others who had joined in the act of cleansing. "You," he said, pointing to Lucius, Julia, and the others, "leave now while you still can. But mark my words—if I find you aiding this man again, you will join him on the hill nailed to a cross."

Lucius clenched his jaw, but Gregory's calm voice cut through his anger. "Go," he said firmly. "This is not the time for defiance. Trust in the message."

Quintus turned to the high priest. "Ensure this place is cleansed of all traces of this man's heresy."

Reluctantly, Lucius and the others obeyed, retreating into the crowd as Gregory was led away. The Custodes marched him through the towering columns of the Pantheon, his head held high, his presence a stark contrast to the heavy-handed authority of his captors. The crowd watched as the impact of what they had witnessed settled over them.

CHAPTER TWENTY-THREE
CLAUSTRA

The iron gates of Claustra groaned open, their ominous weight echoing off the cold stone walls. Gregory stood between two armored Custodes, his wrists bound in cuffs. The fortress loomed ahead, its blackened stone exterior rising like an impenetrable sentinel against the sky. A mosaic of carved deities adorned its facade—Jupiter with his lightning bolt, Mars with his sword, Minerva with her owl—etched reminders of the empire's unrelenting authority and Divine mandate.

The distant clang of iron on iron carried a grim rhythm. Prisoners' voices echoed faintly from within, desperate or resigned, mixing with the heavy tread of guards patrolling the ramparts. Gregory's expression remained calm, but his shoulders bore what might come.

The central processing hall of Claustra was a cold and imposing space. Fluorescent lights buzzed overhead, casting a harsh glow on the cinderblock walls adorned with engraved plaques listing the laws of the empire—an unyielding reminder of Rome's omnipotence. At the center of the room, a clerk typed methodically behind a sleek metal desk. Nearby, an officer in the polished black-and-gold uniform scrutinized a report, his expression unreadable as he reviewed the charges.

"Gregory of the Foreign Faith," the receiving officer announced, his voice cold and impersonal. "You are charged with inciting sedition, defiling sacred space, and undermining the authority of the empire."

Gregory's eyes met the officer's. "I sought not to undermine but to illuminate," he said calmly, his voice steady despite the chains biting into his wrists. "What I did was not rebellion but a call to reflection."

The officer's lips tightened. "Your so-called reflection has cast a shadow on Rome's glory. The Senate will decide your fate. For now, you will remain within these walls."

The guard stepped forward, yanking Gregory toward a narrow corridor. The halls of Claustra were a labyrinth of cold steel and flickering shadows, the walls slick with condensation that carried a faint metallic tang to the air. The stench of unwashed bodies and human waste clawed at Gregory's nostrils, mingling with the acrid bite of disinfectant sprayed in a futile attempt to mask the decay. As they descended deeper into the prison, the temperature dropped, each breath tasting stale and damp, as though the very air had been trapped within these walls for centuries.

Cells lined the corridor, their iron bars coated with rust that flaked off at the lightest touch. Each one was a grim tableau of suffering, holding dozens of prisoners crammed together in unbearable squalor. Gaunt faces pressed against the cold metal, their hollow eyes tracking Gregory as he passed, their expressions a mixture of suspicion, resignation, and faint curiosity. Shouts echoed through the hallway—

angry curses, desperate pleas for food, and cries for freedom, blending into a cacophony of misery. Some prisoners huddled in corners, muttering fragmented prayers to distant gods, their voices a dissonant chant that filled the air with a haunting hum.

The smell was unbearable and clung to the damp air. Each step Gregory took toward his assigned cell intensified the stench, assaulting his senses. When the guard finally threw open the door, chaos and decay greeted him. Inside, the overcrowded cell crammed thirty, perhaps forty men together, all living in abject filth. A single, overflowing toilet stood in one corner while a rust-stained sink dripped sluggishly into a dark pool beneath it. Feces and grime streaked the walls, adding to the oppressive atmosphere of despair.

The prisoners turned their heads as Gregory entered, their gaunt faces reflecting the toll of their confinement. Some clung to the walls, their hollow eyes barely flickering with acknowledgment, while others lay sprawled across the damp floor, lost in restless half-sleep. The dim light from the high, narrow window cast long shadows, accentuating the filth and decay that clung to every surface. Gregory hesitated, his gaze sweeping over the crowded cell, the suffocating reality of his confinement pressing down on him.

The guard unshackled Gregory's wrists with a sharp twist and gave him a rough shove toward the interior. "Pray you find Rome's mercy before it finds you," the guard muttered before slamming the iron door shut behind him. The lock echoed through the corridor, a final, metallic punctuation to Gregory's arrival. The cell fell back into a tense quiet, interrupted only by the occasional cough or shuffle of limbs as the other prisoners shifted in their limited space.

Gregory moved slowly, his steps deliberate as he searched for a place to sit. His eyes scanned the packed benches hugging the wall, where bodies leaned against one another in exhausted slumber or quiet desolation. Finally, he spotted a narrow sliver of space between two dozing men. Carefully, he lowered himself onto the rough wood, his shoulders brushing against theirs. Neither man stirred, their faces pale and slack with exhaustion. The bench creaked under the added weight, and Gregory sat still, his hands resting on his knees. The air was stifling, and the foul odors clung to his skin, but he forced himself to remain calm.

For the first time since his arrest, Gregory allowed doubt to seep into his mind. Had he gone too far? Was he playing a game against forces too vast and too powerful to overcome? He replayed the moments at the Pantheon, questioning every step, every word. The cheers, the whispers of understanding—were they enough? Or had his act of defiance sealed his fate?

Gregory's thoughts darkened as he considered the warnings of the seer. Her words echoed in his mind: "If you perish in this world, it will not only end you but fracture the balance of both realms." He clenched his hands into fists, the chill of the cell's air biting at his knuckles. Could he avoid death in a place designed to strip men of their will? Would this cell be the end of him, his mission, and the prophecy that had brought him here?

His gaze lingered on the grimy floor, then shifted to the faint moonlight filtering through the high, narrow window—a sliver of light amidst the oppressive gloom. The predicament pressed heavily. Chilling words from the senator echoed in his mind: "Aid him again, and you will join him on the hill, nailed to a cross." Crucifixion loomed before him, no longer an abstract punishment but a visceral, inescapable threat. Roman justice offered no room for hope, only the sharp reality of an agonizing death.

Gregory's resolve wavered under the crushing strain of his predicament, the reality settling over him like a shroud. To perish in this world would not only mean the failure of his mission but also risk unraveling the fragile threads of this reality and the one he had left behind. The cost of his defiance loomed larger than ever—a sacrifice that could extinguish the very hope he sought to ignite.

The shuffle of straw against stone drew Gregory's attention. He saw an old man approaching, his movements slow and deliberate. The man's long silver beard was unkempt, hanging in thin strands down to his chest. Wisps of hair clung stubbornly to the edges of a bald scalp, and his skin, lined and weathered, bore the harsh testimony of years spent in hardship. Yet his eyes captured Gregory's focus—piercing blue orbs that were unnaturally bright against the grime of his face, like headlamps cutting through the darkness.

The old man stopped a few feet away, studying Gregory with an intensity that made him feel momentarily exposed. "You don't look like you belong here," the old man said, his voice rough but not unkind. He gestured vaguely around the cell, the motion encompassing the filth, the stench, and the dozens of men crammed into the small space. "None of us do, I suppose. But you… you have the air of a man who still thinks he can leave."

Gregory regarded him carefully before replying, "And you don't?"

The old man chuckled, a dry sound devoid of humor. "Ten years I've been here—for stealing a loaf of bread to feed my grandson. The boy's grown by now, but here I remain. Rome does not forgive, and it certainly does not forget."

Gregory glanced at the cramped bench, his shoulders brushing against the men sleeping on either side of him. He shrugged apologetically, unable to offer more space. "There's nowhere—"

The old man waved a hand dismissively, cutting him off. "Bah, space is what you make of it." Without hesitation, he shuffled closer, wedging himself onto the narrow bench. His wiry frame pressed against Gregory's, and with a surprising burst of force, he nudged one of the sleeping men aside, shifting him a good dozen inches down the bench. The displaced man grumbled in his sleep but didn't stir.

"There," the old man said, settling in with a satisfied grunt. He rested his elbows on his knees, his piercing blue eyes locking onto Gregory's. "So, let's try this again. What crime brings you to this pit?"

Gregory took a deep breath, his hands resting on his knees. "I didn't steal. I didn't kill. My crime, as they see it, is a defiance of pride. I speak of humility, of service. I spread the word of one who teaches a different way."

The old man frowned, his eyes narrowing. "Who is this teacher?"

Gregory turned to face the old man fully, his voice steady but fervent. "He is the Son of God," Gregory said. "Not a god of wealth or war, not one who revels in conquest or demands sacrifice. He calls for love, compassion, and humility. He asks us to see beyond ourselves, to serve others, and to recognize the Divine within all."

The old man's blue eyes narrowed his expression, a mix of confusion and curiosity. "The Son of God, you say," he muttered, leaning closer to scrutinize Gregory's words better. "But which god? Do you mean Jupiter, the ruler of the heavens? Or perhaps Mars, who guards the battlefield? There are gods for every domain—strength, wisdom, even wine. Every god serves a purpose, so what purpose does this son of yours fulfill?"

Gregory's resolve deepened, and his reply came without hesitation. "He is not like the gods of Rome. He does not belong to one sphere or domain or serve any earthly ambition. He embodies Divine love, a light to guide us—not through power but humility and service. His purpose is to teach us that strength lies in compassion and true Divinity is found in lifting others, not dominating them."

The old man's gaze lingered on Gregory, skeptical yet intrigued. "Rome is a city of gods, built on their favor and strength," he said, his voice low and gravelly. "And yet you speak of another—a god who asks for nothing but gives freely? Strange. Very strange." He stroked his beard, his eyes narrowing with doubt. "You'll find no home for this son of yours here. Rome respects gods who conquer, not gods who kneel."

Gregory met his gaze, steady and calm. "Perhaps," he said quietly, "but I've already seen hearts begin to change—people willing to risk everything to stand beside me. Their courage shows that humility can take root even in a city of marble and pride."

The old man leaned back, letting out a weary breath as his calloused hands rested on his knees. His tone carried the force of certainty, edged with resignation. "I'm afraid that's over. You're in their grip now. Rome doesn't bend to whispers of change—it destroys them. They've silenced countless voices before you and do the same to yours. That's how it's always been."

Gregory exhaled as the words settled over him. "Maybe they will," he said softly. "But a seed planted in faith doesn't die with the sower. Compassion, humility, and forgiveness can grow even in the hardest soil. And that's why I began."

The old man shook his head, a faint, wry smile tugging at the corners of his mouth. "You're either a fool or a prophet," he said. "Maybe both. But I'll say this: there's something in your eyes that makes me want to believe you."

Gregory's voice softened, his conviction undimmed. "It's not me you need to believe in. It's the truth of what I speak. Even here, in this cell, where the stench of despair clings to the air, that truth can grow."

The old man fell silent, his gaze drifting to the narrow window where a sliver of moonlight spilled through.

Gregory studied him for a long moment, the faint light streaming through the high, narrow window softening his weathered features. Despite the grime and despair clinging to the cell, there was a flicker of something in the man's eyes—a glimmer of curiosity, perhaps even hope.

"What's your name?" Gregory asked, his voice quiet but clear, cutting through the muffled sounds of the cell.

The man glanced at him, his lips curling into a faint, almost imperceptible smile. "Name's Silvanus," he said, leaning back against the wall. "Not that it's mattered much in here."

Gregory nodded, letting the name settle in his mind. "It matters to me," he said.

Silvanus tilted his head, studying Gregory with renewed interest. For the first time, his skepticism wavered, and a hint of warmth entered his gaze. "Well then, Gregory," he murmured, his voice laced with resignation and intrigue, "let's see if you and your truth can survive in a place like this."

The cell sank into a fragile silence, broken only by the rustle of shifting bodies and the crude sounds of survival—an occasional cough, the faint shuffle of feet on damp straw, or the muffled groan of a restless sleeper. Gregory sat quietly, his thoughts heavy yet resolute, the mission pressing upon him like the shadows themselves. Beside him, Silvanus lifted his weary gaze to the narrow beam of light, his piercing blue eyes searching for answers in the faint glow—answers that seemed just out of reach.

CHAPTER TWENTY-FOUR
FORGIVENESS

Gregory sat hunched on the splintered bench; his head bowed low as the gravity of his circumstances pressed him into a numb haze. The squalor of the cell gnawed at him—the oppressive stench of human decay, the unrelenting cries of desperation, the rough edges of despair that scraped against his soul. His once-steady resolve felt fragile, like a thread stretched too thin. He thought of Lucius and Marcus, their warnings and cautious eyes, and realized they had been right. He had overreached. His mission now seemed doomed to end in this filthy, forgotten sewer of Rome.

One day blurred into the next, a slow erosion of purpose. Gregory's prayers had grown weaker, his words faltering as the shadows of doubt encroached on his faith. He found himself slipping into silence, his heart heavy with regret. Even the faces of the prisoners—men who might have been his flock—seemed blurred now, their suffering a mirror of his own.

One night, when the cell had quieted to a muffled symphony of restless bodies and distant sobs, Gregory fell into a fitful sleep. And then the dream came. It began with silence. Gregory stood alone in a barren wasteland; the earth beneath him cracked and dry, splitting into deep fissures as far as his eyes could see. The air shimmered with a heat that scorched his skin, the sky a pale, oppressive gray above him. There was no sound, no movement, only the stillness of desolation. He felt small, insignificant against the enormity of this lifeless expanse.

As he walked, his bare feet stirring the dust, a soft wind began to rise. It carried a voice—not a sound, but a resonance that stirred his very being. "Gregory," it called, calm yet commanding, reverberating through him like a bell tolling in an empty cathedral. He turned, searching for the source, but found only the endless wasteland.

Then, without warning, a tiny, unassuming seed appeared in his hand. Its surface was smooth and golden. He stared at it, bewildered, when another fell into his open palm and then another until his hands overflowed with them. The wind swirled around him, lifting the seeds upward. They drifted away, settling into the cracks of the parched earth.

Gregory watched, transfixed, as the soil began to tremble. A tender green shoot emerged from each seed, unfurling with impossible speed. The barren wasteland transformed before his eyes. Shoots became stalks, stalks became trees, and the air filled with the scent of blossoms and fresh rain. The sky brightened to a vivid blue, and the sun shone down, warming the lush garden that had sprung forth.

The voice returned, clearer now and full of power. "Even in desolation, life can grow. Forgiveness is the water that nourishes the seeds. Begin, Gregory. Here, in the shadow of despair, you will sow the next seed."

Gregory woke with a start, his breath ragged, his heart hammering in his chest. The damp, rancid air of the cell clung to him, but it could not smother the vivid clarity of what he had seen. He ran his fingers over his palms, expecting to feel the seeds still there. The dream lingered, not as a fleeting vision, but as an undeniable truth. He sat upright, his gaze drawn to the narrow sliver of moonlight streaming through the high window.

This was not the end. This prison, this pit of misery, was not a tomb—it was a garden waiting to be planted. The men around him, with their gaunt faces and hollow eyes, were not beyond redemption. They were the soil, hardened and cracked but ready to receive the third seed of forgiveness.

Gregory closed his eyes, a new strength rising within him. He remembered the faces of Lucius, Marcus, Julia, and the others—their courage, their willingness to risk everything for the truth he carried. Their belief in him had not faltered, nor would his belief in this mission. The voice from his dream echoed once more in his mind—*begin.*

Gregory opened his eyes to the dim cell around him, the moonlight catching the grime-covered walls and illuminating the faces of the men who shared his imprisonment. They were broken and battered by their crimes and the harsh justice of Rome. In the dream's vivid afterglow, Gregory saw them anew—not as prisoners but as souls yearning for release, purpose, and forgiveness. He drew a steady breath, feeling his resolve solidify like stone. If this place were to become a garden, it would begin with a single voice—a single word of hope whispered into the darkness. Gregory straightened on the bench, his eyes meeting Silvanus's. "The seed," he murmured, "must be planted." And with those words, his mission within the walls of Claustra truly began.

At first, his words were soft, shared only with the old man seated beside him on the crowded bench. Despite his initial skepticism, Silvanus seemed captivated by Gregory's stories of love, humility, and forgiveness.

"Forgiveness?" Silvanus echoed, his tone laden with disbelief. "You speak of love and humility, and I can see its value. But forgiveness? How do you forgive men who have broken you, who have stripped you of everything? How do you forgive an empire that grinds men like us beneath its heel?"

Gregory turned to him, his voice calm but resolute. "Forgiveness is not for them, Silvanus. It is for us. To forgive is to free ourselves from the chains of hatred and bitterness. Only then can we truly be free, no matter where we are."

The old man's eyes narrowed as he considered Gregory's words. Around them, the murmurs of the cell faded, prisoners straining to hear the conversation.

"And what of justice?" one man asked from a shadowed corner. His voice was rough, broken by years of anger. "Do we forgive the guards who beat us? The judges who condemned us? Does forgiveness mean letting them go unpunished?"

Gregory shook his head. "Justice and forgiveness are not enemies. Justice serves the world, but forgiveness heals the soul. To forgive does not mean to forget what was done or to excuse it. It means releasing the power it holds over you, choosing not to let anger and vengeance consume you."

The words stirred tension and curiosity in the air. The prisoners, who had ignored Gregory, began to ask questions and share their grievances and hurts. Gregory's corner of the cell slowly became a gathering place, his bench a pulpit. Silvanus sat beside him, sometimes challenging Gregory's teachings and other times nodding along, his skepticism softened by hope.

One day, Gregory invited the men to confess—not to him, but to one another. "Speak your burdens," he urged. "Share what weighs on your hearts. In doing so, you will begin to unshackle yourselves."

The confessions came hesitantly at first, whispered in trembling voices. A thief admitted his shame at stealing from a neighbor he once called a friend. A former soldier wept as he spoke of the lives he had taken in the name of the empire. Even gruff and guarded Silvanus shared his pain—the grandson he had failed to protect, the bread he had stolen, the bitterness that had consumed him ever since.

Gregory listened, offering no judgment, only a quiet prayer for healing. As the men spoke, something remarkable began to happen. They began to forgive themselves and those who had wronged them.

Gregory taught them that forgiveness was a seed; like humility, it needed fertile soil to grow.

Word spread. Men from neighboring cells pressed against the iron bars to listen. The guards, at first dismissive, began to linger near the bars, their stern faces betraying hints of curiosity. Gregory's voice carried through the stone halls of Claustra, a beacon of hope in a place defined by despair. "Forgiveness," he began, "is the hardest seed to plant, for it must grow in the most barren soil—the wounded heart. It is easy to hate those who wrong us. It is easy to let the chains of anger and resentment bind us. But I ask you—what does hatred yield? Does it not only feed the fire that consumes us, burning away our peace and our hope?"

The prisoners listened, their weary eyes fixed on him. Some were skeptical, and others yearned for a reason to believe.

"Forgiveness is not weakness," Gregory continued, his tone firm yet compassionate. "It is the greatest strength a soul can possess. To forgive is to free yourself from the poison of vengeance, to step out of the darkness and into the light. And it is not just for those who harm us but for ourselves. How long will we carry the weight of our anger? How long will we allow it to keep us shackled?"

He paused, his eyes scanning the room, meeting the gazes of the men before him. "We are all prisoners—not just of these walls, but of our pasts, our mistakes, and our pain. I say to you: we can be free, not by breaking these iron bars, but by breaking the chains around our hearts. Forgive not because the offenders deserve it but because you do. Forgive because it is the only way forward."

Gregory's voice softened, yet it reached every corner of the cells. "And yes, forgive those who brought you here—the guards, the judges, the ones who have treated you as less than human. Not because their actions are just but because your spirit is greater than their injustice. Forgive them, and in doing so, reclaim your power, your dignity, your soul."

The prison fell silent except for the faint sound of a few prisoners weeping. Gregory knelt, inviting them to join him. "We will not change the world with hate," he said, his voice a whisper now, full of emotion. "But with forgiveness, we can plant the seeds of a new one."

And one by one, they knelt. The once cold, dark cell became a sanctuary of transformation, where the unlikeliest gardens began to bloom. Gregory's heart swelled. He saw the hardened faces of prisoners softened by the possibility of hope and even the eyes of the guards now glimmering with the faintest trace of understanding. The seed of forgiveness had taken root in the unlikeliest of soils, a light breaking through the suffocating darkness of the Claustra.

For the first time since his imprisonment, Gregory felt a sense of profound purpose settle over him. He had planted the third seed, and it took root. But the mission was far from over. His gaze shifted to the narrow window high above, where the faintest sliver of moonlight shone, a reminder of the world beyond these walls—a world still waiting for the fourth seed of justice.

The path forward would be challenging, but he needed hope. Forgiveness had turned this prison into fertile ground, and now he needed to find a way out—not for his own freedom, but to carry the seeds of change further. With a deep breath, he turned his mind to the challenge ahead, knowing that the strength to overcome it lay not in force but in faith.

CHAPTER TWENTY-FIVE
SEXTUS

For many days, Gregory's voice became the rhythm of life within the Claustra. His sermons, once whispers shared with Silvanus, now echoed through the cells, reaching prisoners and guards alike. The air in the prison began to shift, the suffocating despair lifting ever so slightly. For the first time, laughter and hope flickered among the men like fragile flames in a storm.

The prisoners treated Gregory like one of their own. They offered him what little they had—extra scraps of bread, sips of their precious water. Some even insisted he take their space on the bench when he appeared weary. Aware of his tendency toward pride, Gregory refused their offerings, redirecting their generosity toward one another. Yet, he couldn't ignore the reverence in their eyes or the murmurs when he walked by.

Silvanus leaned close one evening as they sat on the splintered bench. "You see how they look at you," the old man said, his voice gruff but laced with warmth. "As if you're the son of your god himself."

Gregory's expression tightened. "I am no more than they are, Silvanus," he said, his tone firm but tinged with unease. "We are all vessels, and I am but one carrying a message."

"Perhaps," Silvanus replied, his piercing blue eyes studying Gregory. "But your words make you more in their eyes."

Gregory nodded, his gaze falling to his hands. He prayed silently for humility, aware of the familiar temptation gnawing at the edges of his resolve.

Gregory's presence among the guards was a source of curiosity and conflict. Some dismissed him as a delusional preacher, while others lingered near the cell, listening intently to his words. One guard, in particular, seemed drawn to Gregory more than the others. His name was Sextus. He was a younger man, his hardened exterior barely masking the guilt he carried.

Gregory noticed Sextus lingering near the cell more often. His usually stoic demeanor was tinged with an unease that the guard tried—and failed—to hide. Gregory didn't know what weighed so heavily on the man, but he could see the cracks in his composure: Sextus's hands trembled slightly, and the furrow in his brow deepened with each passing day. It was the look of a man haunted by something he could neither escape nor confess.

One evening, as Gregory neared the conclusion of his sermon, his voice rose in quiet defiance of the despair that clung to the prison walls. "Forgiveness is not the erasure of what has been done; it is the healing of what remains," he said, his words reaching every ear in the crowded cell. "To forgive is to unclench the hand that grips anger, to set down the heavy stone you carry—not for their sake, but for your own. Forgiveness does not rewrite the past, but it reshapes the future."

The prisoners listened intently, their gaunt faces illuminated by the sunlight that filtered through the distant window. Even the most skeptical among them had grown silent, their skepticism eroded by Gregory's conviction. "Forgive not only those who ask," he continued, "but those who will never ask. Forgive when it is hardest, for then it is most needed. Blessed are those who forgive, for they will know a peace that surpasses all understanding."

As his voice softened, Sextus stepped forward. The guard's movements were hesitant, and his usual air of authority was replaced with a vulnerability that drew the attention of several prisoners. The cell stilled, and their eyes darted between Gregory and the man in uniform now standing just beyond the bars.

Sextus's gaze met Gregory's, and for a moment, neither spoke. Then, as if compelled by a force beyond himself, Sextus spoke, his voice low but clear. "You say forgiveness frees us. But how does a man forgive himself when the weight of what he's done is too great to bear?"

Gregory's expression softened, and he stepped closer to the bars, his hands resting lightly on the cold iron. "Forgiveness begins with a choice," he said gently. "It is not given because you are free of guilt— it is given because your soul deserves to heal. The weight you carry is not yours to bear alone. Release it and allow the light of grace to take its place."

The guard's face tightened, his jaw clenching as emotion swirled in his eyes. Around him, the prisoners watched in stunned silence, their own burdens momentarily forgotten. Sextus exhaled, his shoulders sagging as though the words had lifted a fraction of his unseen burden. Without another word, he turned and walked away, his footsteps echoing down the corridor.

But he returned the next night and the night after, each time lingering longer and listening more intently. With every sermon Gregory delivered, forgiveness took deeper root in the prisoners and the man who had once oppressed them.

One night, Sextus lingered by the bars. He summoned Gregory closer with the flick of his hand, his voice barely a whisper. "I can get you out of here," he said, his tone urgent. "There's a transfer scheduled for tomorrow—a prisoner they're moving to another facility. I can switch the records and make it seem as though you're the one being moved."

Gregory's heart quickened, but he forced himself to remain calm. "Why would you risk this?" he asked.

Sextus's brown eyes met his, filled with determination and desperation. "Because I believe in your words," he said.

***

The next day passed in tense anticipation. Gregory kept to himself, his thoughts weighed down by the promise of what could come. The hum of the cell, filled with murmured conversations and the occasional shuffle of restless bodies, felt distant to him. Silvanus, ever watchful, caught the subtle shifts in Gregory's demeanor—the distracted glances toward the corridor, the faint, unspoken urgency in his movements.

"You're leaving, aren't you?" Silvanus whispered, leaning closer so his words wouldn't carry to the other prisoners.

Gregory hesitated, his gaze lowering to his hands. "I hope so," he said finally. "There is more work to be done beyond these walls. The seeds planted so far—they are only the beginning."

Silvanus snorted, his expression as sharp as his tone. "You talk like a man who carries the world on his shoulders. You know these men look to you like some savior. If you leave, they will falter; what then?"

Gregory met Silvanus's eyes, his voice steady but soft. "I'm not their savior, Silvanus. I'm just a messenger. What grows here will not depend on me—it depends on them. On you."

The old man's brows furrowed, his weathered face a mask of skepticism. "And you think forgiveness will survive in a place like this? You think these seeds of yours will grow in soil as bitter as mine?"

Gregory lightly touched Silvanus's shoulder, the gesture firm but comforting. "Forgiveness is not a gift you give to others—it's a gift you give yourself. Whether the seeds grow or wither is not up to me. But they are planted, and that is what matters."

Silvanus grunted, his gaze hard but not unkind. "Then go. But don't think you'll leave here forgotten. These men won't forget what you've done."

Gregory smiled faintly, a flicker of gratitude in his weary eyes. "I won't forget them either," he promised. "And neither will the One who sent me."

The two men sat silently for a long moment, their unspoken words settling between them like a shared burden. Finally, Silvanus straightened, his gruff voice cutting through the quiet. "You'll need your strength out there," he said, sliding a small piece of bread toward Gregory. "Take it. Don't argue."

Gregory paused, then reached out to take the offering, his movements deliberate and filled with quiet gratitude. "Let the seeds of forgiveness take root here, Silvanus," he said softly. "And may you find the peace that's been missing for so long."

Silvanus leaned back, a dry chuckle escaping his lips. "Peace?" he muttered, shaking his head. "If you think that's possible in a place like this, you've got more faith than sense, Gregory. But maybe that's exactly what we need."

With that, the conversation ended, but the words lingered in Gregory's mind as he prepared for the night ahead. He knew the path forward would be treacherous, but his resolve was unshaken. Beyond the prison walls, the next seed waited to be sown.

Sextus approached the cell that evening as the guards began their rounds. "Gregory," he said, his voice steady. "It's time for your transfer."

The prisoners watched in stunned silence as the cell door creaked open. Gregory stepped out, his movements deliberate and calm. He turned back to the men, his gaze sweeping over them. "The seeds are yours to tend now," he said softly. "Grow them well."

As Sextus led Gregory down the dim corridor, the prisoners began to rise, their voices lifting in a wave of reverence. Cries of honor and thanks echoed through the stone halls, mingling with murmured prayers like the chant of an army exalting a returning hero. "Bless you, Gregory of the Foreign Faith!" one man shouted, his voice raw with emotion. "Go with God," whispered another, his words trembling with faith. The sound swelled, growing louder with every step, a symphony of gratitude and hope that filled the prison with an energy it had never known.

Gregory's steps faltered momentarily under the overwhelming force of their devotion. He turned, his eyes meeting the gaunt faces pressed against the bars, and felt their faith in him like a mantle placed upon his shoulders. Yet, he carried it gladly—not as a king among men, but as a gardener tending the fragile shoots of transformation. The seeds of forgiveness had taken root in this barren place, and as Sextus led him into the night, Gregory's heart swelled with purpose, his gaze fixed firmly on the road ahead.

They emerged from the suffocating gloom of the fortress into the cool night air. The stars above shimmered like distant promises of freedom. Sextus handed Gregory a rough woolen cloak. "This will keep you hidden," Sextus said, his voice steady despite the tremble in his hands. He hesitated before continuing, his words spilling out in a rush. "I can't stay here. Not after this. I will go with you if you'll have me."

Gregory studied him for a long moment, his expression softening with quiet understanding. "This path will not be easy, Sextus. To walk it is to risk everything. But if you truly feel called, then come."

Together, they approached Sextus's car. Without a word, Sextus slid behind the wheel, his jaw clenched in silent resolve. Gregory pulled open the passenger door, got inside, and glanced briefly at Sextus's determined expression before closing the door behind him.

The fortress loomed behind them, its harsh silhouette shrinking as they pulled away. Gregory breathed deeply, the scent of the cool night air mingling with the resolve in his heart. The third seed had been planted, and its roots had taken hold in the most unlikely soil. But the work was far from over.

As the car rolled along the empty road, its headlights cutting through the darkness, Sextus broke the silence. "You believe in this mission of yours, don't you?" he asked, his voice steady but edged with curiosity.

Gregory turned his gaze toward Sextus, calm but resolute. "It's not belief, Sextus. It's a certainty. The seeds of compassion, humility, and forgiveness are not mine to plant alone. They belong to all of us."

Sextus nodded slightly, his eyes fixed on the road ahead. The moon's faint glow illuminated his face, casting soft shadows that reflected the depth of his thoughts. "Then I'll follow," he said quietly. "Wherever this road leads, I'll follow."

Gregory reached over, placing a hand on Sextus's shoulder. The gesture was firm yet filled with a quiet camaraderie. "The road ahead will not be easy," he said, his voice low but steady. "There is more work to be done—more seeds to plant. Forgiveness has taken root, but the fields of Rome still await the seeds of justice, wisdom, courage, and sacrifice. Each step forward brings us closer, not just to our mission, but to the world these seeds can create."

The car hummed steadily as they drove, the road stretching endlessly before them under the night sky. Behind them, the seed of forgiveness had blossomed, a fragile yet vital beginning. Together, they turned their faces toward the horizon, ready to face whatever lay ahead.

CHAPTER TWENTY-SIX
ON THE RUN

The hum of the car's engine was the only sound in the tense, quiet night as Gregory and Sextus sped along the narrow streets of Rome. The city lights blurred past the windows, casting fleeting shadows across their faces. Gregory leaned back in the passenger seat, his thoughts heavy but his gaze steady, while Sextus gripped the steering wheel, his eyes darting between the rearview mirror and the road ahead.

"Once they realize you're gone, they'll send the Custodes after you," Sextus said, his voice low but urgent. "We have to stay ahead of them."

Gregory nodded, his gaze fixed on the darkened horizon. "Do you have somewhere safe to go?"

"I know a place," Sextus replied, turning down an unmarked side street. "An old studio I used to work in before I took a position at the prison. It's out of the way, quiet. No one would think to look for us there."

They drove in silence for several miles, the tension thick as neither dared to speak. Finally, Sextus turned sharply into a secluded alley, its shadows swallowing the car whole. He parked alongside a rusting dumpster that leaned precariously against the wall of a long-abandoned photography studio. The building's facade, once vibrant and inviting, was now a ghost of its former self, its peeling paint and shattered windows whispering of forgotten memories.

Sextus killed the engine and scanned the alley, his eyes narrowing as he ensured they hadn't been followed. Satisfied, he stepped out and motioned for Gregory to do the same. "Come on," he murmured, his voice low but urgent. Without waiting for a response, Sextus moved toward the studio's side door, its chipped frame barely clinging to its hinges. Gregory hesitated, glancing back as the car vanished into the shadows of the alley, its shape consumed by the darkness, melting away like a phantom, before he trailed after Sextus.

Sextus pushed the door open, its creak echoing like a warning. Inside, the air was heavy with the smell of mildew and decay. Faint outlines of old photography equipment were scattered across the room, blanketed in dust and cobwebs. The interior was sparse, lit only by the pale glow of streetlights filtering through the boarded-up windows. Dust hung in the air, and the faint tangy scent of chemicals lingered, a remnant of its former life. Sextus flipped a switch, and a single bare bulb flickered to life, casting a dim, yellow light over the room.

"This is it," Sextus said, setting his bag on a metal table in the corner. "It's not much, but it's safe. At least for now."

Gregory nodded, lowering himself onto a battered stool. He glanced around the room, noticing the peeling paint and cracked linoleum floor. Although it was far from inviting, it was a sanctuary.

Sextus rummaged through a small cabinet, pulling out bottled water and some aged energy bars, which he offered to Gregory.

"Take it, they're still good," Sextus insisted. "You'll need your strength."

Gregory hesitated before accepting, offering a quiet nod of thanks. As he unwrapped the bar, Sextus leaned against the table, his arms crossed and his expression thoughtful. "I've been meaning to ask," he began, his tone careful. "Where are you from, Gregory?"

The question hung in the air, simple yet layered with complexity. Gregory looked up, meeting Sextus's gaze with quiet intensity. "I was born here, in Rome," he said carefully, his voice measured. "But where I'm truly from… that's not as simple to explain."

Sextus tilted his head, his frown deepening. "Rome, you say? Then tell me this: where were you educated? What you preach and how you speak is not taught anywhere, not in the universities or temples. Your words defy everything they teach us. They're even illegal to speak, let alone to preach publicly."

Gregory's faint smile returned, a flicker of understanding softening his features. "What I've learned doesn't come from the schools or the temples," he replied. "It comes from something deeper—something beyond what most can see or touch. A world I've glimpsed, where humanity rises above its divisions, where justice, wisdom, courage, and forgiveness are not just ideals but truths we live by. It's not perfect, Sextus, but it's a world worth striving for."

Sextus leaned back, the skepticism in his expression shadowed by intrigue. "A world beyond Rome," he murmured, more to himself than to Gregory. "And you think you can bring it here?"

Gregory's gaze remained steady, his voice unwavering. "The seeds of change cannot grow in silence. I speak because I must, not because it is safe. And I speak not to defy but to inspire—to show that another way is possible."

Sextus's fingers tightened around the edge of the table, his doubt warring with a spark of belief. "You're either mad or brilliant," he said at last, shaking his head. "Maybe both. But I'll say this: I've never met anyone like you, Gregory. And you think you can bring that here? To this world? To people who only know how to fight and take?"

"I believe so," Gregory said firmly. "And belief is the first step to change. The seeds we plant now may not bear fruit in my lifetime, but they will grow. That is why we must act."

Sextus leaned forward, his voice dropping to a near whisper, his eyes sharp with curiosity. "You talk like you've seen a better world. Is it real? Or is it just some dream you've conjured up?"

Gregory hesitated, his gaze steady but guarded. "It's real enough to guide me," he said slowly. "Real enough to show me what must be done. But it's not a world you'd recognize, Sextus. It is not built on the stones of men or their empires but on something greater. A Divine truth."

Sextus folded his arms, his expression a mixture of intrigue and doubt. "You speak with such certainty, Gregory, but you don't understand what you're asking. The gods aren't just marble statues or stories told to children. They are Rome. They are in every action we take, every law we uphold, every prayer we offer. Our victories, failures, and struggles all lead back to the gods. To dismiss them as myths is to dismiss the foundation of our lives."

Gregory's gaze remained steady, his voice calm but resolute. "I do not dismiss your life, Sextus. But I challenge the shadows that obscure the light. The Roman gods are woven into your world, but that does not make them true. They are convenient explanations and reflections of human desires and fears. They demand tribute but offer no answers. They thrive on division and conquest but cannot bring peace to the soul."

Sextus's jaw tightened, his breath uneven as he wrestled with the enormity of Gregory's words. "Do you think I haven't doubted them?" he said, his voice low, almost a whisper. "Do you think I haven't cursed Jupiter's name when I prayed for mercy and heard nothing in return? But how can you be so sure they are empty? What gives you this certainty, this truth you speak of?"

Gregory leaned closer, his voice softening but losing none of its intensity. "Because the truth I carry does not come from temples or sacrifices. It comes from the one God—one who does not demand but invites, who does not punish but forgives. This God does not dwell in marble halls but within the human heart. I have seen what happens when this truth takes root, Sextus. It heals, it uplifts, and it unites."

Sextus shook his head, his hands trembling as he ran them through his hair. "But everything—everything in Rome—is built on the gods. How do you replace that? How do you tell people that everything they've known and trusted is an illusion?"

Gregory's gaze softened. "By showing them something greater. By planting seeds of love, justice, and forgiveness. This truth is not an enemy of the Romans, Sextus—it is their liberation. It is not about tearing down what is, but lifting what could be."

Sextus sighed, the impact of Gregory's words pressing on him. "You talk like you've seen this better world," he murmured. "As if it's more than just an idea."

Gregory hesitated, his expression thoughtful. "I have seen it, Sextus. But it is not a world built by conquest or rule. It is built by hearts willing to forgive, love, and seek justice even in the face of cruelty. It is not easy, and it may not come in our lifetimes. But it is worth striving for."

Sextus was silent for a long moment, the tension in his frame gradually easing as recognition flickered in his eyes. "Rome is harsh," he admitted quietly. "Its rule is unforgiving. Maybe… maybe there's room for something more. Something better." He glanced at Gregory, his voice tinged with uncertainty. "I don't know if I can believe in this God of yours. But I believe in you. And for now, that's enough."

He hesitated, his brow furrowing before a new thought took shape. "In the prison," Sextus said, his voice carrying a tone of awe, "I saw how those men looked at you like you were something more than human. Like you were Apollo, walking among us in the flesh. What's it like, Gregory, to have so many desperate souls look to you with such reverence? To see you as their light in the darkness?"

Gregory's lips pressed into a faint smile, but his eyes held a solemn depth. "It's not me they revere, Sextus. What they see is hope—hope reflected at them through the words I carry. I am not the source of that light, only the mirror that casts it. What they admire is not me but the truth that moves through me."

Sextus nodded slowly, his expression one of quiet amazement. "Still," he murmured, "to see a man held in such high regard—it's rare. Inspiring, even. You've stirred something in them, Gregory. Something that Rome itself could never ignite."

Gregory placed a hand on Sextus's shoulder, a gesture of quiet solidarity. "Then let us stir something greater together, Sextus. There's still much to do and many seeds to plant."

The city buzzed faintly beyond the cracked studio walls, oblivious to the quiet exchange within. Gregory's gaze shifted to the faint light spilling through the window, symbolizing the road ahead. Justice was the next seed, and he knew the journey to plant it would be as perilous as the truths he had just shared.

CHAPTER TWENTY-SEVEN
SANCTUARY

The dim studio light flickered faintly overhead as Gregory and Sextus sat at a worktable. With a deliberate motion, Sextus reached into his pocket and pulled out a map of Rome, unfolding it carefully onto the table. The paper was frayed at the edges, its surface marred by streaks of dirt and oil. Streets and alleys crisscrossed the map in intricate detail, each line drawn with meticulous precision, though time had faded many markings.

Gregory leaned over the map, his eyes narrowing as his fingers traced its lines. At first glance, it resembled the Rome he knew—its broad avenues, intricate alleys, and towering landmarks forming a familiar web. Yet, the more he studied it, the more subtle, unsettling differences emerged. Buildings loomed in places where none had stood before, while others, once iconic, were conspicuously absent. This map belonged to a Rome that had followed a parallel path, a reflection distorted by time and unseen forces.

Despite these differences, the city's remarkable engineering, crafted over two millennia, was unmistakable. Its streets were carefully organized, its landmarks purposefully positioned. It was awe-inspiring to see how the vision of Rome's early planners had withstood the test of time, their understanding of power and permanence etched into the very bones of the city. The sweeping avenues, converging at key locations, spoke of a city built to command and endure, a testament to its unmatched history.

Yet, this Rome bore the weight of something else—an unfamiliar vision layered upon its foundation. Gregory felt both awe and unease as he absorbed the sight before him. This city reflected the ambition and precision of its architects but whispered of a history rewritten, of power and purpose reshaped in ways he had yet to understand.

The Tiber River, winding elegantly through the city's heart, was familiar, but the historical landmarks that once defined the Rome of his world were unrecognizable. He saw an expansive office park where, in his world, the grandeur of the Vatican and St. Peter's Basilica stood. A sense of profound loss settled over him. The spiritual epicenter of his Rome, the sacred seat of Christendom, had been erased and replaced with something utilitarian, devoid of its Divine essence.

Gregory sat back, his eyes lingering on the map. "This Rome," he murmured, "the place of my birth is a stranger. Walking its streets offered glimpses, but this…" He gestured to the map, his tone heavy with awe and sorrow. "This view is a revelation—a city unrecognizable."

Sextus frowned, leaning closer, his brow furrowing in confusion. "I'm sorry, but I don't understand," he said slowly, his voice tinged with curiosity and skepticism. "This is Rome. It's always been Rome. The streets, the Forum, the Colosseum—they've stood for centuries. How can this city be a stranger to you?"

Gregory met his gaze, his thoughts reflected in his somber expression. "What you see here," he said, gesturing to the map, "is not the Rome I know or knew. The Rome I come from bears some resemblance. But in my world, this city was shaped by something greater. Faith. The Vatican and St. Peter's Basilica were the beating heart of a Rome dedicated to Christendom, a center for all Christ's teachings and a beacon of hope for the faithful."

Sextus tilted his head, the lines of confusion deepening on his face. "The Vatican? St. Peter's Basilica? I've never heard of them. Rome has always been devoted to the gods, to Jupiter, Mars, and the rest. Your faith… it doesn't exist here, Gregory. But how could it?"

Gregory hesitated, his fingers brushing the edge of the map as though trying to grasp the enormity of the truth he was about to reveal. "Because, Sextus," he began, his voice low and steady, "I am not from this Rome. Not this version of it, at least. I come from a world parallel to yours, where history unfolded differently. In my world, the Roman Empire collapsed, and this city became the cradle of Christianity. The gods you revere were abandoned long ago, and in their place rose a faith that united nations, built cathedrals, and guided millions."

Sextus blinked, his breath catching as he tried to process the revelation. "Are you saying you're not from this world?" he asked, his voice barely above a whisper.

Gregory nodded, his voice calm but resolute. "I don't know how I came to be here," he admitted, "but I believe it was for a purpose. To plant seeds of change and to show this Rome that there is another way. A way that doesn't rely on the old gods or the unyielding grip of empire. These seeds can ignite a change this world has never seen."

Sextus stared at him, disbelief etched across his face. He let out a dry laugh, shaking his head. "Do you hear yourself, Gregory? You speak as though this is some fanciful tale from a science fiction novel. A parallel universe? Another Rome? That's impossible."

Gregory nodded, his expression heavy with understanding. "I know how impossible it sounds, Sextus. How could two worlds, so similar yet so different, exist simultaneously? It defies logic and everything we think about the nature of existence. And yet, here I am, standing before you. I don't claim to understand, but I cannot deny the truth of it."

Sextus ran a hand through his thick hair, his confusion deepening. "So, what? There's another Rome somewhere out there? Another world? With people like us walking streets like these? How could such a thing be? How could a man cross from one to the other? This isn't just impossible—it's absolute madness."

Gregory sighed, his voice steady but gentle. "I don't expect you to believe me, Sextus. I hardly believe it myself. But I know this: the Rome I came from and my life there was real. And I was brought here for a reason. Perhaps it's not for me to understand how or why. Perhaps the only thing that matters is what I do with this moment, with this opportunity."

Sextus's skepticism didn't waver, but his eyes betrayed a flicker of something else—curiosity, perhaps, or the faintest hint of hope. "And you think these seeds, these ideas of yours, can change a world as entrenched as this one? A world that worships its gods and its empire above all else?"

Gregory nodded, his gaze unwavering. "I don't just think it, Sextus. I believe it. And belief is the first step toward change."

Gregory's words hung in the air, the gravity of their implication settling heavily between them. Sextus leaned back, his arms crossed, his skepticism evident but softened by an undercurrent of intrigue. "You speak as though you've seen this change before," Sextus said, his voice quieter now, almost thoughtful. "As if these seeds you talk about aren't ideals but truths you've witnessed."

Gregory allowed a small, reflective smile to touch his lips. "In a way, I have," he said, his tone steady and almost reverent. "To understand why I believe strongly in their power, you must know where I came from and the journey that brought me here."

Gregory leaned back slightly, his voice steady but tinged with the depth of memory. "I was born in Rome, yes, but not this Rome. The world I come from is both like and unlike this one. It is a place where something called Christianity blossomed and where the teachings of Christ shaped an empire into something different—a flawed but striving reflection of God's will."

Sextus frowned but said nothing, his attention rapt. Gregory continued, his voice steady, yet each word carried the depth of a lifetime. "In my world, I ascended through the ranks of the Church, dedicating myself entirely to the one God. First, I was ordained a priest, ministering to the faithful and offering guidance in their times of need. From there, I was appointed a bishop, entrusted with the care of a diocese, guiding both clergy and laity under my charge."

He paused, his gaze distant, as if reliving the moments. "Eventually, I was elevated to the rank of Cardinal, a role that called for spiritual leadership and deep involvement in the governance of the Church. It was a position of both influence and burden, as I stood among those responsible for shaping the future of our faith."

Gregory's voice grew firmer, resonating with the gravity of his following words. "And then, through the will of the College of Cardinals and God Himself, I became Pope—the shepherd of souls for millions, the successor to Saint Peter. It is the highest office, one that carries immense responsibility and profound isolation. Every decision I made bore spiritual implications and significant worldly consequences. The weight of it was unrelenting, yet I carried on because I believed in the mission. To guide, heal, and protect the flock entrusted to me."

Sextus leaned forward slightly, his expression a mixture of awe and curiosity. Gregory's journey, so foreign to him, was painted with both the majesty and the cost of leadership.

Sextus tilted his head, skepticism creeping into his tone. "And how did you end up here, in this Rome?"

Gregory hesitated, choosing his words carefully. "I don't know how it just happened. But I believe I was called here for a purpose. To plant these seeds, to show this Rome a path it has yet to see."

Sextus furrowed his brow. The skepticism hadn't left his face, but there was something else now—a quiet resignation, perhaps, or the beginnings of an uneasy acceptance. He shook his head slowly, a faint smile of disbelief tugging at the corner of his mouth. "You speak with such conviction, Gregory," Sextus said finally. "Maybe too much conviction for a sane man. You expect me to believe you were a… what did you call it? A Pope? In some other Rome?" He chuckled dryly, but the sound lacked mockery. "It sounds like the ramblings of a madman, if I'm honest."

Gregory met Sextus's gaze, his expression steady. "It doesn't matter what you believe, Sextus. What matters is the mission. What matters is that we try to plant these seeds, to show this world something it hasn't yet imagined."

Sextus nodded, his jaw tightening as he looked down at his hands. "I threw away a good life to help you, you know. That position at the prison—it wasn't just a job. It was stable and respectable. It came with good benefits and helpful connections. And now, I've traded all that to run with a man who speaks of a mysterious god and a parallel world." He let out a long breath, his voice softening. "And yet, here I stand.

Why? I can't say I fully understand your story or your claims. But I've seen how people look at you, how your words stir something deep within them. Maybe that's enough. So, I'll follow you, Gregory. Not because I believe in your talk of a parallel universe, but because I believe in the man standing before me."

Sextus shifted in his seat, his words hanging in the stillness between them. He rubbed the back of his neck, his gaze flickering toward the dim light overhead as though searching for clarity in its faint glow. The air in the room felt charged, thick with unspoken thoughts and the shared burden of uncertainty. Gregory watched him quietly, sensing the turmoil within—a man caught between the life he had left behind and the unknown path before him.

Finally, Sextus exhaled, his voice breaking the silence. "These seeds you speak of," he said, his tone contemplative. "Compassion, humility, forgiveness… What comes next, Gregory? What seed do we plant now?"

Gregory straightened, his gaze steady but thoughtful. "Justice," he said. "The fourth seed is justice, but not the kind Rome knows—the justice of empire, built on fear and domination. This justice is different. It seeks not vengeance but restoration. It is blind not to truth but to prejudice, and it values the dignity of every soul above the power of any institution."

Sextus frowned, trying to grasp Gregory's words. "Justice," he echoed, his voice skeptical. "I've fought wars in the name of Roman justice. I've seen men die because someone decided it was 'just.' What makes your justice any different?"

Gregory leaned closer, his voice calm but resolute. "True justice, Sextus, does not seek to punish—it seeks to heal. It does not divide—it unites. It does not crush—it lifts. It's not about enforcing the will of the powerful but restoring balance and dignity to the powerless. Justice, as I've come to know it, is not an act of strength but an act of courage."

Sextus sat back, his brow furrowed with thought. "And how do you intend to plant this seed of justice in Rome? A city where the law bends to those in power, where the weak are crushed beneath its weight?"

Gregory leaned forward, his hands resting lightly on the map between them. "By starting with those who have the least. Rome's laws protect the powerful, but true justice favors the powerless. We will go to the outcasts—the slaves, the beggars, the laborers in the shadows. We will show them justice is not a privilege reserved for the elite but a right bestowed upon every soul. They will be our foundation."

Sextus shook his head, the doubt in his eyes plain. "You can inspire them, Gregory, but what good will it do? The law is a tool of Rome's might, not its mercy. You cannot simply preach justice into existence. The system itself is too entrenched, too vast to be swayed by the cries of the weak."

Gregory's gaze didn't falter, his voice growing firmer. "That is why the system must change, Sextus. The purpose of governance is not to protect the powerful but to level the playing field and ensure everyone can live a worthy life. Rome's laws must be turned against their makers, used to protect those they were designed to oppress."

Sextus leaned forward, his voice low and urgent. "Do you realize what you're saying? You're speaking of turning Rome against itself. You're talking about uprooting centuries of tradition and power. Even if you could stir the masses, do you think the Senate will let this happen without a fight?"

Gregory nodded solemnly. "I know the cost, Sextus. But justice is worth the struggle. Rome's strength has always been in its order, its ability to adapt. That same order can be redefined—not through rebellion but transformation."

Sextus's jaw tightened, his skepticism battling with a flicker of hope. "Transformation… And you think the oppressed will lead this change? That the voices of the forgotten can be heard over the roar of Rome's mighty legions?"

Gregory smiled faintly, his confidence unshaken. "Not alone. We will need allies—men like you, Sextus—who know the system's strengths and flaws. You've served Rome and seen its might firsthand. Now imagine that same might redirected—not to conquer, but to uplift. Justice is not about erasing Rome's power but redefining its purpose."

Sextus sighed, rubbing the back of his neck. "It's a noble vision, Gregory, but noble visions don't often survive contact with reality. Still, I've already thrown away my life for you. Perhaps there's something to this mission of yours. If justice is to mean anything, it must start somewhere.”

Gregory nodded, his gaze steady and filled with resolve. “We will show Rome that justice is not weakness but the greatest strength of all. But we cannot do this alone. There are others—men and women like you—who understand the cost of this mission. Caius, for example, an ex-soldier like yourself. His heart beats for something greater than conquest, something more meaningful than following orders.”

Sextus raised an eyebrow, his interest piqued. “Caius? What’s his story?”

Gregory’s voice softened, tinged with admiration. “Caius once led legions—a man of discipline, a tactician who mastered the art of strategy. But war left its scars, and he began questioning the cost of Rome’s victories. When he left the military, he sought purpose beyond conquest. He became one of my most trusted supporters when he found me.”

Sextus leaned back, his brow furrowed in thought. “And how does he help you plant these seeds now?”

“He brings order to chaos,” Gregory replied. “He knows how to rally others, even under the Custodes’ watchful eyes. Caius has turned his strategic mind toward this mission. With his help, we’ve established a secure communication network. Messages go out to our supporters, reaching them quickly and discreetly without raising suspicion. He’s vital to what we’re building.”

Sextus nodded slowly, letting Gregory's words sink in. "And you trust him?"

"With my life," Gregory said without hesitation. "Caius no longer fights with weapons. Though convincing him of that was a struggle. His mind and his heart are his tools now. Men like him—and like you—are essential to this mission."

Gregory leaned forward, his eyes locking with Sextus's. "We'll need Caius and the others here, Sextus. Justice can't grow in isolation. It takes minds as sharp and hearts as resolute as those who've stood with me before."

Sextus exhaled, his fingers drumming lightly against the table. "Getting word to them won't be easy. The Custodes are watching anyone connected to you."

"That's why I need you," Gregory said firmly, his voice steady but imploring. "You know how to move unseen, how to outthink them. This place will be our sanctuary, the heart of the mission. Bring our people here, and we'll plan the next steps together."

Sextus rose, his resolve visibly hardening. "I'll get word to Caius and the others. But, Gregory," he added, his voice edged with caution, "if we're going to do this, we need to be sure. One mistake, and it won't just be us who pay the price."

Gregory met his gaze, unwavering. "I am sure, Sextus. Justice isn't just for us—it's for those who have lived their entire lives under oppression. It's for Rome's future, even if Rome can't yet see it."

Sextus gave a slight nod, his jaw tightening. "Then I'll make it happen." He turned toward the door but hesitated, glancing back at Gregory. "You'd better have a plan ready when we return. This seed you're planting needs firm ground to grow."

As Sextus disappeared into the night, Gregory allowed the faintest smile to cross his lips. The road ahead was treacherous, but hope lingered in the air. Justice would take root—not through the strength of one, but through the shared resolve of many.

CHAPTER TWENTY-EIGHT
JUSTICE

The Grand Basilica of Maxentius stood solemnly, its arches stretching like stone guardians into the night sky, illuminated by the soft glow of a crescent moon. The basilica's imposing facade loomed over the plaza below, a stark reminder of centuries of judgments passed within its walls—verdicts that had fortified the powerful and crushed the powerless. Tonight, however, this monolithic symbol of Rome's authority was surrounded by an energy it had never known. The plaza swelled with humanity, the crowd spilling far beyond its boundaries and flooding the adjoining streets and alleyways. Lights flickered like constellations in the sea of faces, casting shadows that danced across the massive stone walls.

The air buzzed with murmurs of curiosity, hope, and trepidation. Word of Gregory's mission had traveled swiftly, messages amplified by whispers and viral tales of his previous acts. The teeming mass of spectators—slaves, merchants, laborers, and even veiled patricians—created a tableau, a living tapestry of Rome itself, converging to witness what promised to be a moment of transformation.

The first two seeds of compassion and humility, sown in whispers and small gatherings, had taken root in the hearts of many, spreading like fire through Rome's diverse populace. The transformative event at the Claustra, where Gregory preached forgiveness to prisoners and the guards alike, had become the cornerstone of the viral movement. Videos of his words, captured by unseen hands, circulated across every platform, each share and comment adding to the tidal wave of awareness. Stories of hardened men weeping openly and chains dropped in symbolic acts of release had pierced the heart of a city accustomed to brutality. Rome would hold its breath tonight, its collective focus drawn to a movement that no longer lingered in the periphery but stood boldly in the light of the basilica.

As Sextus surveyed the swelling crowd from the basilica steps, he could feel the significance of what Gregory of the Foreign Faith—now spoken of in whispers as *Gregorius Fidei Externae*—had created. The flickering lamps of the plaza lit the faces of every kind—slaves with scarred wrists, merchants clutching the edges of their cloaks, veiled patricians standing with uneasy anonymity. This was no mere assembly; this was Rome, shaken from complacency and hungry for something more. Sextus found himself momentarily overwhelmed by the scale of it all. He turned to Gregory, his voice subdued but reverent. "This… this is no longer just an idea," he said quietly, the awe in his tone unmistakable. Gregory met his gaze, his calm composure unbroken, yet his eyes carried the unspoken acknowledgment that this was their moment to seize.

"Justice," Gregory murmured, his voice calm but tinged with the gravity of the moment. "Tonight, we give it form."

Using Tabularium, Sextus sent precise instructions to the followers. The messages were simple: *The plaza is the stage. Lanterns will light the way. Be ready to speak the truth.* These directives were enough to set the movement in motion.

Gregory's followers moved purposefully through the crowd. With his tall, imposing frame, Lucius carried lanterns that glowed with warm, flickering light, arranging them to cast the perfect illumination over the makeshift stage. Julia, her grace akin to a seasoned performer, distributed masks and props from her satchel, her sharp gaze ensuring everything was in place. Caius coordinated with the team, his voice low but firm as he directed Decimus and Felix to assemble the crude stage from wooden planks and crates. Octavia knelt, her hood casting a shadow over her focused expression as she prepared her chalk, while Silvanus unfurled bolts of linen fabric to create a backdrop for the set that would command attention.

Gregory's followers moved with quiet efficiency, but the crowd surprised them. The energy was electric, charged with a shared curiosity and hope that transcended class. The basilica plaza had transformed into a theater, buzzing with life and expectation.

The performance began subtly, as planned, with the actors portraying the familiar story of Rome's triumphs. They wore masks emblazoned with symbols of power: coins for wealth, swords for strength, laurels for victory. Their rigid, ceremonial movements mirrored the calculated grandeur of imperial pageantry. The crowd watched passively, their expressions marked by a distant familiarity with such displays.

But then, as if on cue, the tone shifted. One by one, the actors cast their wooden masks to the ground. The hollow clatter echoed across the plaza, cutting through the murmurs of the audience. The actors' movements grew fluid, unbound by the rigid symbols they had shed. The crowd leaned in, captivated by the transformation unfolding before them.

Lucius stepped forward, his wrists wrapped in chains that clinked softly as he moved. His deep voice resonated through the plaza. "I am Justice," he declared, his words deliberate and heavy. "Shackled not by law but by the greed of those who wield it."

Julia followed, her presence commanding as she raised a chalkboard inscribed with Dignity. "I am Dignity," she proclaimed. "Stripped from those who labor without reward, silenced by those who fear our voices."

Caius stepped into the light, carrying a board marked Truth. His words cut through the air like a blade. "I am Truth, buried beneath the lies of those who seek to keep their power unchallenged."

One by one, Octavia, Decimus, Felix, and Caius took turns, their voices ringing out with conviction. "I am Mercy." "I am Integrity." "I am Equality." "I am Honor." Together, they formed a circle around Lucius, their presence a tableau of the ideals Rome had forgotten.

Octavia knelt and began drawing on the plaza stones with her chalk. Her strokes were deliberate, creating an image of balanced scales that glowed faintly in the lantern light. The simple symbol, imbued with defiance and hope, challenged the injustices etched into the basilica's history.

Then Gregory stepped forward. The light caught the edges of his robe, casting a long shadow over the crowd. He ascended the stage with slow, deliberate steps. When he spoke, his voice carried the gravity of the moment, slicing through the night like the strike of a hammer. "Citizens of Rome," he began, "this plaza, this basilica, has long been a fortress for the powerful. It has silenced the cries of the oppressed, wielding justice not as a shield but as a weapon. Tonight, we reclaim it. True justice is not the privilege of the few but the birthright of all."

The crowd fell silent, his words sinking into them like seeds into fertile soil. A young man, his wrists scarred from years of bondage, stepped forward hesitantly. "What justice can there be for a slave like me?" he asked, his voice trembling. "Will it free me from my chains?"

Gregory descended the stage and knelt before the man. "True justice does not shatter chains—it renders them meaningless. It begins with truth: the truth that your life, your voice, and your spirit matter. Tonight, we sow the seeds of that truth."

The plaza held its breath as Gregory's words settled over the crowd. Some wept openly, their tears catching the glow of the lanterns. Others stood frozen, their faces marked with awe and determination.

Then, in the distance, the unmistakable rhythm of marching boots shattered the fragile moment. Sextus, ever watchful, caught the streams of searchlights scanning the plaza. With a quick gesture and a low, urgent tone, he signaled to Gregory. "The Custodes are coming."

Gregory rose slowly; his movements deliberate as if to imprint the final image of his defiance on the crowd. His eyes swept across the mass of faces, each reflecting hope, fear, and determination. "The seed is planted," he said with quiet certainty. "They will carry it forward."

The performers moved swiftly; their retreat rehearsed to precision. Lucius extinguished the lanterns, plunging the stage into shadows, while Julia efficiently gathered the remaining props. Caius directed the dispersal, his military instincts ensuring no pattern could be traced. Octavia erased the chalked scales with swift strokes, her hands steady despite the growing tension. Burdened with fabric, Caius disappeared into the darkened alleys like a ghost. Sextus brought up the rear, ensuring every path they took split unpredictably, leaving no trail for the Custodes to follow.

The crowd, too, seemed to dissolve as if by some unspoken agreement. Slaves melted into the night, laborers returned to their quarters, and the veiled patricians slipped into carriages waiting at the plaza's edge. Whispers of what they had witnessed filled the air like embers carried on the wind. When the Custodes stormed the plaza moments later, they found nothing but the empty stage, the discarded masks, and the faint outline of scales still visible on the stones.

As the performers regrouped in Sextus's hidden sanctuary, their adrenaline gave way to cautious relief. Gregory spoke quietly, reinforcing the night's triumph. "We have given them more than words; we have given them truth."

***

The following day, Rome was ablaze—not with fire, but with conversation. The city awoke to headlines that refused to be ignored. Photos of the performance dominated the front pages, capturing the haunting tableau of unmasked actors encircling the glowing scales. "Justice is not a privilege," one headline proclaimed in bold letters. "It is the birthright of all."

Social media platforms exploded with shares, comments, and reposts of the event. Some praised Gregory's audacity, while others condemned his defiance as dangerous sedition. Online forums buzzed with debates, some calling for reform and others demanding Gregory's capture. The viral nature of the event ensured that the message could not be contained.

The Roman Herald, the city's leading newspaper, published an in-depth exposé, amplifying Gregory's words and the performance's symbolism. The stark contrast between the basilica's history as a tool of oppression and the ideals presented that night resonated deeply. Scholars dissected the implications, and street corners became impromptu stages for discussions about the future of justice in Rome.

The Custodes doubled their patrols, determined to find those responsible, but the movement had already outpaced them. What had begun as a performance had become a spark igniting hearts across the city. Gregory's message was no longer confined to the basilica—it was everywhere, carried by the very people who had stood in the plaza and those who had only heard the whispers. Justice had been declared, and Rome would never be the same.

CHAPTER TWENTY-NINE
THE PRAYER

In the quiet of the abandoned studio, Gregory hunched over the manuscript, its ancient pages illuminated by a dim, flickering bulb. The room was sparse, its walls streaked with peeling plaster. Across the room, Sextus lay on a makeshift cot, his breathing steady in the stillness of the night. They had agreed to meet Lucius at dawn to chart their next move, but Gregory's mind refused the solace of rest.

Gregory's fingers lingered over the cryptic symbols etched into the manuscript, his mind straining to decipher their hidden message. Each line alive with an enigmatic energy, hinting at truths yet unveiled. Compassion, humility, forgiveness, and justice—the seeds he sought to plant—hovered in his thoughts, their potential tugging at his resolve. Yet he wrestled with uncertainty: could these virtues genuinely take root and thrive in the fractured soil of Rome's tumultuous society?

He could sense their growth beneath the surface, hidden yet unyielding, as they sought sustenance in a world starved of truth and love. The impact was not visible in grand revolutions but whispered through subtle transformations: a laborer daring to hope, a guard rethinking the value of mercy, a slave realizing his worth. These seeds were more than virtues; they were roots extending silently, persistently, binding the fractured ground of a society drowning in pride and oppression.

Yet, as Gregory reflected on what he had accomplished, the burden of what remained weighed heavily on his heart. Wisdom, courage, and sacrifice loomed before him; not as abstract ideals to preach but as living challenges to embody. Wisdom would require confronting the entrenched philosophies of a society built on conquest and hierarchy, demanding that he navigate a battlefield of minds as sharp and unyielding as blades. Courage would call him to stand unwavering in the face of inevitable opposition, to embrace danger not as a threat but as a necessary cost of transformation. And sacrifice—sacrifice was the shadow that loomed largest of all. What would it demand of him? His life? His soul? Or something he had yet to comprehend?

As he traced the manuscript's delicate lines, Gregory realized the path ahead was not simply treacherous but uncharted. His seeds had taken root, but growth was fragile, vulnerable to the relentless forces of doubt, fear, and resistance. He closed his eyes, searching for clarity amid the uncertainty. Could he endure the mission? Would the message he carried, fragile and profound, prove stronger than the systems and ideologies that sought to crush it? And if he faltered, what would become of the Rome he sought to change—or the Rome he longed to return to?

In that moment of reflection, Gregory resolved that the only way forward was through unwavering faith, not just in the gospel he preached but in the transformative power of love and truth. His fingers left the page, but the significance of its prophecy remained, etched deeply into his soul.

Gregory leaned back, his eyes drifting to the cracked ceiling above, though his mind strayed further. He thought of the world he had left behind, where Christianity thrived, and where he, as Pope, had shepherded countless souls in his over sixty years since becoming a priest. There, the gospel was a foundation, a known truth. This fractured Rome moved like a flame catching dry timber—wild, unpredictable, and fiercely contested.

His thoughts turned dark as the seer's ominous warning swarmed his mind. Her words clung to him like a shadow since they were first spoken: "The failure would not be yours alone. The fracture you've caused will widen. This Rome and the Rome you left behind will begin to unravel, colliding until both are lost. To linger here is to risk unmaking both realities."

The prophecy and its implications pressed down on him. If he failed to plant the remaining seeds and faltered, the cost would be immeasurable—not just for himself or this world but for all he had ever known.

Gregory turned toward the window, his silhouette outlined by the faint moonlight spilling over the sprawling streets below. The city slumbered, yet he knew that his followers were at work somewhere in its depths, their faith in his mission steadfast. Their belief was a constant source of strength, but tonight, Gregory's own resolve felt fragile, shadowed by doubt.

Could the wisdom he carried truly withstand the entrenched philosophies that defined Rome? The city's worldview, steeped in power and pride, was as unyielding as its stone edifices. However, he had seen cracks in its foundation—moments when compassion, humility, forgiveness, and justice had taken root. But would wisdom, the next and perhaps most profound seed, be able to flourish against such opposition?

He thought of Quintus and his Custodes, their watchful eyes ever vigilant. Rome had not been kind to those who challenged its authority, and Gregory's mission was nothing less than a challenge to its very soul. The enormity of his task pressed down on him. Purpose had carried him this far, but the path ahead seemed narrower, the stakes higher.

Quietly, Gregory turned back to the room, his gaze lingering for a moment on the faint outline of Sextus. The young man shifted slightly in his sleep, the cot beneath him groaning softly under the weight of restless dreams. The dim glow of the moon painted long shadows across the floor, each a reminder of the trials yet to come. Gregory lowered himself to his knees beside the manuscript, his hands clasping with trembling resolve.

At first, his words came quietly, a whisper barely audible in the stillness. "Lord, guide me," he murmured, his voice steadying as he spoke. "Let Your wisdom be my voice, courage my strength, and sacrifice my salvation. If this is to be my world, let it be Yours first." His fingers tightened around each other as if drawing strength from the very act of prayer.

He bowed his head further, the silence enveloping him like a sacred shroud. The room held its breath, the faint hum of the city beyond its walls fading into nothingness. The burden of his mission pressed heavily upon him—the seeds of wisdom, courage, and sacrifice waiting to be planted in the unyielding soil of a world that did not yet understand their need.

As the first pale fingers of dawn crept through the cracked windowpane, Gregory lifted his gaze to the manuscript. Its ancient script came alive in the dim light, each word a thread tying him to his purpose. The room brightened ever so slightly, the rising sun offering quiet affirmation and a silent promise of the battles to come and the strength he would need to endure.

Gregory stood slowly, the ache in his knees grounding him in the present moment. He looked again at Sextus, whose features softened in sleep, and felt a flicker of gratitude for his companions who shared in his mission. The day ahead loomed with uncertainty, but for now, Gregory allowed himself one final whispered plea: "Let me be worthy of the path You have set before me." Then, steeling himself with the resolve of the prayer, he was ready to face the trials of the new dawn.

CHAPTER THIRTY
DEBATE AT THE FORUM

The sun blazed over the Forum, casting its golden light across the vast plaza teeming with life. A sea of Romans filled the square, spilling into adjacent streets and alleys. The crowd was a living mosaic of togas and tunics, senators and merchants, laborers and slaves—all drawn by the promise of a philosophical duel that threatened to reshape their understanding of Rome's virtues. Among them were journalists, writers, and artists, poised with implements, eager to document the event for posterity.

The Forum's marble columns stood tall, framing the stage for this historic confrontation. Vendors lingered at the edges, hawking sandwiches and drinks to the spectators. Above it all, the bronze statue of Jupiter gazed down, its inscrutable expression suggesting that even the gods awaited the outcome.

As Gregory stepped forward, he was struck by the sheer size of the gathering. The Forum was overflowing, a mass of humanity stretching far beyond what he could have imagined. Every step he took drew more eyes, every breath of the air heavy with anticipation. The whispers of his teachings had spread like wildfire, igniting not just the curiosity of the commoners but also the fervor of scholars, merchants, and wealthy patricians who now lined the marble steps.

Lucius, Sextus, and Marcus stood at the edge of the throng, their faces grim with concern. Lucius gripped Gregory's arm. "I'm having second thoughts. You cannot go through with this," he said urgently. "Quintus and the Senate don't want a debate—they want your head. They've planted agitators in the crowd to ensure the people turn against you."

Gregory glanced at Lucius, but his gaze soon returned to the crowd. This was not a gathering of the disinterested or the indifferent. He could see faces young and old, some weathered by years of toil, others untouched by hardship. Men and women from every corner of the empire had come—not merely to witness but to listen. His words, his presence, had resonated with them in ways even he hadn't yet fully grasped.

"The Senate may want my head," Gregory replied, his voice calm yet firm. "But look at them, Lucius." He gestured toward the crowd, his hand sweeping over the sea of faces. "They don't. They're here for something more—something the Senate cannot silence with swords or schemes. This isn't about me anymore. It's about the truth they're yearning for."

Gregory glanced at the raised platform, where Quintus stood flanked by the Senate's star orator, Gaius Tertullius. His jaw tightened as he replied, "If I refuse now, we concede the fight before it even begins. Silence won't be seen as wisdom—it will be seen as surrender."

Sextus stepped forward, his composure cracking. "Even if you speak, Tertullius will twist your words. He's Rome's greatest orator. He'll turn your call for compassion, humility, forgiveness, and justice into weapons against you. Don't you see? These ideals, noble as they are, make Rome appear weak to those who worship strength and conquest. The people will see them not as virtues but as vulnerabilities that threaten the gods, the traditions, and the might that have kept Rome unchallenged for centuries."

Gregory turned to the platform, his gaze unwavering. "If Rome cannot grow, it will crumble from within. It is not weakness to embrace compassion or humility—it is strength. But strength comes at a cost. This moment is not about guarantees, Sextus. It's about planting the seeds of truth and hope, even if the soil is rocky and harsh. If one person hears me and carries these ideals forward, it will be worth the risk."

Marcus sighed, his voice heavy with resignation. "Just remember, Gregory, even the purest seeds can take generations to bear fruit. Don't make us dig your grave before they've even begun to grow."

As Quintus stepped forward, the crowd erupted. His toga flowed like a banner of authority, its pristine white folds glinting in the sun. He raised his arms high, commanding silence with a presence that filled the vast Forum. When he spoke, his voice rolled out like thunder, carrying conviction and urgency to the furthest edges of the plaza.

"Citizens of Rome!" he cried, his tone sharp and unyielding. "Look around you! Behold the majesty of our empire, the pillars of our civilization that have stood firm for over two millennia! Do you not feel pride in the roads we've built, the cities we've raised, the lands we've conquered in the name of order and prosperity? We gather here today not as mere spectators but as guardians of a legacy forged in the fires of discipline, sacrifice, and devotion to the gods who watch over us."

He pointed an accusatory finger toward Gregory, his expression darkening. "And yet this man—this Gregory of the Foreign Faith—dares to stand here in the heart of our greatness and question the very virtues that have made us strong. He does not revere the gods who gave us victory. He does not honor the ancestors who bled so we could thrive. Instead, he brings foreign ideals that would weaken our resolve and unravel the unity that holds our empire together."

The crowd stirred, murmurs growing louder as Quintus's words fanned the embers of their loyalty into flames. "This man," Quintus continued, his voice rising, "would have you believe that love and humility are the path to greatness. But tell me, citizens, did love defeat Pyrrhus and his war elephants? Was it humility that built our aqueducts, our roads, our laws? No! It was strength! It was discipline! It was the unshakable belief in our destiny to rule as the gods' chosen people!"

Quintus stepped closer to the platform's edge, his arms outstretched to embrace the crowd. "Rome is eternal because we honor the traditions that bind us, the gods who guide us, and the discipline that tempers our might. If we abandon these virtues for soft ideals, we risk becoming weak—fractured. I ask you, citizens, will you allow this man to sow division in the heart of our empire? Will you let him tarnish the legacy of Rome?"

The crowd erupted into cheers and jeers, their passions ignited by Quintus's fervor. He let their voices swell for a moment before delivering his final blow. "Let the foreigner speak, then, so his folly may be exposed! Let him show all of Rome that no words, no ideals, can stand against the strength and unity of the greatest empire the world has ever known!"

The Forum shook with the force of the crowd's roar, a tidal wave of emotion surging in Rome's favor. Quintus stepped back, his expression triumphant. He turned to Gregory, the faintest smirk playing on his lips.

The jeers from the crowd swelled, their anger stoked by Senate loyalists scattered strategically throughout the throng. Gregory climbed the steps to the platform, his plain robes stark against Quintus's opulence. As he ascended, he scanned the crowd. His followers—Lucius, Julia, Caius, Decimus, Felix, and Octavia—were scattered among the sea of faces, their steadfast gaze a quiet reassurance.

Just then, Tertullius emerged at the far end of the platform, his crimson toga trimmed with gold. He moved with the grace of a practiced debater, his piercing gaze sweeping the crowd. Quintus raised a hand for silence.

"Tertullius," he began, his voice dripping with disdain, "is this man's philosophy not a threat to Rome?"

Tertullius paused, his voice smooth and calculated. "Indeed, Senator. Gregory speaks of foreign virtues with words that would strip us of our strength. Rome was built on piety, discipline, and honor. These virtues have made us great. Tell us, Gregory, what does your truth offer that could compare?"

A murmur rippled through the crowd, a mix of agreement and disdain. "Rome's greatness cannot be undone!" someone called out, earning a wave of applause. Another voice shouted, "What do these foreign teachings know of our glory?" Sharp and biting laughter followed, emboldening the murmurs of skepticism.

Gregory stepped forward, his voice steady. "Yes, Rome's virtues have brought order, but at what cost? Fear and conquest cannot be the foundation of eternity. The truth I bring—love, compassion, and humility—does not seek to destroy your virtues but to transform them into something greater. Through understanding, we build not empires, but a united humanity."

The crowd murmured, a restless tide of curiosity and doubt rippling through the plaza. Some nodded, captivated, while others exchanged skeptical glances. Tertullius stepped forth, his smirk cutting through the tension like a blade. "Love and humility?" he sneered, his voice ringing with disdain. "Rome has thrived on strength, not sentiment. Compassion did not conquer Hannibal and the Carthaginians. Would you have us lay down our swords and pray love shields us from annihilation?"

Gregory stood unmoved, his calm presence strikingly contrasting Tertullius's vehemence. He raised his voice, firm but resonant, carrying over the crowd. "Strength without compassion breeds tyranny. Discipline without love becomes cruelty. You worship gods of vengeance and ambition, but they are not greater than the unity that binds humanity. What if Rome's destiny is not to rule through fear but to inspire through virtue?"

Tertullius's face darkened, his voice rising with indignation. "And what of duty? What of loyalty to the gods and ancestors who demand our devotion and sacrifices? Your virtues would unravel the discipline that forged Rome's might and hold it together."

The tension crackled like a storm about to break. The flickering street lamps painted stark shadows on their faces, each word an ember thrown onto the fire of the crowd's emotions. Gregory stepped forward, his gaze unwavering, and let silence hang for a beat, a weapon more powerful than words. Then, in a voice that pierced the air, he replied, "Rome's true strength lies not in its legions but in the hearts of its people. Inspire them, and Rome will endure for eternity. Fear may conquer lands, but only love can conquer the soul."

The crowd fell silent, the impact of his words settling like the first rumble of an earthquake. Even Tertullius hesitated, his rebuttal momentarily lost in the tide of awe Gregory's defiance had unleashed.

Gregory turned to the crowd, his voice rising. "Duty without love is slavery. Devotion without understanding is idolatry. True loyalty to

Rome means helping it grow—not chaining it to fear but freeing it with wisdom and love. The cost is courage, but the reward is a Rome that does not conquer but enlightens."

Tertullius's face twisted into a scowl, his voice ringing through the Forum. "Rome has lasted for over two millennia without faltering. Our empire stands as the pinnacle of strength and order, unmatched by any other civilization in history. What you offer, Gregory, is weakness cloaked in false virtue. You would have us trade discipline for sentiment, power for passivity. Is this what you call progress?"

A man from the crowd shouted, "What if this talk of love makes us weak?"

Gregory raised a hand, commanding silence. "Love is not weakness. Love is the greatest strength, for it demands the highest courage—to forgive, heal, and stand together when it would be easier to divide. Fear binds; love liberates. I do not ask Rome to abandon its greatness. I ask it to fulfill it."

Tertullius sneered, stepping closer to Gregory. "And what of those who resist this vision of yours? Those who cling to the old ways, the old gods? Will you silence them in the name of your so-called unity?"

Gregory's reply was swift, his voice like a blade. "Unity does not silence—it listens. It welcomes. It grows stronger through diversity of thought, not weaker. Rome's true greatness lies not in crushing dissent but in embracing the voices that call it to be more."

The crowd erupted, voices clashing in a cacophony of argument and agreement. Gregory stood firm, his presence unwavering even as Tertullius leaned in, his tone venomous. "You speak of love, Gregory, but love cannot hold an empire. It cannot command armies or bend enemies to its will."

"No," Gregory said softly. "But it can heal the wounds that armies leave behind. It can build bridges where fear has torn them down. And it can create a legacy that no sword or empire could ever match."

Before either man could say another word, the tension snapped like a taut string, plunging the Forum into chaos. Spectators from both sides surged forward, their ideological fervor spilling over into shouts and blows. Vendors scrambled to protect their wares as fists flew and bodies collided. The Custodes waded into the fray, barking orders and raising shields to separate the warring factions. But the sheer size of the crowd made their task impossible.

"Enough!" Gregory's voice rang out, sharp and commanding, cutting through the din like a bell. He climbed atop the nearest marble platform, his arms outstretched. "Violence is not the answer! You dishonor the very ideals we debate by resorting to brute force. Stop this madness!"

For a brief moment, some in the crowd hesitated, looking up at Gregory as though his presence alone could restore order. But others, emboldened by rage or fear, ignored his pleas, their shouts drowning out his words.

Quintus stepped forward. His face was as cold and immovable as the statues that surrounded him. "Custodes!" he roared. "Seize him!"

The soldiers hesitated for a fraction of a second, gazes flicking to Gregory, who stood above the chaos, a solitary figure of calm amidst the storm. But Quintus's authority left no room for doubt. They surged toward him, shields raised, their path clearing as Marcus, Lucius, and Sextus were shoved aside.

Gregory did not resist as they grabbed his arms and pulled him down. He kept his gaze steady and locked eyes with Quintus, who approached with measured steps.

"You speak of peace," Quintus said, his voice low enough that only Gregory could hear, "yet your words bring chaos. This city has no place for a man like you."

"And yet the people heard me," Gregory replied, his tone calm despite the soldiers tightening their grip. "You can silence me, Quintus, but you cannot unmake the questions now burning in their hearts."

Quintus sneered but said nothing. He raised a hand, signaling for the guards to escort Gregory away. As they moved through the tumultuous crowd, Gregory turned his head, his voice rising one last time above the chaos. "Rome does not need fear to endure! It needs courage! It needs—"

A shove silenced him, his words swallowed by the cacophony as he was dragged from the Forum. In his wake, the chaos began to subside, though the ripples of his words lingered, an echo that would not fade.

CHAPTER THIRTY-ONE
THE EMPEROR

Gregory was thrust forward, his feet dragging across the polished marble floors of the imperial court. The grandeur of the space was suffocating: towering columns carved with scenes of conquest, tapestries dyed in rich purples and gold depicting the gods in triumph, and an expansive, intricate mosaic floor that glittered with images of Rome's vast dominion. At the far end of the hall, seated on an elevated throne of ivory and gold, was Emperor Tiberius Magnus Aurelius.

Tiberius was a man whose presence alone commanded silence. His dark eyes burned with an intensity that pierced through any mask of pretense. His thick, streaked gray hair was styled in the traditional Roman manner. His muscular frame, draped in a toga bordered with imperial purple, hinted at a life of privilege and rigor. A gold laurel wreath adorned his head, its gleaming leaves reflecting the flickering light of the hall's massive chandeliers.

Shackled and flanked by two Custodes, Gregory felt the intensity of every gaze in the room. Senators, generals, and advisors stood in rigid formation, their faces a mix of curiosity and disdain. This was a trial in all but name—a spectacle meant to solidify the Emperor's authority and crush the seeds of rebellion Gregory's words had sown.

"So, you are the man who dares to challenge the will of Rome," Tiberius said, his voice a deep, measured cadence that resonated through the hall. "You speak of a god unknown to us, of virtues that weaken the soul, and of a future that undermines our strength. Tell me, foreigner, why should I not have you crucified as an example to all who would disrupt the order of my empire?"

Gregory raised his head, his composure unbroken despite the tension in the air. His voice, though quiet, carried an unshakable resolve. "Because courage is not found in crushing those who dissent, but in listening to the truth they speak."

The room erupted in murmurs. Tiberius leaned forward, his expression unreadable. "You accuse me of lacking courage?" he asked, a dangerous edge to his tone.

"Not courage of the sword, but courage of the heart," Gregory replied. "You are a man who has conquered lands and subdued nations. However, true courage lies not in domination but in understanding. In daring to look beyond one's own power and see the humanity in others."

Tiberius's eyes narrowed. "Bold words for a man in chains. Perhaps you mistake bravery for recklessness."

Gregory took a step forward, his chains clinking with the movement. "Your empire is mighty, but even the strongest walls crumble without the foundation of compassion and justice. The people who follow me do so not because they see a light in the darkness. That light is not rebellion; it is hope. To snuff it out would be to declare war on the very soul of your people."

Tiberius's gaze sharpened as he leaned forward on his throne, the force of his authority pressing down on the court. The murmurs that had briefly stirred among the gathered officials and nobles quickly hushed as he rose to his full height. His movements were deliberate, each step echoing through the grand chamber like the toll of a bell. The golden embroidery on his robes caught the light, lending an almost otherworldly aura to the Emperor as he descended the steps toward Gregory.

The tension in the room thickened, palpable and unyielding. Heads turned, some with curiosity, others with fear, as the court watched their ruler approach the foreigner in chains.

Tiberius stopped mere inches away, his piercing eyes flickering with intensity as if attempting to penetrate the layers of secrecy shrouding the man before him. His commanding presence magnified the silence that gripped the room. His voice, both measured and demanding, cut through the stillness. "Who are you, stranger, and what brings you to my Rome?"

Gregory straightened as best he could, the chains binding his wrists, clinking softly like a muted bell. He met the Emperor's penetrating gaze with unflinching resolve. "I hail from a world that exists alongside your own," he said, his tone steady yet infused with urgency. "I have come not as a conqueror, nor as a rebel, but as a messenger of hope. My mission is to sow the seeds of a future where light and understanding guide your people. But know this, Emperor: should I fail, the repercussions will ripple across both our worlds, ruining all."

The court stirred uneasily at his words, whispers of disbelief and alarm spreading like wildfire. Tiberius's brow furrowed as he studied Gregory, his expression a mask of intrigue and caution. A slow, faint smile touched his lips, though its meaning remained enigmatic. "Grand declarations," he murmured, his tone laced with a mix of skepticism and curiosity. "But they come from a man shackled and powerless. Tell me, Gregory, do you confuse courage with folly?"

Gregory lifted his bound wrists, the cold metal glinting in the torchlight. "True power," he said, calm yet unyielding, "is not forged in the weight of chains or the sharpness of swords. It resides in the hearts of those who dare to hope when the world seems lost."

He turned his gaze toward the gallery, his words resonating through the silent hall. "Your empire's walls are mighty, but even the strongest fortresses will fall once the Seven Seeds are sown. Those who walk with me are not driven by fear but drawn by a light that offers not conquest but the hope of a brighter tomorrow."

Gregory's voice grew firmer, imbued with the strength of conviction. "That light is hope, Emperor. To extinguish it would not simply silence me; it would be to wage war against the very soul of your people. Once hope has been released, it cannot be caged, nor can it be conquered. It is the foundation upon which all enduring power must stand."

A surge of murmurs erupted within the court, the voices swelling in volume until they resembled the rumble of an approaching storm. Tiberius lifted a hand, and silence swept over the assembly like a sudden gale. Standing before Gregory, the Emperor's towering frame loomed over him, his presence like a tempest meeting an unyielding mountain. Fire sparked in his gaze as it met Gregory's steady, steel-like resolve. "You speak of hope and courage, yet you defy the gods who have blessed this empire. Tell me, Gregory of the Foreign Faith, would you stake your life on it if your courage is so great?"

Gregory met the Emperor's gaze, unwavering. "I would stake more than my life. I would stake my soul, for courage is not the absence of fear but the willingness to face it for the sake of others."

Tiberius's lips curved into a faint smile, though whether it was one of amusement or respect was unclear. "Very well. Let us test your courage." He turned to the assembled court. "This man claims to possess a courage greater than the might of Rome. We shall see if his deeds match his words."

The Emperor gestured to the Custodes. "Take him to the Colosseum. At dawn, he will face the Trial of the Gods. If his courage is true, let his God save him. If not, let the beasts decide his fate."

The court erupted in cheers and gasps, the Emperor's decree sending a surge of anticipation through the gathered crowd. Gregory's gaze lingered on the Emperor for a fleeting moment as the guards seized him. The rattling of his chains merged with the cacophony of the hall. He was dragged toward the grand doors, the weight of his fate heavy but his steps steady.

As the doors shut behind him, the sound reverberated like the tolling of a bell. Gregory did not look back, but in his mind, he saw the Emperor's face—a mask of power veiling the faintest shadow of uncertainty.

***

That night, the cold stone floor of his cell pressed against his knees as Gregory prayed. His breath, visible in the chilled air, came in steady, deliberate whispers, his voice trembling with urgency.

"Grant me strength not only to endure but to prevail. I do not ask for mercy; I ask for the will to survive—for hope must not die with me." His words hung in the silence, his plea rising like a flame against the darkness.

The hours stretched on, the passage of time marked only by the occasional shuffle of guards and the muted murmurs of the restless city outside. Gregory's mind drifted to what lay ahead—the Colosseum. He had known of its grandeur, its infamy, a symbol of Roman might and human suffering. He knew it as a place where lives ended amidst the deafening roars of a mob thirsty for blood and spectacle. To be brought there was to become a pawn in a narrative far greater than oneself—a stage where courage, faith, and mortality would clash under the scrutinizing gaze of thousands.

The thought weighed heavily upon him for what his trial represented. He was undoubtedly no gladiator, no criminal. He was a man chained by the convictions of a world foreign to this one, standing against an empire that prided itself on strength above all else. Would the crowd see his defiance as folly? Or would they glimpse the flicker of something more—a hope that could not be silenced, even by death?

Gregory raised his low but firm voice as a guard passed his cell. "You there?" he called, his words cutting through the stillness. The guard paused, his features obscured by shadows. "Please tell me about this Trial of the Gods."

The guard hesitated, glancing down the corridor before stepping closer. "It is the Emperor's decree," he said. "A test not of strength, but of Divine favor. The gods will judge you, foreigner, through beasts, fire, or blade. If you survive, it is said that the gods themselves have chosen you. If not…" His voice trailed off, and he stepped back as if the very act of speaking to Gregory was forbidden. "Pray to whatever god you serve," he added, his tone softer now. "You will need more than courage when you stand in the arena."

The guard turned and walked away, leaving Gregory alone once more in the silence of his cell. Gregory closed his eyes, the guard's words sinking deep into his heart. "More than courage," he whispered to himself. "Faith, then. And hope—for them."

As the first pale light of dawn crept into his cell, Gregory rose with a groan, his knees stiff but his spirit unyielding. The roar of the Colosseum reached him even here, a distant rumble that seemed to resonate through the very stones beneath his feet. It was not merely noise but the sound of an empire bearing witness, a chorus of voices ready to judge.

The guards arrived, their faces impassive, their steps heavy. Gregory's hands remained bound, but he walked with a steadiness that spoke of purpose rather than submission. Each step carried him closer to the arena, where history, destiny, and faith would converge. The trial awaited, a crucible not just for his body but for the soul of an empire— a moment where seeds of courage might find purchase, even in the unlikeliest of soils.

CHAPTER THIRTY-TWO
TRIAL OF THE GODS

The heavy scent of sweat, blood, and damp stone hung in the air as Gregory stood in the dim tunnel leading upward to the Colosseum's arena. The muffled roar of the crowd above reverberated through the stone walls, a constant reminder of the spectacle that awaited. Around him, gladiators clad in gleaming armor paced like restless predators, their muscular frames coiled with anticipation. Amused glances and whispered jests cut through the tense air, mocking the man in the simple linen robe whose only weapon was his faith.

Gregory's hands trembled, but his voice remained steady as he prayed aloud, the words flowing in quiet defiance of the chaos surrounding him. "Lord, guide my steps and steady my heart. Let me be a vessel of your light, even in the shadow of death." His prayer vanished beneath the rising swell of the crowd, their voices merging into a fevered chant, eager for the spectacle that would mark the start of the day's brutal games.

The gate before him groaned as it rose, revealing a sliver of golden light that expanded until the arena was fully visible. Gregory stepped forward, his bare feet meeting the coarse sand as a wave of sound crashed over him. The Colosseum was packed to capacity, every tier brimming with spectators whose faces blurred into a kaleidoscope of

"

excitement, disdain, and curiosity. The enormity of the offering took his breath away—a vast amphitheater that stretched endlessly upward, its grandeur both awe-inspiring and oppressive.

The sun blazed overhead, casting stark shadows that danced against the towering walls. The arena floor was a canvas of past battles; its sand stained with reminders of the lives it had claimed. Gregory's chest tightened as he took in the scene, the magnitude of the moment sinking in with every beat of his heart. Yet even amidst the cacophony, his lips moved in practiced prayer. "Though I walk through the valley of the shadow of death, I will fear no evil. For you are with me."

Above him, the Emperor sat enthroned in the imperial box, his expression as inscrutable as ever. His golden laurel wreath glinted in the sunlight, a stark reminder of the absolute power he wielded. To his left, the high priest of Mars stood with his ceremonial staff, his gaze fixed on Gregory with disdain and curiosity. Beside them, senators and nobles leaned forward, their faces alight with expectation—some hungry for blood, others eager for vindication.

The crowd's roar rose like a living beast, deafening and unrelenting, vibrating through the very stones of the Colosseum. Gregory stood alone at the center of the vast arena floor, the sheer scale of the amphitheater overwhelming him. The walls, tiered with thousands of spectators, stretched toward the heavens, making him feel as small and fragile as a lone reed in a storm. The sun blazed high above, its light pouring down like molten gold, searing his skin and casting long, ominous shadows across the sand.

He had prayed for an audience—a multitude to hear his words—but now, faced with this colossal sea of humanity, he felt its enormity tighten around his chest. All eyes were locked on him, glaring like daggers: some with genuine curiosity, some with open hatred, and others with a cruel hunger for brutal entertainment. The noise of the masses washed over him in waves—cheers, jeers, and chants blending into a single, oppressive wall of sound that threatened to drown him.

Gregory turned slowly, taking in the spectacle, his heart pounding like a war drum. His bare feet pressed into the coarse sand, each step an act of will against the trembling in his legs. He could feel the ghost of every life that had ended here—gladiators, slaves, martyrs—their echoes lingering in the suffocating air. The arena was a monument to suffering, its splendor a cruel mask for the horrors it had witnessed. And now, he was its latest offering.

The crowd's roar reached a fever pitch as the Praeco Maximus raised his staff. Amplified by the arena's acoustics, his voice sliced through the chaos like a blade.

"Gregory of the Foreign Faith," he proclaimed, his words heavy with scorn and finality. "You stand here to face judgment. By decree of Emperor Tiberius, your courage and faith shall be tested in the Trial of the Gods. May the will of Jupiter be known!"

A hush fell over the arena, sudden and eerie. It was as though the very air had been sucked from the space, leaving only silence and the pounding of Gregory's heart. He felt it then—the enormity of the moment, the collision of worlds unfolding here in the sands of Rome. This would be no ordinary trial; this was a spectacle for eternity, a message written in blood on stone.

Gregory swallowed hard, his throat dry as dust, and lifted his gaze to meet the imperial box. Tiberius sat unmoving, his dark eyes fixed on him, unreadable but unrelenting. The high priest smirked, confident of the outcome. Gregory's gaze shifted to the crowd—a sea of faces, strangers all—and he searched for something more in their tumult. A flicker of understanding. A glimmer of doubt. A single soul willing to hear.

Desperation clawed at the edges of his thoughts as he scanned the masses. He searched for his friends. Lucius, Sextus, Marcus—any followers who had walked beside him and believed when belief was most burdensome. But it was all a blur. The faces in the Colosseum were a frenzy of bloodthirsty spectators, their cheers and jeers mingling into a torrent of noise. Their expressions were a grotesque mix of excitement, apathy, and hunger for spectacle, as if humanity had been drained from them, leaving only shadows of what they once were.

There were no friendly faces here—no allies, no voices of support. He was alone, a solitary figure on an endless stage, where the cruel theater of Rome played out with him as the central act. Yet even in that isolation, he clung to the faintest hope that someone, somewhere among them, might hear.

"Lord, let them see," he whispered, his words lost in the roar. "Let them remember."

Drawing a deep breath, Gregory dropped to his knees in the center of the arena, the movement shocking in its sudden humility. He clasped his hands together, lifting his voice in prayer that rang through the silence, soaring above the pull of expectation.

"Lord, let me not falter. Let these thousands not see a man but a message. You have brought me to this place, and so long as I have breath, I will bear your light. Give me the strength to endure, for their sake—for both worlds—and for the hope that must not die."

The arena, moments before alive with bloodlust, now held its breath. The silence was absolute, as though even the wind dared not stir. Gregory stood then, the sand shifting beneath his feet, and his voice rose, strong and clear, carrying to the very edges of the Colosseum.

"People of Rome! You gather here for spectacle—a test of life and death—yet what do you truly witness? Not strength of flesh or force of blade, but the strength of the spirit. You call me a foreigner, a stranger, but I come not to divide but to remind you of what has been forgotten. For these walls of stone will one day fall, but the courage to hope will outlast empires."

He turned slowly, his gaze sweeping across the sea of faces, searching for the flicker of humanity beneath the mask of spectatorship.

"What is it you seek in blood? Triumph? Glory? The righteous gods do not speak through suffering—they speak through mercy, through courage that does not conquer but lifts others. Have you become so hardened that you cannot see this? Even the strongest among you were once children who dared to dream. That dream—that light—still lives within you. Do not extinguish it."

Murmurs rippled through the crowd, faint but growing like an ember catching fire. Senators shifted uneasily. Even the high priest's smug demeanor faltered, his knuckles whitening around the staff. From his place in the imperial box, Tiberius watched Gregory with a gaze sharpened by something unreadable—not anger, not mockery, but curiosity.

Gregory raised his arms wide, palms open, as though offering himself to them. "Courage is not the absence of fear. Courage is standing when the world demands you to kneel. Courage is speaking the truth when it is easier to remain silent. I stand here not as a man seeking escape but as a witness to something greater than myself. If my life is the price to plant this seed, then so be it—but I say to you: let it grow. Let courage bloom in your hearts, for in that bloom lies your salvation."

Silence followed, deeper than before, the impact of his words pressing down upon the masses. Somewhere, someone clapped—a single echoing sound that broke like thunder against the stone walls. Another followed. Then more. The applause spread in fits and starts, mingling with hushed voices and the glint of something unfamiliar on the faces of the crowd—reflection, perhaps, or the first stirrings of doubt.

Gregory lowered his arms, his gaze again lifting to meet Tiberius's. The Emperor's expression remained unreadable, but his grip on the armrest of his throne had tightened.

"This is only the beginning," Gregory whispered, his voice carried away by the winds. The seed had been planted. He could not yet know whether it would take root, but he felt the earth shift ever so slightly beneath him for the first time since his arrival.

The sunlight caught in the dust as it swirled around him, haloing Gregory like a figure from legend. For a heartbeat, the arena held its breath—as if the pagan gods themselves paused to listen—and Gregory pulled back his shoulders, ready to face whatever trial awaited him.

The massive bronze gate across the arena creaked open, its gears grinding like the prelude to an execution. From the shadowy depths emerged a lion, its golden eyes gleaming with feral intensity. The beast's low growl rumbled through the air, sending a wave of anticipation through the crowd. Gregory stood motionless, his gaze upward, his voice rising in prayer that defied the chaos around him.

"Grant me strength, Lord, not for my sake but theirs. Let them see your light even in the darkest hour."

The lion began its slow, deliberate approach, its powerful muscles rippling beneath its tawny coat. The tension in the arena was palpable, and each step of the beast drew the crowd closer to the edge of their seats. Its golden eyes, sharp and ancient, locked onto Gregory with an intensity that pierced through the physical and into something far deeper—something timeless. Yet, Gregory did not stir.

As the lion prowled forward, Gregory felt the instinctual chill of fear coil in his gut, his body aching to flee. The beast embodied primal power—a creature untouched by the artifice of men, a link to a world humanity had long forgotten. But beyond its fearsome exterior, Gregory saw something more: a being in tune with forces unseen, forces humanity had buried beneath ambition, war, and pride. Where man had turned away from the spirit, the lion remained open to it, listening to the whispers.

As the lion coiled to strike, the air grew taut and heavy with anticipation of violence. Its muscles surged beneath its tawny hide, and its roar shattered the Colosseum's cacophony into silence. The beast launched forward, a blur of feral power, its claws outstretched to rend.

At that moment, Gregory moved—not with panic but with purpose. His hand darted beneath his robe, seizing the chain around his neck. With a swift, resolute pull, he tore free the cross that hung there, raising it high in a straight-armed gesture of defiance and faith. The gleam of the cross caught the sunlight, casting a flash that cut through the arena's shadowed tension.

"Peace conquers the fiercest heart," Gregory intoned, his voice calm yet commanding, resonating above the hushed crowd.

The lion skidded to a halt, a spray of sand marking its sudden submission. Its eyes locked on the cross, not with rage, but with an almost unnerving stillness. The growl in its throat softened into a low rumble, its head tilting as though hearing an ancient melody only it could comprehend. Slowly, the beast turned, pacing away, leaving Gregory unscathed.

A collective gasp rippled through the arena, disbelief washing over the thousands of spectators. Gregory's gaze never wavered as he turned toward the Emperor, lifting the cross higher as if to present it to the heavens. The Emperor's face contorted with fury, his clenched fists trembling as he leaned forward, his voice a venomous snarl.

The Emperor's anger erupted, his voice thundering through the Colosseum. "You dare defy Rome's will with your tricks?!" he roared, his words dripping with venom, echoing into the stunned silence of the crowd.

Gregory's grip on the cross tightened, its gleaming surface reflecting the waning sunlight. He raised his gaze, calm yet resolute, and spoke with unwavering conviction. "I offer no tricks, Caesar. Deception belongs to the Adversary, the true Prince of Shadows. What you witnessed is not the work of man nor devil, but the light of truth—an enduring force no empire can extinguish."

His voice carried a quiet power, reverberating through the hearts of those gathered. The Emperor scowled, but the crowd's silence grew heavier, as though Gregory's words had struck deeper than any blade.

Gregory turned slowly to face the lion, his movements measured, exuding a calm that belied the rising tension in the arena. The creature's golden eyes bore into his, unblinking and intense, as though it sought not the man's body but the essence of his spirit. For a fleeting moment, Gregory believed the lion was not a predator but a vessel for some more profound understanding.

The beast advanced once more, each step deliberate and feline. Its massive paws pressed into the sand with a muted grace. The murmurs of the onlookers faded into silence, replaced by a charged stillness. Every gaze was locked on the surreal confrontation unfolding before them.

The lion's gaze remained fixed on Gregory, sharp yet devoid of malice, as though appraising the man who dared stand unarmed before it. Gregory drew a deep breath, steadying the storm within, and raised a hand—not to ward off the beast, but to offer peace. The lion came to a halt, its breath warm and steady as it ruffled against the fabric of Gregory's robe.

The creature let out a low, resonant rumble, neither a growl nor a roar, but something akin to acknowledgment. Slowly, it lowered its head, its thick mane brushing against Gregory's extended palm. Tentatively, Gregory let his fingers weave through the coarse fur, the grounding and electric sensation. The crowd gasped in unison, their disbelief palpable as predator and man stood in communion.

The lion remained poised, its raw power evident, yet it yielded to the moment, forming a bond between them that transcended fear or dominance. In that instant, the primal laws of the arena dissolved, replaced by something far more profound—a shared recognition of spirit that left the crowd breathless.

At that moment, the arena ceased to exist. The roar of the crowd, the thousands of eyes, the grandeur of the Colosseum—all of it faded into nothing. Only Gregory, the lion, and the quiet understanding transcended words. The beast, once a symbol of terror and judgment, had become a living testament to the harmony humanity had lost.

From the imperial box, Tiberius rose slowly, his expression frozen in astonishment. Beside him, the high priest clutched his staff with a force that betrayed his shock; his mouth parted in speechless disbelief.

Whispers rippled through the Colosseum like a sudden gust of wind, carrying with them awe, confusion, and fear. The Emperor's voice broke the stillness; his tone edged with something unfamiliar—reverence.

"The gods have spoken. Gregory's courage is true."

The arena erupted into chaos again, but the cheers carried awe instead of bloodlust. The crowd—hungry moments ago for death—had been silenced and then transformed, if only for a fleeting moment. Gregory stood amidst the noise, his gaze lifting to meet Tiberius's. In that silent exchange, he saw the Emperor's doubt and the faint glimmer of something more—an understanding yet to be realized; a door left ajar.

The gate to the arena opened, and Gregory was led away, his steps steady, his heart lighter. As he passed beneath the towering arches, he looked back one final time at the lion, still watching him, still listening.

"They have forgotten, but you remember," Gregory whispered under his breath. "Let them remember, too."

The Trial of the Gods was over, but the true test—the seed of sacrifice—was still to come.

CHAPTER THIRTY-THREE
REFLECTION

The iron doors of the imperial palace groaned open, and Gregory stumbled through, flanked by stoic guards. His steps, still unsteady after the Trial of the Gods, echoed in the cavernous corridor. Shafts of light from towering windows splintered across the marble floor, but to Gregory, it all seemed a blur—the colors, the figures of distant servants, the ever-present scent of incense masking something colder beneath.

He was alive. That much he knew. Yet survival brought little comfort when weighed against what still lay ahead. The lion's wisdom had stirred something in the hearts of those who bore witness, but Gregory could feel the thin line upon which he walked. The seed of courage had been planted, but the seventh—the seed of sacrifice— loomed like a shadow across his thoughts. *Must it come to that?* he wondered, his heart pounding as his feet dragged forward.

They brought him to a small chamber—a gilded prison of sorts— with a single bench and a basin of water. The guards locked the door and left him in silence. For a long while, Gregory sat motionless, staring at his trembling hands. He could still feel the lion's breath against his fingertips as though some ancient understanding had passed between them.

The door creaked open, breaking the stillness. Gregory looked up to see Marcus standing there, his scholarly robes pristine, his face lined with worry.

"Marcus," Gregory breathed, relief cracking his composure.

The door closed behind Marcus with a heavy, final thud. He stood there momentarily, his eyes fixed on Gregory, his face a storm of worry and unspoken fear. When he finally spoke, his voice trembled on the edge of urgency.

"They're calling it a miracle, Gregory," he said, almost in a whisper, as if speaking it aloud would make it more real. "The lion—what happened in the arena—is all anyone can discuss. They say the beast bowed to you. Bowed! And now the streets are alive with whispers, with questions. They don't know what you are but know you're something more."

Marcus took a shaky breath, his gaze sharp, his words quickening under the strain he bore. "The Emperor was humiliated. Before the entire Colosseum, before all of Rome, his gods were silent, and his power—his absolute power—was shaken to its core. He will not forgive. Not in his court. He will lash out. He has to, or risk losing control."

He stepped closer, his voice softening, almost pleading. "You've planted something—courage, doubt, I don't know—but whatever it is, it terrifies him. And terrified men are the most dangerous of all."

Gregory exhaled, the truth settling in his chest like a stone. "Tiberius will act soon, won't he?"

"Yes." Marcus sat beside him, his voice dropping to a whisper. "There are rumors that the Emperor, to reassert his power, will order your crucifixion at the dawn of the Saturnalia. It is a holiday reminding Rome that no man stands above its gods or ruler."

Gregory flinched as if struck. Crucifixion. The word alone was enough to send fear gnawing at his resolve. *Is this the final seed?* The thought rattled through him like an unrelenting tide.

"You mustn't do this, Gregory." Marcus turned to him, his tone pleading. "The people have seen your courage. You've planted doubt in their hearts—perhaps even in Tiberius himself. That's enough. Denounce your beliefs, even if only in word. Live, Gregory. Live to see what comes next."

Gregory swallowed hard, turning to meet Marcus's gaze. "And what would become of the seeds, Marcus? The prophecy demands all seven. If I falter now and turn my back on this path, everything—the hope we've kindled—will wither. The consequences stretch beyond this Rome, beyond even this world. The seer warned me: failure will fracture both realms."

Marcus's expression tightened, disbelief flickering across his face. "You speak of prophecy and worlds I cannot fathom, but what of your life, Gregory? What of the countless lives you've touched already? What good is a message if its messenger is silenced forever?"

Gregory closed his eyes, his voice faint but steady. "A message born of sacrifice carries more weight than a thousand sermons spoken in safety. The seeds must be sown, and the seventh—sacrifice—must bloom where it is most needed. If my death is the price, then so be it."

Marcus leaped to his feet, pacing furiously across the small room. "This is madness! Rome has no mercy, Gregory. They will take joy in your suffering. And the people? They will cheer or look away, as they have done for centuries. Do you think your death will change that?"

"Not my death," Gregory replied softly. "The meaning behind it. Sacrifice does not end in suffering, Marcus—it begins transformation. It breaks the chains of fear and forces even the hardest hearts to ask why. That is how a seed takes root."

"I don't understand you," he murmured. "I've spent my life studying this empire—its power, pride, and gods—and I cannot see how one man's death can turn it upside down."

Gregory rose to his feet, his weariness evident but his resolve unshaken. "Then perhaps it is not for you to understand," he said, quiet but unyielding. "Perhaps it is for those who will come after us—those who will see, in sacrifice, the first fragile bloom of something greater."

Marcus turned, his expression torn between anger and admiration. "And what if you're wrong?" he asked, almost desperately.

Gregory stepped forward and rested a steady hand on Marcus's shoulder. "If I am wrong, I will have given all I have for my beliefs. And belief in something greater—something good—is never in vain."

For a long moment, the two men remained silent, the tension of the unspoken hanging heavy in the air. At last, Marcus sighed, his shoulders slumping. "You're a fool," he said, though his tone lacked malice. "But I will not abandon you."

Gregory offered a faint, weary smile. "Nor will He abandon us."

Marcus turned to leave, his hand lingering on the doorframe. Something held him back, and after a moment, he looked over his shoulder, his gaze heavy with curiosity and something deeper—concern, perhaps. "Gregory," he said softly, "if… if you succeed in this mad journey—if you return to your world—what will you be?"

Gregory blinked, surprised by the question. Marcus stepped closer, his voice quiet but insistent. "You've told me of your life before this—Pope Gregory, the shepherd of millions, the symbol of your faith. But after everything you've seen here after this world has tested you, changed you… do you think you can go back to who you once were?" He hesitated, searching Gregory's face. "Or will you be different? Can anyone walk through fire and emerge unchanged?"

Gregory's expression softened, his eyes distant as he considered Marcus's words. "I don't know," he admitted, his voice calm. "The man I was lived in certainty, in a world where the path was clear. But here…" He gestured faintly to encompass the alien Rome, the Colosseum. "Here, I've learned faith is not a shield against doubt. It's the strength to walk through it."

He paused, his gaze meeting Marcus's. "If I can return, I will carry this with me. I must. A shepherd cannot lead his flock unless he knows what it means to be lost. Perhaps that is why I was sent here—not to change this world, but to be changed by it."

Marcus stared at him for a long moment, something unreadable in his eyes. At last, he nodded, a hint of understanding crossing his features. "Then maybe there's hope for both of us," he said quietly. Turning back to the door, he added, "The Emperor will summon you soon. I'll see what I can do, but Gregory—if this is truly your path— may your God be with you."

The door creaked as it closed behind him, leaving Gregory alone. The faint echo of Marcus's question lingered in the air as Gregory sank to his knees, hands clasped tightly in prayer. He did not yet have all the answers, but he knew this much: the man who would return would not be the same one who left.

CHAPTER THIRTY-FOUR
THE GOLDEN CROSS

Gregory was led through an arched doorway into the Emperor's private chambers, where power lingered in the air. The vast room stretched before him, its vaulted ceiling draped in blood-red banners that hung like silent sentinels, each embroidered with symbols of conquest. Gilded relics lined the walls—tributes to Rome's might—while restless shadows danced across towering statues of the gods, their marble faces frozen in pitiless judgment. Tiberius reclined on a chaise at the chamber's heart, the golden laurel upon his brow catching the flames like a crown forged from sunlight and fire. His presence filled the space. He was a man who was both ruler and symbol, his gaze sharp enough to cut through any defiance.

Tiberius leaned forward, his dark eyes fixed on Gregory like a predator observing prey. "You stand here before the heart of Rome," he began, his voice low but unrelenting, each word echoing across the chamber. "You've stirred rebellion in the hearts of my people, Gregory of the Foreign Faith. You've planted seeds of doubt where there were none. And now you will answer for it."

Gregory remained silent, his breathing even, his hands clenched just enough to still their trembling.

The Emperor rose slowly, the crimson folds of his robe spilling around him like blood pooling on the marble floor. His voice, measured and deliberate, cut through the silence like the blade of a gladius. "Do you see the magnanimity I extend to you?" Tiberius said, his gaze sharp, unyielding. "Acknowledge your offenses. Pay homage to the truth. Seek absolution under my authority." He paused, his tone steeped in calculated scorn. "Do you not revere the virtues of piety, honor, and loyalty? Here is your moment to show the gods that you live by the principles you claim to uphold."

Tiberius paused, letting his words settle like iron weights. "Do this, and I will spare you the cross." He stepped closer, his imposing figure looming over Gregory. "But resist me, and you will not be remembered as a martyr. The people will forget your name in time, as they always do with men who claim greatness and find only their end nailed to wood."

The room was silent, and the tension was so taut that it felt as though it might snap like a frayed cord. Gregory stood motionless, the moment pressing heavily against him. His chained hands rested at his sides, and though his robe now lay tattered from the trials of the arena, its fabric still clung to him, bearing the marks of his journey.

Slowly, deliberately, Gregory raised his shackled hands to his chest, each movement steady, defying the heaviness of the air. The metallic clink of the chains reverberated through the chamber, silencing even the faint whispers of the guards. All eyes were upon him—curious, suspicious, waiting.

The guards shifted uneasily, their fingers brushing the hilts of their swords as though expecting defiance. A faint but tense murmur threaded through the room, like the first drops of rain heralding an oncoming storm. Yet Gregory's gaze did not waver; his movements were precise and purposeful.

With a slow, reverent motion, Gregory raised his shackled hands, presenting not an object but himself—a man unbroken, a vessel of unwavering faith. The cross, already revealed to the lion and the arena, was no longer needed as proof. The power it symbolized now resided wholly within him, a beacon without form, shining through his presence alone.

"I stand unarmed," Gregory said, his voice calm yet resonant, carrying through the chamber like the first notes of a hymn. "Not with gold, nor with chains, but with faith—an offering no sword can shatter." His words hung in the still air, a challenge to the silent authority of the Emperor himself.

"What is this mockery?" Tiberius's voice cut through the tension like the snap of a whip, though it wavered beneath its fury.

Gregory stepped forward, his chains dragging with a deliberate rhythm echoing like bells. His voice, steady and unwavering, carried across the room. "This is no mockery, Caesar. This is my truth."

The Emperor's fists clenched, pale knuckles stark against the crimson folds of his robe. "You dare defy Rome with your talk of truth? With your mark of the condemned?"

"I dare because truth demands it," Gregory replied, his words ringing with clarity. He raised his bound hands higher as though lifting an invisible banner. "You would have me kneel, confess, and repent. And I will—but not for myself. I kneel for Rome. For you."

The Emperor's lips curled, his fury bubbling to the surface. "By Jupiter's wrath!" he spat, his voice trembling with uncontained rage.

"No," Gregory said, his tone sharp and cutting. "No, it's a revelation. Your gods are silent. They offer no answers, no peace. But this faith you scorn is not a mark of defeat. It is a promise. A promise that something greater than fear, greater than power, exists. And it cannot be silenced, no matter how many you crucify."

A ripple ran through the guards and attendants—a murmur of disbelief, anger, and something more insidious: doubt. It spread through the chamber like a crack in a dam, Gregory's words carrying a force that shook the very foundation of the Emperor's authority. Tiberius's face darkened further, but the room seemed to hold its breath, awaiting a truth it could no longer ignore.

"Enough!" Tiberius roared, his voice cracking like a storm's wrath. He pointed a trembling finger at Gregory, his composure crumbling. "Take him back to his cell! Prepare the crucifix!"

The guards hesitated, if only for a moment, before surging forward. They seized Gregory's arms, wrenching him backward with a brutal force that sent his head snapping forward. The chain around his neck strained against the motion, the gold cross dangling precariously. As the struggle intensified, the chain gave way, slipping over his collarbone and sliding free. It tumbled to the ground, spinning once before landing with a sharp metallic chime echoing endlessly, cutting through the tense silence. Gregory's gaze, however, never faltered. He met Tiberius's glare with unflinching resolve, his defiance as unwavering as the faith embodied by the fallen cross.

As the guards dragged him away, his voice rang out, clear and unwavering. "You fear the cross," he called, his words slicing through the silence. "Not because it condemns men, but because it frees them."

Tiberius said nothing, but his eyes remained locked on the cross—its gold glittering on the marble floor like a ghost that refused to disappear.

As the doors slammed shut behind Gregory, the echo lingered in the chamber, hollow and unrelenting. Tiberius turned away from the space where the cross had fallen, but its image remained burned into his mind. For the first time, the Emperor of Rome, ruler of the world, felt a splinter of doubt—tiny but spreading like a crack in an empire's foundation.

From the darkness of the corridor, Gregory whispered to himself, his breath steady despite the burden of the chains. "Let the seed be sown."

CHAPTER THIRTY-FIVE
LAST RESPECTS

The morning light barely pierced through the narrow slit of Gregory's cell, muted and gray, as though the heavens themselves wept for the hours yet to come. The stone walls, slick with lingering night chill, pressed in closer with the weight of the moment. Gregory sat upright, his breath visible in the cold, his fingers lightly tracing the edges of the manuscript tucked safely in his robe. The parchment crinkled faintly under his touch, a fragile whisper amidst the silence—a reminder of the prophecy that had carried him to this grim and inevitable hour.

A guard's keys rattled in the distance, and moments later, the iron door groaned open. Marcus entered first, followed closely by Lucius and Sextus. The three men hesitated as they took in the sight of Gregory—a hollow-eyed yet calm figure. For a long moment, no one spoke.

"It feels colder than it should," Lucius murmured, breaking the silence, his voice rough with restrained emotion.

Marcus stepped forward, holding a bundle wrapped in fine cloth. "I brought these," he said softly, unwrapping Gregory's pontifical vestments. First, he revealed the white cassock—simple yet immaculate, its ankle-length fabric symbolizing purity and humility. Resting atop was the white zucchetto, a soft skullcap that signified the

Pope's devotion and spiritual authority. And finally, he unveiled the red leather shoes, polished to a quiet sheen, a striking symbol of the Pontiff's willingness to walk the path of sacrifice, recalling the blood of martyrs and Christ's journey. The garments lay before them, glowing pale and resolute against the oppressive gloom of the cell, as though untouched by time or the world beyond.

Gregory regarded the robes for a long moment, something unreadable flickering in his gaze before he nodded. "Thank you, Marcus."

"You'll wear them?" Sextus asked, his tone uncertain.

Gregory's smile was faint but steady. "I will face them not as a prisoner but as the man I was sent here to be."

Sextus looked away, his hands clenching at his sides, frustration simmering beneath his stoic facade. "You shouldn't have to face them at all," he muttered. "This doesn't have to happen."

Lucius stepped forward, his brow furrowed in thought. "Gregory," he began cautiously, "what if the seer's omen is true? Did she not warn you—if you perish in this Rome, it could unravel the fabric of both worlds? Perhaps…" He hesitated. "Perhaps there is still a way to escape this fate."

Gregory's gaze softened as he turned toward Lucius. "And if I run, what then? The seventh seed remains unplanted. The prophecy undone. Sacrifice is not mine alone—it belongs to the hope we have ignited. If I falter now, everything we've built will wither before it takes root."

"But if you die," Marcus interjected sharply, his voice cutting through the room, "what becomes of this hope? Dead men plant nothing, Gregory. You cannot water the seeds of transformation with your blood."

Gregory turned his gaze to Marcus, unflinching yet gentle. "Have we not already seen the truth of sacrifice?" he asked. "The lion bowed. The Emperor trembled. The people are beginning to understand."

Words hung heavy in the cell, settling like a stone in each man's chest. Sextus turned abruptly, pacing to the far side of the room. "This isn't faith," he spat, his voice trembling. "This is madness. You talk of seeds and prophecies as though they're facts carved in stone. And yet"—he stopped, turning to face Gregory, his expression pained—"you're just a man. A man who deserves to live."

Gregory rose slowly, his movements deliberate as the chains on his wrists clinked softly. "I am just a man," he said quietly. "But a man can become a bridge. A man can be the vessel through which something greater takes shape." He paused, his gaze sweeping over them. "The prophecy lives in all of us now. You've seen it—you've felt it. When I am gone, the seeds will sprout and grow."

Marcus exhaled harshly, his hands running through his hair in frustration. "Then why did the seer warn you not to die?"

Gregory's gaze remained steady, his voice calm. "Perhaps her warning was not about death itself," he said slowly, "but against dying without fulfilling all Seven Seeds. Only then can it ripple into something eternal."

The room fell into silence again; each man lost in the wisdom of his thoughts. Gregory reached for the white robes, his fingers running along the edge of the fabric. "If this is to be my final act, then let it be one of truth. Let it be a light that cannot be extinguished, even on the cross."

Lucius cleared his throat, his voice heavy with resignation. "And what of the seventh seed? Is this truly it?"

Gregory nodded. "Sacrifice. The seventh seed has always been sacrifice. Perhaps it is not merely mine but all of ours. The final seed taking root is the choice to stand witness and carry this forward when I am gone."

Marcus opened his mouth to protest, but the words never came. Instead, he dropped heavily onto the stone bench beside Gregory, his voice low and hoarse. "You're asking too much of us."

Gregory placed a steady hand on Marcus's shoulder. "I ask only what you already know you must give. The choice will not be forced upon you. It will come when you are ready."

Sextus turned his back to them all, his shoulders rigid as though he fought to contain something unspoken. "If you're wrong..." he said quietly, his voice barely above a whisper. "If none of this matters..."

"Then I will have given everything for the belief that it does," Gregory replied, his voice unwavering. "And belief, no matter how small, can change the course of the world."

The cell grew quiet once more, save for the distant hum of life in the prison beyond.

At last, Marcus stood and gathered the robes, handing them to Gregory. "Then wear these," he said softly, "and let them see the man you are."

Gregory accepted them with a quiet nod. He turned to Lucius, who clasped his arm tightly, and then to Sextus, who lingered in the shadows, his expression unreadable.

"Will you be there?" Gregory asked.

Lucius nodded first. "We will stand with you."

Sextus hesitated, his jaw tight. "To the end," he muttered finally.

As the guards returned, Gregory stood tall, his white robes draped over him like light in the darkness. The manuscript remained tucked safely in his robe, the Seven Seeds held close to his heart.

He stepped forward, the weight of the cross yet to come heavy in the distance. Behind him, Marcus, Lucius, and Sextus watched, their hearts heavy but resolute.

The seed of sacrifice was ready to be sown.

CHAPTER THIRTY-SIX
CAPITOLINE HILL

Capitoline Hill loomed ahead, its jagged silhouette etched sharply against the silver expanse of a storm-laden sky. A place steeped in history, where justice often masqueraded as spectacle, its ancient stones bore witness to countless punishments meant to humiliate and break. Today, its focus was narrowed to one man—Gregory of the Foreign Faith.

The open-air wagon groaned over the uneven cobblestones; each jolt a sharp reminder of Gregory's frailty. Shackled in iron that bit into his wrists and ankles, he sat hunched; his body bowed under the crushing weight of exhaustion and pain. His white cassock—once a proud symbol of dignity—was now a sullied shadow of its former self, smeared with mud and filth from the wagon floor. The crimson sash at his waist hung heavy and damp, its vibrant hue dulled by grime. Even his zucchetto, that last stubborn relic of his office, clung resolutely to his head despite the wind's relentless attempts to wrench it free. Every fiber of his vestments, every blemish upon them, spoke not just of indignity but of a man being paraded as a spectacle, dragged through the streets like prey for a baying mob.

Flanking the wagon were Roman soldiers, their armor glinting dully beneath the overcast sky, a testament to the ancient traditions they upheld. These were not ordinary guards but executors of Rome's most somber rituals, men who had carried out the grim duty of crucifixion since the earliest days of the Republic. Hardened by years of discipline and death, their faces betrayed no emotion as they marched in unyielding precision. Each step, each movement of their spears, seemed a continuation of a history etched in blood and iron. For them, this was not cruelty but duty—a task carried out with the cold efficiency of those who had long abandoned the luxury of moral conflict.

Though Gregory carried the burden of their indifference, he could feel the presence of history in their measured movements, in the unspoken understanding that he was now another thread in the vast tapestry of their grim tradition. He lowered his eyes, not in submission but in an attempt to steel himself against the enormity of what lay ahead. The soldiers, unwavering in their purpose, kept their march steady, forming a wall between Gregory and a world that had already condemned him.

His body throbbed with pain—his muscles screaming from the contorted position forced by the shackles, his skin raw where metal scraped flesh. The jeers of the crowd were unrelenting, a storm of venom that struck deeper than the cold rain falling from the heavens. Rotten eggs burst against his chest, their stench mingling with the rain-soaked air, while overripe tomatoes splattered his robes in visceral smears. Each projectile struck with precision, aimed not only to injure his body but to shred his spirit.

Gregory lifted his gaze, his bloodshot eyes sweeping across the crowd, not in defiance but in search of something—someone—that might anchor him amid the chaos. The jeering faces blurred together, a storm of scorn and rage, but scattered among them were others—still, solemn, and filled with unspoken sorrow. A woman clutched her shawl, her tears falling unnoticed in the cacophony. Nearby, a man surged forward, his raw voice cracking as he cried out, "Enough!" The soldiers moved swiftly, shoving him back into the faceless throng. Still, the word lingered, reverberating with defiance, a fleeting shield against the tide of hatred surrounding Gregory.

Gregory's heart twisted as he scanned the crowd, searching desperately for the faces of those he trusted. Where were they? Marcus, Sextus, Lucius—they had promised. Julia, Decimus, Caius—none were there. The absence of his followers gnawed at him, sharp as the pain in his limbs. Had they abandoned him, left him to shoulder this alone? Doubt mingled with despair, tightening its grip on his mind.

The wagon climbed higher, each creak of its wheels announcing their ascent up the ancient hill. The road grew steeper, the incline pressing Gregory's already bruised body against the iron bars. Rain began to fall more heavily now as if the heavens wept for him. Droplets slid down his face, mingling with sweat, blood, and dirt, masking the silent tremor of his breath. With each turn of the wheels, Capitoline Hill came closer.

Then he saw it.

The crosses.

Two of them silhouetted against the storm-heavy sky; their forms loomed larger with every turn of the wheels—stark, merciless, weathered beams of blackened, blood-soaked wood. The sight struck him hard. Fear seized his chest, and Gregory's hands trembled visibly in their chains for the first time. His breath came shallow, and his resolve flickered.

The wagon reached the crest, grinding to a halt. Gregory's chains clattered as the soldiers hauled him roughly to his feet. He staggered, his knees weak, his white robes wet, and clung to his legs, trying to hold himself upright. The wind howled through the clearing, tugging at the fabric and whipping it like a banner of defiance.

On the mud-ridden ground before him lay the cross—his cross— its long, dark frame drinking in the damp earth. Unyielding and heavy, it thrummed with silent gravity, its presence an inescapable omen cast at his feet.

The murmurs fell away, swallowed by heavy stillness. Even those who had come to jeer and mock were silent now, their eyes locked on the man in white, their faces unreadable. A strange stillness settled over them as though they awaited something unknown, something dreadful.

Gregory faltered. His breath hitched, ragged and shallow, as he stared at the cross. No longer a distant promise whispered in dark corners, no longer an abstract torment for his faith to endure. It was here now, real and unrelenting. His body trembled—a betrayal of the fear he could no longer suppress.

He looked up at the sky. The clouds churned in shades of gray and silver, parting just enough to reveal the faintest glow of light beyond. Gregory inhaled sharply, his trembling hands clenching at his sides. He lifted his head higher, meeting the gaze of the heavens. "Lord," he whispered, his voice raw but steady, "please let this seed bear fruit."

The soldiers seized Gregory by the arms, dragging him off the wagon and onto his feet. One knelt to unlock the heavy chains binding his wrists and ankles, the iron biting one last time into his raw skin before clattering to the ground. Gregory stood unsteady, his body trembling from exhaustion.

The soldiers gripped Gregory tightly under his arms, dragging him the final steps to the cross. His feet scraped against the rain-slicked ground, leaving faint streaks in the mud before they forced him to his knees.

Gregory's chest rose and fell with each shallow breath, the cold air biting at his lungs. The blackened and splintered wood before him smelled of damp earth and old pain. Rain traced lines down his face, mingling with dirt and sweat, but his gaze remained steady.

"Lay him down," a voice ordered.

Two soldiers lowered him onto the beam, his body heavy against the sodden wood. His arms were wrenched outward, and thick ropes were wrapped around his wrists and ankles, coarse fibers biting into his skin. Each knot was cinched tight, tethering him in place. Gregory winced, the strain tugging at his limbs, but he made no sound. Above him, the clouds churned—dark and restless, as though the heavens themselves refused to look upon what came next.

The hammerman approached, his movements slow and deliberate. The crowd stilled. Gregory turned his head, catching a glimpse of the man—a laborer with a grim, unreadable face, a heavy hammer in one hand, and a long, sharpened spike in the other.

The man knelt beside him. Gregory's eyes lifted to the heavens, the thick gray clouds rolling like waves in a restless sea. His lips parted, and his voice escaped in a low, trembling whisper. "Grant me strength to endure and the wisdom to see the path you have set before me. Do not let me fail in this final hour—guide my steps, carry me if You must, for I cannot do this alone."

The prayer hovered in the air for a moment before being carried off by the wind as Gregory took a slow, steady breath.

The first strike came—a single, deafening crack of the hammer. Pain exploded through Gregory's wrist, white-hot and blinding, as the spike drove deep through flesh and bone and into the wood. His body arched reflexively, but the ropes held him down. He exhaled sharply, a cry caught in his throat, his teeth gritted as the sound of the hammer rang again and again, each blow punctuated by the splintering of wood and the cries and groans of the crowd.

The hammerman moved to his other side. The hammer rose and fell, each strike louder than the last, as if the heavens pounded in unison. Blood streaked the beam beneath Gregory's hands, dark and pooling. When the final spike was driven, silence descended—deep and unnatural, broken only by the patter of rain on the cross and the sobs from the crowd.

Gregory's breathing came in shallow gasps, the agony radiating like fire. Yet still, he did not yield. His eyes fluttered open, and he looked to the crowd—a sea of faces, some twisted with hate, others marred by something else: fear, pity, disbelief.

The soldiers stepped back, and the cross shuddered as they hoisted it upright. Ropes groaned, wood splintered, and Gregory's body sagged under his own weight. For an endless moment, he hung there, arms stretched wide, his white robes stained where rain mingled with blood.

The sky darkened further, and thunder rumbled in the distance. Gregory's head tipped forward, and his voice was a whisper carried by the wind. "The seventh seed… has been sown."

And still, he endured—unbowed, unbroken.

The pain was excruciating, though he refused to cry out. Through the haze of his suffering, his gaze settled on familiar faces—a lifeline amidst the torment. He saw Marcus, his brow furrowed in helpless anguish. Sextus stood beside him, his hands clenched into trembling fists as though restraining himself. Lucius was there, his eyes glistening with silent tears, a battle between faith and despair etched into his features.

And then the others appeared, their forms just beyond the blur of agony. Julia, Decimus, and Caius carried grief like a shroud, their faces streaked with tears. Gregory's breath came uneven as he looked upon them, their silent anguish as tangible as the burden of the cross. In their eyes, he saw more than pain—he saw love, unwavering loyalty, and a sorrow that mirrored his own.

Their presence steadied him, even as his body rebelled. For this—for them—he endured.

The sky darkened further, clouds swirling like restless shadows, their presence pressing heavily on the hillside below. Thunder grumbled—a low, mournful sound that rippled through the heavens. A single bolt of lightning split the sky, casting Gregory's silhouette against the gray expanse in a flash of cold fire.

A tremor followed as it ran through the earth beneath him, subtle at first, then stronger, as though the world had begun to stir. Gregory's eyes, half-lidded with pain, turned toward the horizon, where the sun strained against the darkness—its feeble light swallowed by the gloom.

Marcus fell to his knees, his cry choked with grief. Lucius turned away, his fists clenched to hold back his torment. Sextus stood frozen, his gaze locked on Gregory. His lips trembled, and words failed him.

Time slowed, stretching endlessly between the thunderclaps, and in that stillness, Gregory's final thought emerged clear and steady.

The seed has been sown. Let it take root.

His breath shuddered one last time as he closed his eyes, surrendering himself to the pull of destiny.

CHAPTER THIRTY-SEVEN
RISEN

Gregory's eyes fluttered open. His breath came sharp, ragged—like a man pulled from drowning. He lay still, his mind suspended between dream and waking. The silence of the papal apartments pressed around him, broken only by the faint flicker of a candle on his desk. Its flame wavered as if bearing witness to his return.

Slowly, Gregory sat up. He winced, his breath catching, expecting the sharp lance of pain—expecting the fiery agony of spikes cleaving through flesh and bone. But it did not come. Instead, his limbs obeyed with eerie ease, mocking the suffering he knew had been real.

His heart pounded, wild and uneven, as if it, too, doubted its place in this restored body. Trembling, Gregory turned his hands upward, his breath hitching as his eyes fell upon them. They were smooth and untouched. There were no jagged wounds, no torn skin, no streaks of blood to mark his torment. And yet, he felt it.

The phantom ache gripped him like a vice—raw, visceral, undeniable. He could hear the groan of wood under strain, the grinding of spikes being driven into place, each strike shaking him to his core. His shoulders tensed under the memory of his own unbearable weight as he hung from the cross, its beam clutching him like the burden of all existence.

Gregory's hands curled into fists as he gasped for air, the sensation overwhelming him. The tearing of flesh. The shudder was deep and tremorous, as spikes punctured skin and shattered bone. It was still there—beneath the surface of his unmarred wrists, as though his body had betrayed the truth while his soul refused to forget.

Gregory glanced at the crucifix above the fireplace, its carved figure half-lit by the flickering candle. The eyes of Christ, carved and still, seemed softer now, almost knowing. But a silence screamed between them, and an understanding passed without words.

He exhaled shakily, his hands trembling at his sides. "I was there," he whispered hoarsely, the words breaking the stillness like shattered glass.

The flicker of the candle faltered for an instant, the flame bending in a breathless pause as if the room itself bore witness to his confession. Gregory pressed a hand to his chest, where his heart now beat steadily— a rhythm at odds with the fractured memories clawing their way back into him.

He should not be here, whole and breathing, untouched by scars. But the truth was undeniable.

He had hung there.

Tears gathered at the edges of his vision. It was real.

The memory came crashing down—the journey to Capitoline Hill, the jeers of the crowd, the hammerman's strikes, the agony as he hung high above the world. And yet, within that suffering, he had seen something beautiful. The faces of those who wept. The man who cried out, "Enough!"

And those he had left behind.

Gregory's thoughts turned to Marcus, Lucius, Sextus, Julia, Decimus, Caius, Silvanus, and the others who had looked to him with hope, their faith fragile yet unyielding. Did the Seven Seeds take root? Did his sacrifice on the cross shift their perception of it? In that Rome, where the Divine was a distant echo and the cross a mere instrument of cruelty, had they begun to see it as something more? A symbol not of death but of transformation?

The vision of his followers—his friends—wavered before him. He had left them with Seven Seeds, but what of their harvest? Would this Rome change? Could it, without the Divine narrative he had known in his own world?

A pang of guilt rippled through him. Had he abandoned them? Or was his sacrifice the final act they needed to believe and transform? His fingers curled into his palms as he stared at the flickering flame, its unsteady glow mirroring his inner turmoil. Faith was never a certainty but a hope in the face of the unknown—fragile, trembling, yet unyielding. That hope bore down on him relentlessly, pressing into his chest like an unshakable force, constricting his breath until the dam of restraint finally broke. Gregory's chest heaved as tears streamed freely down his face. He buried his head in his hands, his shoulders shaking with the intensity of his release.

The memory of their cries surged back—how they hailed him as Messiah. A flicker of pride stirred, but shame quickly consumed it. He had let their adoration fill him, nourish him like wine to a parched tongue. *How misguided I was*, he thought bitterly. His ego had mingled with his purpose, clouding the truth of what he had been sent to do.

"Lord," he whispered, his voice thick with emotion. "What have I become?"

Gregory rose to his feet, his legs unsteady, and crossed to the window. He threw back the heavy drapes and the faint light of dawn spilled into the room. The Vatican below lay calm and silent, oblivious to the man standing above them, who had been nailed to a cross and walked a path that echoed Christ's own.

"Was it enough?" he asked aloud, the faint breeze stirring his cassock. "Did I save them? Did I save Rome?"

Gregory's hand drifted to his pocket. His fingers curled around the rough leather and withdrew the manuscript. When Gregory first discovered the ancient tome in the shadowy depths of the Vatican Archives, it seemed impenetrable—a relic so shrouded in mystery that its text felt like a dead language, its meaning buried under the weight of centuries. Dust clung to its cracked leather cover, and its brittle pages carried the faint scent of decay. But now, as he stood on the precipice of revelation, the book seemed almost alive in his hands, a palpable reminder of its secrets.

Gregory opened the book with trembling fingers, its parchment whispering as it yielded to his touch. At first, the markings blurred, shifting like smoke on the edge of his comprehension. Then, as if summoned by an unseen force, the words began to sharpen, arranging themselves with a clarity that defied reason.

His breath caught as his eyes moved across the page:

"When the seventh seed takes root, the harvest will follow. Do not look to the heavens for salvation, for it will come from the earth. From the unseen, the forgotten, and the lost."

The words struck him like a blow, settling heavily in his chest. He could feel the resonance of their meaning as though the book had been waiting for this moment—for him—to reveal its truth. The room around him blurred, and for a fleeting second, Gregory wasn't sure whether the text had spoken to him or whether the words had been whispered into his mind.

The passage revealed a truth far deeper than Gregory could have anticipated. The seventh seed was not simply an act of sacrifice—it was the culmination of a transformation, a turning point that could birth something entirely new. However, the text offered an unexpected shift: salvation would not come from the heavens, Divine miracles, or celestial power, but from the earth—from humanity itself.

Gregory closed his eyes for a moment, letting the revelation settle over him. The words were not just an answer but a challenge—one that called for faith not in the unreachable Divine but in the resilience of the human spirit. This shift in perspective was radical, almost heretical by the Church's standards, yet it resonated with a truth Gregory could not deny. To embrace this path meant restoring what had been lost and planting the seeds of a new beginning that would rise from the very soil of suffering and despair.

The *"harvest"* would not simply restore what was broken but allow something new to emerge, rooted in the hidden strength of the unseen, the forgotten, and the lost.

Gregory's sharp exhale reflected the enormity of this realization. The manuscript's wisdom transcended a single Rome, a single reality. It spoke of every world, every Rome—those that had fallen, those that endured, and those still struggling to find their way. The seeds were a prophecy and a blueprint for redemption that spanned realms and time.

The unseen were the souls cast aside or silenced. The forgotten were the downtrodden, the invisible, the overlooked corners of society—their potential buried like seeds beneath soil, waiting to bloom. And the lost? The lost searched for purpose, light in the darkness, and truth beyond their reach.

Gregory now understood that his journey was not merely a trial of faith or a test of endurance. It was a commission, a directive. The seeds he planted would bear fruit—not through Divine intervention but through the hearts and actions of those who carried them forward. Salvation was not to descend from the heavens; humanity's hands and hearts were called to do the work—to heal the earth and one another.

Gregory realized that his role was not to impose salvation but to ignite it, to inspire it from the forgotten depths of every Rome.

He turned again toward the crucifix above the fireplace. In its carved face, he saw no judgment—only quiet understanding. Gregory stepped closer, staring at the figure of Christ. "I walked where You walked," he murmured. "I bore the weight of the cross. I felt their hatred, their love, their scorn. I know now what it cost You."

The room was still, save for the faint hum of the world awakening beyond his windows. Gregory rose, his resolve hardening. This experience—this monumental journey—had changed him. He had borne the burden of sacrifice not for himself but for others.

"Seven seeds," he whispered, turning back to the window. "I planted them in one Rome. Now, I must plant them here."

The Church, his Church, had strayed. It had grown rigid in its power, stagnant in its traditions. This world, too, was fractured, he thought. But it can be made whole.

Gregory pressed his palm flat against the windowpane, staring out at the vast expanse of the Vatican. The bells began to toll—slow, deliberate, their chimes rolling across the city like waves. *They did not know I was gone, and they did not know I had returned.*

But they would know soon. Gregory's hands tightened around the manuscript, its presence anchoring him. He had returned, and his purpose was clear.

He would bring the Seven Seeds into this world and remind the Church of its true purpose—not dominance or control but service to the unseen, the forgotten, and the lost.

For every hand that mocked him, there had been another reaching for hope. For every jeer, there had been a tear shed in silence. Pope Gregory's path would be difficult—of that, he had no doubt—but he would not falter. He had walked the road of sacrifice once before.

And he was reborn; he would walk it again.

With the first rays of dawn lighting his face, Pope Gregory turned from the window, his voice soft but certain. "The season begins now."

He tucked the manuscript beneath his cassock, opened the door to his chambers, and stepped into the waiting halls of the Vatican.

The bells rang louder as the world stirred to life, unaware that a shepherd of souls—renewed and unbroken—was ready to lead them.

THE END

ABOUT THE AUTHOR

Neil Perry Gordon approaches storytelling as more than a craft—it's his passion and purpose, a means to explore the extraordinary and bring it within reach. Through his writing, he masterfully intertwines the threads of history, metaphysics, and speculative inquiry, crafting immersive narratives that uncover hidden truths and resonate deeply on a human level. With over a dozen books, including the widely acclaimed *The Seven Seeds: Shepherd of Souls,* Neil has dedicated himself to creating stories that inspire reflection, wonder, and a deeper understanding of life's mysteries.

Neil's creative journey began at the Green Meadow Waldorf School, where imagination flourished, and the arts were experienced as living, transformative forces. These formative years profoundly shaped his approach to storytelling, instilling in him a reverence for the power of narrative to connect, uplift, and challenge. His stories are rich tapestries where history, metaphysics, and "what if" scenarios collide, inviting readers to explore alternate realities and the untapped potential of human existence.

For Neil, storytelling is more than a pursuit—it's an act of discovery. Each book is a canvas upon which he explores the complexities of life, blending past, present, and future to reveal the beauty and fragility of our shared humanity. Neil crafts intellectually engaging and spiritually enlightening narratives through vivid prose and emotionally resonant detail.

Whether delving into the depths of the human experience, posing speculative questions that challenge the imagination, or drawing readers into the intricate interplay of history and metaphysics, Neil's work strives to entertain and inspire. His stories are an invitation to see the world—and ourselves—in extraordinary ways, offering a feast for the mind and spirit that lingers long after the final page.